WITHDRAWN
TORONTO PUBLIC LIBRARY
OFFERS THIS ITEM FOR SALE

D1038903

LOST BOYS

LOST BOYS

James Miller

Little, Brown

LITTLE, BROWN

First published in Great Britain in 2008 by Little, Brown

Copyright © James Miller 2008

The right of James Miller to be identified as author of this
work has been asserted by him in accordance with the
Copyright, Designs and Patents Act 1988.

*All characters and events in this publication, other than those
clearly in the public domain, are fictitious and any resemblance to
real persons, living or dead, is purely coincidental.*

All rights reserved.
No part of this publication may be reproduced, stored
in a retrieval system, or transmitted, in any form or by
any means, without the prior permission in writing of the
publisher, nor be otherwise circulated in any form of binding
or cover other than that in which it is published and without
a similar condition including this condition being imposed
on the subsequent purchaser.

A CIP catalogue record for this book
is available from the British Library.

ISBN 978-1-4087-0088-4

Typeset in Palatino by M Rules
Printed and bound in Great Britain by
Clays Ltd, St Ives plc

Little, Brown
An imprint of
Little, Brown Book Group
100 Victoria Embankment
London EC4Y 0DY

An Hachette Livre UK Company
www.hachettelivre.co.uk

www.littlebrown.co.uk

LOST BOYS

. . . he distinctly remembered a youthful desire to return to the tree-tops, and with that memory came others . . . that he had lain in bed planning to escape as soon as his mother was asleep . . .

J. M. Barrie, *Peter Pan in Kensington Gardens,* 1906

. . . a few weeks before . . .

– Nothing, I said nothing, I told them nothing . . .

   – But what did they ask you?

   – They must have asked you something.

   – No, no, they didn't. They just seized me. They pushed a gun into my face and bundled me into a pick-up. Like I've said. But I didn't tell them anything. They asked me nothing.

   – Nothing?

   – Yes, that's what I said.

   – You're sure?

   – Of course I'm sure. They didn't know who I was. I don't think they even knew why they had taken me. It was a mistake. It was just a mistake. That's all. I thought I was going to die . . . I thought I would end up like the others . . . I thought they would kill me like they killed all the others.

   – Yes, you were lucky.

   – Very lucky.

Arthur Dashwood rubbed the sweat from his face. He had said all he could say. All he wanted now was to see his wife and his two darling boys again. Throughout the ordeal, in the heat of the room, with the dirty hood over his face and the ropes binding and cutting his wrists . . . and with the other things, the terrible things they did to him . . . all he could think, all that had kept him going, was his beautiful family: Susan, Timothy and Harry. But he couldn't tell them what had happened. He couldn't tell anyone. Throughout those dark hours, the thought that he might not see them again had been unbearable, a torture worse than anything. And that was why. He looked at the men with him now in the room. They were trying to be kind, but couldn't hide the fact that this was also an interrogation of sorts. Only two of the men present spoke to him. The first, Mr White, said he was from the Foreign Office. Arthur vaguely knew the other one, Mr Curtis. He was head of security for the company – the bad-news manager – a short, rough-tongued man with a shaven head and thick dark eyebrows that met in the middle. He chain-smoked as Arthur talked, plumes of blue smoke circling upwards.

Nothing – nothing – nothing. I said nothing. I told them nothing.

It's very important you realise.

Nothing.

The other two men sat at the back and they too said nothing. One made notes. The other one had asked for clarification on a couple of answers Arthur had given earlier, and he had an American accent. Arthur assumed they must be intelligence officers – CIA, MI6, that sort of thing. A tape recorder sat on the table, capturing his every denial. He couldn't shake the fear that they didn't believe a word he was saying. A small camera mounted on the ceiling watched them all. Arthur just wanted to see his family.

– How much longer will I have to put up with this? My wife has been worried sick.

– Your wife didn't know what had happened until you were found again, Mr Curtis spoke through a cloud of smoke.

– You weren't gone for long.

– She didn't have time to get worried.

– Well, she was worried when they told her. I was gone for long enough. You should have been there, in that room. It's easy for you to say.

Arthur wiped some of the sweat from his face. He didn't know why he felt so hot.

– I've told you all I know. I can't stay in this room much longer. I'm sorry. I'm exhausted. I've hardly slept in days.

– And you're sure you never saw their faces?

Back in the Green Zone, the Americans had shown him a great many pictures of men, none of whom Arthur had ever seen before, and they had played him recordings of voices, some speaking Arabic, others English, or languages that didn't even sound like anything he had heard before. But he hadn't recognised any of those either. Then they showed him footage and photos of torture camps and insurgent bases: hidden rooms with bars on the windows and chairs stained with blood, with bloody palm prints and crude messages scrawled on the walls. Any of them could have been the same room; he couldn't say for certain.

– No. Like I said, the only guy I really saw was the one who seized me and I hardly remember it now. I gave the best report of what he looked like back in Iraq. Like I said, he was just a guy, an Iraqi-looking guy. I told you all this. I don't even know if he was a Sunni or a Shia. I can't tell. I can't remember anything very clearly. I was scared. It's not easy to remember, is it, when you're scared?

– And you didn't tell them anything? You didn't reveal

any information about your work over there? You know many things.

Nothing.

I said nothing. I told them nothing.

At last they let him out. In a private room in a strange part of Heathrow his family were waiting. His wife had never looked so beautiful and his boys had never been so precious to him. Rising together at the sight of him, they seemed bathed in a radiant light, like treasure from a distant world. The worry in Susan's eyes turned into a curious troubled sort of delight. He had been away for just two weeks, but it felt like so much longer. With a stifled sob, she was in his arms and he brought her close, inhaling the sweetness of her hair. Trying not to let his hands shake too much, he hugged his sons, one arm around each. He suddenly felt very weak. With some effort he was able to control his emotions. He did not want to frighten them. He had been so scared. The worst thing would be to break down now and start crying. They must never know that he'd thought he might die, alone and wretched, in that black hot room. They must never know what it was like to have such a thought, and what it might make you do. Seeing them all, he felt overwhelmed with love, a feeling so strong and tender it seemed almost to crush his heart.

'Daddy, you're back!' said Harry.

It was impossible to speak.

'Why did we have to wait so long?' Timothy wanted to know. He was older, almost thirteen, and sensed more than he understood.

'Daddy had to talk to some special people,' said Susan. 'He's an important man. You must remember that.' She touched Arthur's arm as she spoke. He avoided the look he knew she would give him, and smiled again at his boys.

'I'm back now,' he said. 'Don't worry.'

Susan drove them home from the airport. As their Range Rover moved onto the motorway, Arthur gazed at the cool grey English sky and the sleek vehicles speeding safely past. He tried to feel calm. There was nothing now to worry about. He was home.

'I think I'm going to take the week off,' he muttered, suddenly aware of just how tired he was.

'That's a good idea,' Susan said, gently patting his leg.

Later that evening, after the au pair had put the children to bed, Arthur sat in his living room. The TV was on, but he wasn't watching anything. A glass of wine that he wasn't drinking rested by his arm.

'Are you going to tell me what really happened?' His wife's beauty was like a mask sometimes, a barrier between her appearance and everything inside.

'Nothing really happened. What's to tell?'

'But I thought they kidnapped you?'

'I wouldn't use that word. They were just some people. They weren't important. They didn't know who I was. If they kidnap you it's deliberate, isn't it? They just held me for a few hours. It was frightening, but I'm okay. I don't know why everybody made such a fuss about it all.'

'You were lucky.'

'Well. I knew that already,' he replied, reaching forward to kiss Susan. She accepted his caresses without response.

'You won't tell me.'

'There's nothing to say.' He moved away from her. 'That's the truth.'

'Don't ever go back there.' She trembled as she spoke. 'Don't you dare. Don't you ever go back.'

'I won't.' Her hand was so much smaller than his. She moved to the other side of the room.

He opened his eyes.

tell me their names write their names each one write them down or we will

we will

your wife

please I

your family

. . . I

watch you on the television on the news watch you die

nothing I told them nothing I

do you want to die we will kill you like this *infidel*

He could hear the pitter-patter of tiny feet running up and down the corridor.

I'm sorry

Heart pounding, taste of the hood, dirty fabric gummed up thick in his mouth. He could hear them, moving around the room, whispering things to each other. The jolt of pain as they touched his body . . .

screaming and biting his tongue, white spots in the darkness, taste of blood filling his mouth, shaking limbs running with sweat, weak legs buckling . . .

pissing . . . sobbing

. . . his wife his children all the dead children all the black oil . . .

He got out of bed. The clock read twelve past five. Susan was lying on her front, breathing softly, her face buried in the pillow. He went into the corridor, looking for them. He heard it again, a faint scratching, scampering noise. Downstairs.

In the hotel he kept on seeing them: the small boys disappearing down the long corridors, running just out of sight.

The French doors at the back of the house were open. He walked into the small garden. The gate into the larger communal garden beyond hung open. He went through, the grass cold and wet on his bare toes. He shivered. He was dirty from crawling in the mud. No sign of the dawn to lighten the dark sky. 'Forgive me,' he sobbed, the tears falling now. He saw them, huddled under the damp trees, faces hidden with scarves and masks. Waiting.

THE BOYS

Friday

Timothy Dashwood opened his eyes. The dream was fading, dissolving like an aeroplane trail lost to the sky. Sitting up, he pulled back the curtains and shivered at the wet December morning. Outside, in the communal gardens, the tall trees were empty, their branches barren of leaves. In the dream the boy had sat in the upper branches, beckoning him with a silvery flourish of his hand, his shining brown eyes promising great new adventures. Always, in those dreams, it was summer, the air always warm and sweet with the perfume of a thousand open flowers. *Come with me, Timothy* he called in words spoken in no language that Timothy knew, words like colours and strong as feelings, words he understood more clearly than his own thoughts. *Come with me, Timothy* and the boy put his flute to his lips, that light, clear sound touching cool glass to his bones, such a sharp and endless yearning in the light rise of those notes. One day, promised the boy, one day they would fly away together, to a place far from here and far from now.

But this morning those branches outside were empty,

and a tired winter rain fell steadily. The dream was gone, the day about to begin. His bedside clock said 6.55. In a minute Veca, the au pair, would knock on his door and cry, 'Time to get up, sleepy Timmy.' Straight after that she would knock on Harry's door. His brother was only nine and such a deep sleeper that Veca often had to go into his room to help him with his buttons and tie.

All too fast, Timothy's memory of the dream was disappearing, remaining glimpses of it becoming dilute, disconnected and meaningless, like small drops of ink in a great bowl of water. Each time he awoke he feared that the boy would never come again, that his promises were empty, that there was nothing – only this – after all. And now . . . school. At least it was Friday, and after today there was only one week left before the three-week release of the Christmas holiday. He couldn't wait. To be away from that place and their awful taunts, the way they said it: 'Wishy-washy Timmy-wimmy,' squeaking his name and flapping like demented crows, bending their wrists and fluttering their eyes and laughing as his cheeks flushed and his eyes burned with tears. He didn't know why they had turned against him so – just because he was new, and poor at sports, and quiet.

Wishy-washy Timmy-wimmy.

His father would be awake already, maybe on the phone or computer or else watching the business news on TV. Sometimes he did all three at once. That was if he hadn't already left for work. Most days, his father was gone before he'd even got up. He wouldn't be home until long after Timothy had gone to bed and was supposed to be asleep. 'Working for the Wizard,' he said, working in his great white tower in the Docklands. No one teased his father, no one dared. *Yes, Mr Dashwood, of course, Mr Dashwood, right away, Mr Dashwood, sir*. His Mummy preferred to stay in bed because she wasn't 'good' in the mornings, she said. Sometimes she would descend midway through breakfast, hair piled up on top of her head, dressing gown lashed around her waist and her face, free of make-up, oddly pale and empty, as if she couldn't quite decide who she was supposed to be. She would appear in time to kiss them both goodbye, the quick brush of her lips dispensing a dismissive blessing, before Veca would put them in the car and drive them to school. Muffy, of course, was always awake and ready to see them, dropping her big hairy face into Timothy's lap as he ate breakfast and wagging her tail. 'Dear old Muffy,' said Harry. 'Big silly dog!'

Two minutes past seven.

Veca came pattering up the smooth wooden stairs. She was slightly early. Then the sharp knock. 'Good morning, Timmy, rise and shine.' Ten seconds later, the knock on Harry's door, the sound of her going in. The day had begun.

Never enough time: get up, get dressed, eat breakfast, brush teeth, wash face ('You don't want spots, Timmy'), pack school-bag, get in car, go to school, school – school – more school, then back into the car and Monday night was extra French, Tuesday piano practice, Wednesday special maths tuition (Timothy *hated* maths), Thursday swimming, only on Friday did they get to go straight back home, but there was always prep, essays and compositions, assignments and projects, coursework, sums and equations. Next week he was free of extra classes, thank goodness, and could indulge himself, reading, watching TV or fighting on the side of the insurgents in his favourite computer game.

In the car, stuck in traffic, Timothy up front next to Veca.

They weren't moving, no one was, only the people, crowded on the pavements, their heads down, streaming to work, faces turned against the morning. A grey pall overhung the city, as if God had covered the sky with concrete. Veca kept tutting at the congestion, but he didn't mind. They could stay in traffic for ever. The day ahead was nothing to look forward to: House Assembly, then double maths – nearly two hours of Dr Moxton, his sarcastic tongue lashing across the classroom in search of targets – *'The answer, Dashwood, that's what I want, not an excuse, an answer!'* – and that tension, that tight queasy feeling in his stomach as he had struggled to swallow his boiled egg and toast. 'Not hungry, Timmy?' Veca had asked and, feeling the concern in her big blue eyes he had managed to eat, if only to please her. The car was different. Between places his thoughts could drift a little.

Although he had not been living in the city for that long, Timothy knew that there was a second city – another London – all around the first, a brother city squatting in dirty shadows, waiting. It could wait a long time, this second city; it was very patient. Not many people were aware of it; only in dreams did it become clearer. They agreed about that. The boy helped them to see: he showed them that there was another place, a somewhere-better place, and another, much worse place, and that the way it was did not have to be the way it always would be.

Timothy was new to the school. His only real friend was another new boy called Edward Morgan, who had also started in September. Edward had been living in India, where his father was a diplomat and he said they had bars on the window of their house to keep out the monkeys. According to Edward the boy's name was Krishna. But Timothy didn't know what he was called: he thought the boy must have a thousand different names, names different for every boy who dreamed him. They had to be careful talking about him, they had to watch what they said. The Radley brothers overheard them once. 'You dream about boys,' they jeered. 'You fucking queers.' Once they cornered him in the changing room and hit him with their rugby boots on his back and legs. The studs left red marks that stung for ages. He tried not to cry as they hit him and the other boys stood around, watching and laughing. 'Don't cry Timmy-wimmy, don't cry.' 'Fucking queer!'

'Traffic is terrible today,' said Veca, more to herself than to them. 'So many cars.' She glanced back at Harry. 'Have you got your rugby kit, Harry? Your lunch?'

'Yes, Veca.' Harry was a small boy, dwarfed by his red trimmed blazer and school cap, his owlish eyes magnified behind big, round glasses.

Traffic eased through Earl's Court, a dark flood of suits and coats surging in and out of the Tube station. A bus pulled in front and they came to another halt, commuters dodging the stalled cars. A record they all knew came on the radio. Veca tapped out the beat on the steering wheel. Lights changed from green and back to red again and nothing moved. She made a sighing noise through her teeth. 'Look at this,' she said. 'We will be late.'

Timothy didn't care. He didn't mind being late. He could easily miss House Assembly, with its tedious enumeration of the week's sporting triumphs. Linacre – his house – was renowned as a sporting house and whatever the sport Linacre usually came top. Timothy was useless at sport. He loathed games – the oafish masters, the bruising tackles that knocked him into the cold mud. He always dropped the ball. He never scored. The housemaster, Dr Cawl, took sport very seriously indeed. Shoddy showing in a house championship could result in detention, the negligent squad forced to lap the playground for hours. Bookish boys were no good for the House and Dashwood was never going to be a name carved on the mahogany boards commemorating sporting achievements in the grand hall. Not that he cared about that, he didn't want anyone to remember his name. He wanted to move quietly and unnoticed. Most of the time he wished he could just disappear.

Teeth gritted and tongue lashed as the traffic halted once more. Timothy closed his eyes, oblivious to Veca's frustration. He felt sleepy. The music on the radio was so dull and relentless. He struggled to remember the gentle summons of the flute, sweet and pure. When he opened his eyes again he saw a woman with a brightly coloured headscarf wrapped around her face, moving between the cars, one hand outstretched, the other holding a tightly wrapped baby. He pressed his palm against the glass in return, the cool dampness seeping through him. Removing his hand, he stared for a moment at the imprint left behind, strangely fascinated by the lines revealed by his palm, the intricate whorls on his fingertips, a hand in negative, a reverse self. These thoughts had hardly started before the image had faded, the city easing back into focus. Traffic started again, and they drove on.

Today was different: there was no House Assembly.

The form teacher, Mr Clarke, appeared distracted, quietly adding Timothy's name to the register without mentioning the fact that he was nearly ten minutes late. The acerbic remarks normally used to subdue class were absent and instead he announced that House Assembly was cancelled and said the headmaster had something to say to them all. Timothy didn't have a chance to talk to

Edward, but a quick glance suggested he had no idea what was happening either. An uneasy feeling filled the classroom, and even Jason Radley managed to stay silent. A prefect entered the class and said something to Mr Clarke. Then Mr Clarke summoned the pupils to their feet and ordered them to follow him into the Old Hall. Timothy assumed their year was in trouble for some vague, communal lapse of standards, a failure to tuck in shirts or tie ties properly, an excess of public swearing or playground spitting. Entering the capacious hall, he was surprised to find most of the school gathered already, from juniors to sixth form.

Prefects ushered their class to seats in the middle of the hall.

On the high stage Timothy saw Dr Scott, the headmaster, Mr Walker, the deputy head, and all the Heads of Year. Dr Scott looked particularly uncomfortable this morning, perched by the lectern like a man impatient for his bus, one hand twitching. They sat, while the remaining classes arrived, masters and prefects taking positions against the wall, seats scraping and knocking as students sat down, wildfire chitter-chatter flaring up among the different years.

'What's going on?' Timothy whispered to the boy beside him.

'I don't know.'

'Who are those two?' A strange man and woman were sat on stage next to Mr Walker.

'*I don't know.*'

'Do you think—'

'Chaps,' began Dr Scott. 'Now chaps – boys – gentlemen, would you be quiet, please, do you mind.' The restless chatter continued, sweeping back and forth across the hall.

Mr Walker, clearly exasperated, shot the headmaster a look, stood up and bellowed 'SILENCE' at the top of his voice. Famously strict, and rumoured to have been an officer in the Guards before joining the school, his command had an immediate effect.

'Thank you,' said Dr Scott. Bracing himself against the lectern, he leant forward on his right arm, his hawkish eyebrows frowning and his bald head gleaming, waiting as the final ripples of conversation petered out. Satisfied, he straightened up – Timothy knew the familiar pantomime of his movements, everybody did – and grasped the lectern firmly with both hands, his half-moon glasses catching the light that filtered down from high Gothic windows. Someone coughed. Someone always coughed. The strange man sitting beside Mr Walker appeared to be checking his mobile phone.

Dr Scott waited.

Dr Scott began: 'Okay, chaps.' His voice, as always, wavered a little before he got into his stride. 'This assembly has been called because of a very serious matter. With me are Detective Inspector Grant and Detective Sergeant Kennedy, from Chelsea police station.' He gestured, ever so slightly, to the strange man and woman. The man – the detective inspector – had put away his phone and now sat back, arms crossed. He wore a blue suit, slightly baggy and a fraction more fashionable than anything the masters wore. Almost bald, the detective had buzzed what remained of his hair into a thin, macho fuzz. Timothy thought he looked rather like a boxer, about to bust into the ring. The detective sergeant, in contrast, looked more like a teacher. She had the same sort of practical haircut and sour expression. Only she wore trousers and there was something about her that was much tougher. Timothy wondered if she kept her CS spray in the large handbag beneath her seat.

The headmaster was talking: 'Chaps, Inspector Grant will speak to you in a minute. I ask that you all listen very carefully to what he has to say. It concerns us all.' *Police.* Perhaps another sixth-former had been caught selling cannabis again. It had happened at the start of term. Five boys had been expelled and letters mixed with threats and assurances had been sent out to parents. Dr Scott began: 'First, I would have you remember that here, at Royal Brompton College, we believe in certain values . . .' It certainly sounded like drugs, the way Scott was starting with the ever-so-pious tone that always entered his voice when he lectured the school about sex or drugs or not playing enough sport. 'As you know, we believe in respect for ourselves, for each other and our community. We believe in restraint, moderation and hard work of course, but also in good cheer, honesty, common sense, teamwork, and having fun. As you know and, indeed, your parents know, we are a proud school, with a long tradition of decency and achievement.'

Dr Scott slapped the side of the lectern and gazed around. 'Chaps, as I'm sure you are all aware we have a duty to watch out for each other, to look after each other. You are all upstanding young fellows. You have a duty to the school – remember, Brompton boys, we always stick together!' He slapped the lectern again for effect. 'Boys from Royal Brompton have gone on from here to make many notable achievements. Many have had illustrious and important careers. Need I remind you how many old boys have become great men – captains of industry, politicians, diplomats, innovators, inventors, scholars, even – dare I say – artists, musicians and actors?' He paused, looking left, looking right. Someone coughed. 'Chaps, it saddens me to declare that an extremely worrying situation has arisen.' He hesitated for a moment. 'Now, I expect you all to pay great attention to what Inspector Grant has to say. But first, remember what I said. Now, I will hand you over to the police.' Someone tittered at the headmaster's non sequitur, causing Mr Walker to glare fiercely in the general direction of the disturbance. Standing back, Dr Scott tugged at his black gown and nodded for the inspector to come forward.

The inspector surprised everyone by being the first person to address Royal Brompton College in at least one hundred years who not only stood away from the lectern but kept his hands in his pockets and, while speaking, strolled quite casually from one side of the stage to another. 'Right, gents, I'll be as brief as I can. Some of you know Thomas Anderson, in class 3-F. Some of you don't.' He sniffed loudly. 'Well, on Wednesday, Thomas didn't come home. And he didn't come home yesterday, either. Well, now ... what do we make of this, then?' He shrugged, as if it was no big deal. Then he put his hands back in his pockets and continued talking. 'His parents are worried, I can tell you that for starters. They don't know where he is and, what is more, we – the police – are also worried and so is the school. We are now officially conducting a missing-person inquiry.' Inspector Grant paused and scratched his chin, letting his words settle a little. Thomas Anderson. 3-F. From the year above. Timothy had never spoken to the boy, but he thought he knew what he looked like. In his mind he saw a slight dark-haired fellow with glasses, an ordinary sort of boy, not that popular, but not an obvious victim either, not a troublemaker and not a swot, just ordinary.

'We know Thomas left school on Wednesday and entered South Kensington Tube station, as he does every day when going home. We have CCTV footage of him entering the station. That is the only footage we have. Normally, Thomas would leave the Tube at Warwick Avenue station and walk the short distance home. But we know he never exited from that station. We don't know anything else.' The inspector sniffed and walked over to the right-hand side of the stage. Timothy watched the teachers watching him. *A boy had disappeared!* 'Somehow, somewhere, between entering the Tube at South Kensington and coming out at Warwick Avenue, Thomas vanished. We are speaking to his friends – and some of his teachers – privately, to find out if they know anything. But I want to appeal to all of you. Like your headmaster said, you are a community and you've got to watch out for each other. That's what makes a community. Now we need to know, did any of you see anything unusual? Did you see, for example, anyone strange waiting around outside school? We know a lot of you use that Tube station. Did you see Thomas? Were you on the same train as him? Did you see him leave the train? Did you notice anyone unusual at the Tube station? Have any strangers approached you recently, tried to take you somewhere, or make you do something?'

Another pause, another sniff. 'Now, I need you all to think very, very carefully about the last few days. Those of you who use the Tube, especially the Circle or District Line between South Kensington and Paddington, try and remember if you saw anyone suspicious, anything unusual. Anything, gents, no matter how small or inconsequential it might seem to you, however silly, could help us. Don't be shy. If in doubt, just come see us. Sergeant

Kennedy and I will be at school all day. We plan to talk to as many of you as possible.'

Timothy knew that ruled him out. He *never* went on the Tube. Veca was always there, in the Volvo, to take them everywhere. Mummy hated the Tube and had forbidden them to travel on it, except with Daddy on the occasional weekend excursion to Oxford Street or Covent Garden. She was convinced he would get mugged if he went down alone, 'by black boys from the *estates*,' she warned, boys who would take his money or his trainers or his life and 'thank God' she wouldn't let him have a mobile phone because they'd take that in a flash. Anyway, that was without worrying about fires, accidents, mechanical breakdowns 'or terrorism'. Mummy lived with an impending sense of the apocalypse, especially when it came to the Underground.

'One other thing, gents: it is possible that Thomas has just gone away somewhere to be by himself and think about things. He might be perfectly safe. I remember what it was like, at your age. You get fed up. These things happen. But it could be more serious than that. Now, I'm telling those of you who walk home, or get the Tube, or the bus, do not travel alone. Go with your friends. Watch out for each other and keep your eyes open. If you have phones, make sure you keep them to hand. Most of all, don't speak to any strangers. If someone tries to bother you, call the police immediately. We don't want any more disappearances. Thank you.'

Detective Inspective Grant sat down, allowing Dr Scott to resume his habitual pose and tone, rambling on for a bit about something before the Reverend Fowler took over, leading the school through a droning hymn and then a mumbled rendition of the Lord's Prayer. All the time

Timothy was wishing he were somewhere else, somewhere other than here. He tried to return to the memory of last night's dream, the boy in the trees so close and yet just too far away and the sound of the flute drifting through a hot, still afternoon. His hymn book slipped from his fingers, banging loudly on the floor. Jolted awake, Timothy blushed and quickly picked it up. In front of him, another boy absently-mindedly scratched at the spots on the back of his neck.

At lunchtime Timothy had a chance to catch up with Edward. During the winter term, especially when the weather was bad, pupils were allowed to remain indoors during the lunch hour. Confronted with sleety grey rain outside, the two spent the long hour pacing the white-washed corridors between the great hall and the old library. Although most pupils stayed in their classrooms, there was an unspoken agreement between Timothy and Edward that it was safer to stick to the corridors. Confined lunch hours packed into sweaty classrooms were a chore for even the best-behaved pupils and outbursts of mob violence, taunting and abuse were common ways of alleviating the boredom, especially when the Radley brothers held court. Regular patrols by teachers and prefects made the corridors marginally safer territory, and the pair had found that absenting themselves from the malicious gaze of the Radley brothers was a wise strategy for self-preservation.

'Did you dream about him again?' Edward asked.

'I think so. It's hard to remember. Yes.'

'So did I. It reminds me, you know, these dreams . . .' Edward's voice trailed off.

'Yes.'

'India,' Edward said firmly. 'The more I think about it,

the more certain I am. He wants to take me back to India.'
Edward was always talking about India, but Timothy
didn't mind so much. They passed the back toilets, a notorious smokers' hang-out, the faint aroma of excessive
aftershave and Marlboro Lights filling the air. Edward continued, 'In fact, I'm sure I met him – Krishna – when we
lived in Delhi. One of the gardeners, he often had his son
with him, helping with things. He was about my age. I
remember watching them working throughout the midday
heat. He never wore anything but a white cloth around his
waist and flip-flops on his feet. He was so thin and his skin
was so dark and his hair was as black as midnight. I often
wondered where they lived, where they went at the end of
the day. The poor people live everywhere in India, you
know, sleeping under trees, on roundabouts or living in
shacks next to sewers and railway lines. I'm sure it's
him . . . There were so many places in India, places we
could never go . . .'

For a while nothing much more was said and the pair
doubled round, passing again the dining hall, the
staffroom. Mr Walker marched past them: he was always
striding around, officiously removing bags that blocked the
way.

'What do you think happened to the boy who disappeared?' asked Timothy.

'Andrew and that lot said some weirdo came up to them
on the Tube yesterday.'

'Really? Andrew's full of shit.'

'Yeah.'

'Is he going to tell the police?'

Edward shrugged.

'He's full of shit,' repeated Timothy.

'Yeah.'

They reached the library again and paused for a moment. 'Is it worth going outside?'

'We could see how the rain is.'

'We could.' Back down the stairs. 'What did Andy say about this weirdo?'

'I don't know. I don't think it was anything.'

'But what if that boy has been kidnapped?'

'Where's the ransom note? There's always a ransom.'

'What if he's dead?'

'Where's the body? They would have found his body in the Tube.'

'Unless there are secret tunnels, and secret entrances.'

'Under London?'

'Under London,' Timothy confirmed.

'I guess . . . probably you are right.' Edward didn't go on the Underground much either and it was a place of some mystery for them both.

'He said there was a mountain . . .' Now Timothy was trying to remember what the boy had told him.

'The mountain?'

'In the dream. I told you.'

'Maybe . . .' Edward didn't seem quite so sure.

'I would go to the mountain. There was a castle, high up above the snow. Beautiful. With gardens and fountains, so peaceful.'

'I think I've seen it . . . India has lots of mountains, you know – they have the Himalayas.'

'They go out from the mountain. They serve him.'

'Yes . . . I see . . .'

'They have amazing weapons.'

'Yes.'

'Throwing daggers . . .'

'Yes.'

'Swords that can cut through rock . . .'

'Yes.'

'Poison darts . . .'

'Yes.'

'Arrows with eagle feathers . . .'

'Yes, yes.'

'He can make you invisible.'

Now Edward joined in: 'They will teach you how to walk on water.'

'Climb walls with your hands.'

'Go for days without food or water.'

'Long black knives . . .'

'Yes.'

'That cut like that and like that . . .'

'Yes! Yes!'

'They go down from the mountains, they walk for days . . .'

'They hide and no one can find them—'

'Not all the governments of the world . . .'

'And when they find their enemies.'

'They cut them—'

'Cut their throats!'

'And then they are gone!'

'Vanished!'

'Like the morning mist.'

'Gone where no one can find them.'

'And they lie awake, in their beds, at night,'

'Their enemies,'

'With bloody hands,'

'And they cannot sleep,'

'Oh, the bitterness!'

'So many sleepless, anxious nights,'

'Because they know—'

'Because nowhere is safe, not even their beds, their government beds,'

'Not with all their bodyguards!'

'And all their bombs!'

Timothy and Edward smiled simultaneously at each other. The bell rang for afternoon school. With their spell broken, both boys hurried back to class.

The rest of the afternoon went slowly. Timothy wondered what his teachers had written in his end-of-term report. He knew he was supposed to be what they called 'a good boy' and a 'diligent student'. But really, deep down, he didn't want to be anything like that. Last period and they were all given a letter that explained the disappearance to parents. To the disappointment of everyone the police did not visit their class. At four o'clock Timothy trailed out of the school and crossed the road, picking out Veca and the Volvo amid the habitual crush of Range Rovers, BMWs and Mercedes.

'Hello, Timmy. How was your day? Was it good?'

'Yeah, I s'pose.'

'How was school?'

'Okay.'

'Only okay?'

'A boy disappeared.'

'Disappeared?'

'Yeah, in the year above.'

'But this is terrible! When – not at school?'

He groaned. 'I dunno. I've got a letter in my bag about it. The police spoke to us in assembly.'

'Lord! The police!' Veca slapped the steering wheel in disgust. 'I will read it when we get home. What happened?'

'They don't know.'

Veca made a whistling noise and shook her head as she

always did when something appalled her. A lot of things that happened seemed to appal her. Harry, in the back, was asking questions, but Timothy ignored him. He didn't feel like speaking at the moment.

The Dashwoods had only recently moved to the city.

Before that they had lived for six months in the country-side, in a large house with gloomy rooms and draughts that was surrounded by the tallest trees. It always seemed to be windy in that place, especially at night, and now, when they went for walks on windy days in Kensington Gardens, the dry rustle of shaking leaves gave Timothy a strange and rather sad nostalgia for that house, which he had never much liked and his mother had particularly loathed. That sound, like the sighs of a great paper ghost, brought with it such a peculiar yearning, and he would remember the hint of freedom suggested by the barren fields that stretched past the house, and the faint, bluish hills in the distance. In his mind it was always autumn in that house – dead leaves blown across the garden and fields like faded photographs, sad memories of spent summer all russet and ochre. Although his mother would talk of the wonderful walks that were supposed to exist somewhere beyond the field, they never explored them. The weather was almost always bad, so they never really went anywhere. His mother hated the countryside, the mud, the great nothingness, miles from what she called 'decent shops'. Timothy remembered her bitter complaints to his father, and all those empty afternoons she spent pacing from room to room, as if she would find in one of them what was missing from all the rest. Timothy remembered some mornings, when his father was away, how she could hardly even get out of bed and how sometimes – this was always the worst – she would go into the garden alone to shout and scream her frustration at the trees. He remembered once having to go and fetch her – her dressing gown wet and muddy, her face smeared with tears and dirt. But he didn't really think much about that any more.

At the time, of course, it was only meant to be the most temporary of moves while his father tried to decide if they should go back to Saudi Arabia or remain in England. 'Back to Saudi.' Timothy remembered the intense heat, the sun so bright and hot that it turned the sky into a vast molten dome. He remembered the low white buildings in the compound and the bright blue swimming pool that was comfort-cooled on those searing hot afternoons when Mummy sent them smothered in sun cream and wearing their floppy hats back inside. And the dry orange dust of the landscape and the endless, soothing drone of the air-conditioning machines in the compound and that night when the power went off and didn't come back on for hours and his father sat vigilant with a phone and torch in case 'something' was happening.

Only now did Timothy realise how rarely they actually left the compound and then it was mainly to go to the airport, to fly back to England. He remembered the long straight motorway with palm trees on either side, regular as street lamps against the flat horizon. And the gates at the entrance to the compound – they used to fascinate him so – high fences topped with wire and spikes and the concrete walls that kept out the rest of the world. He used to wonder, constantly pestering his mother about them, what would happen to someone if they got caught on those spikes. Most fascinating of all were the guards with their machine guns and eyes hidden by sunglasses, men who checked his mother's pass and stuck strange metal poles underneath the car. Sometimes he would play at 'guards and intruders' with other children in the compound, chasing around and pretending to shoot each other.

Timothy made no connection back then between the gates, scanners and guns, and the pool, the compound shopping mall and the little compound school with its pictures of American presidents hanging on the walls. Only now, when he really thought about it, did Timothy begin to wonder if he was beginning to see what had been waiting all along, beyond those high compound walls.

Timothy's mother put down the letter from the school and sighed. 'Well, I'm not sure we should tell your father about this. He'll only worry. He has enough on his mind.' She tweaked at her wedding ring the way she always did when she felt anxious. 'Have you seen this, Veca?'

'Yes, Mrs Dashwood. Tim told me.'

'That's what happens, I suppose, if you let your children travel unaccompanied on the Tube.' She shook her head to show she couldn't believe how wicked some parents could be. 'Well . . .' Her lips twitched as if she was about to say something else. The letter went into the bin.

Timothy's mother could be very busy when she wanted to be, planning dinners for his father or else decorating rooms in the house or going to the gym. 'Mummy's homework,' she called it, not that Timothy could see much of a parallel. 'Now, Veca, have you seen my address book? I must call Adele. You will be in, won't you, next Thursday?' Following Veca into the kitchen, she touched the top of Timothy's head, the briefest possible caress and yet ever so tender, like a curator allowing herself the smallest of intimacies with her finest exhibit.

Timothy was left alone in the living room. He turned off

the light to see outside better, and pressed himself against the window. The glass was cold. The trees in the communal garden were lost in the gloom. Outside. A boy had disappeared, he thought. A boy was gone.

Saturday

Timothy found himself in a park. The boy sat under a tree, cross-legged and waiting, his face wrapped in a long white scarf. Only his eyes were visible, peeping between a slit in the cloth. He had such beautiful eyes, filled with adventure.

'You are late.' The boy's breath plumed around him in the cold as he spoke.

'I'm sorry. I didn't realise.'

'How much longer will you stay here? You're almost ready, don't you know?'

Sensing the boy's frustration, Timothy kept quiet. He wasn't sure what to say.

'How can you stand it? Does it not sicken you? Don't you wish you could escape while you still have a chance?'

Timothy nodded. It was difficult to meet those eyes, so certain and defiant.

'Soon you must choose. The longer you wait, the weaker you grow. Soon they will have won and you won't even notice.' He reached into his cloak and pulled out a long curved dagger. The blade gleamed like fresh ice. The handle was beautifully carved, with fine silver designs. 'I can't give this to you yet. But soon.'

Talking to the boy gave Timothy a funny feeling in his stomach, a sort of happy vertigo. He yearned to stay with the boy. The thought of going back was hateful.

'Come.' Now they stood by an ornamental terrace topped with Grecian urns. Beyond the balustrade was an expanse of flat grey water that stretched onwards through the park. 'Here, across the water. This is the way. This is where you must go.' The boy pointed across the water. *The Serpentine*, Timothy thought to himself. *Kensington Gardens, this is where I am.* 'You must cross over. You must break through. You must follow the others who have gone before you. You must join us. Don't think of *them*, they won't help you. Empty your mind of them – your father, your mother, your friends, your teachers, your country. Most of all your country. Forget all these things.' He paused for a moment. The air was cold. When he spoke again his voice was so quiet and sad. 'It was so beautiful over there, before it started. Now the war is everywhere.' There was a weeping willow in his heart. 'We will come, silently, in the dead of night.' He sat close, holding up one finger. 'We must do this. There is no choice left any more. They lie and then they lie again. They have no heart, only a desert of thorns. War is everywhere.'

'I understand.'

When Timothy awoke it was hard to recall what the boy had said. Gazing across the wintry garden, all that he could distinctly remember was the boy's fierce sadness, like an icicle slowly melting inside him. *Not long now*, he thought.

Over breakfast, Mrs Dashwood declared that she wanted to go shopping in Knightsbridge for a new outfit. A special dinner was planned for next Friday, and all the directors of the company Timothy's father worked for were invited. 'You want me to look my best, don't you?' she stated, challenging his father to disagree. When he was at home and not away on business, Timothy's father never liked doing much at the weekend. He took breakfast slowly, lingering with the *Financial Times* and a plate of toast, marmalade and a pot of coffee. Sometimes breakfast could drag on until lunchtime. His father ruffled the paper and peered at his wife. Timothy knew the look he gave her was meant to tell her that she already had enough nice new expensive clothes. His mother put her cup down rather hard, causing a little tea to spill over into the saucer.

Timothy quietly finished his eggs, wondering what chance he had of persuading someone to come with him so they could take Muffy for a walk in the park together. It was a gloomy, chilly morning and he knew there was no point asking his mother, while his father had been opposed to Muffy from the start and refused to have anything to do with the dog. His mother wouldn't want them dragging round the shops with her either, and with his father certain to disappear into his study Timothy guessed he'd be left alone for the rest of the morning. Veca was supposed to have Saturdays free and she usually stayed in her room until lunchtime to make sure his mother wouldn't find any sneaky extra jobs for her to do. If he wanted to go to the park he'd have to ask her.

His father, spreading marmalade on a fresh slice of toast, said, 'Honey, you know I have far too much work to be going anywhere. I have an entire report to check by Monday.' He used the same knife for butter and marmalade. His teeth made a crunching noise, slicing through the toast. Timothy's mother spilt a little more tea and went upstairs. Shortly afterwards she reappeared in a gleaming black coat and boats, her hair tucked under a red woolly hat and her face half submerged behind enormous Gucci glasses. Timothy found his Mummy a little frightening sometimes, as if he couldn't quite believe she belonged to them.

'Goodbye, my lovely darling,' she chimed, removing her glasses to kiss Harry on his forehead and ruffle his hair. 'Oh Mum.' The boy scowled. 'Timmy . . .' Her fingers held his chin lightly, tilting his head up so he had to look at her. For a moment, her eyes seemed to cloud over and Timothy faltered, worried that she was going to embarrass them all with some strange display of emotion. 'My special boy,' she began and then, to his relief, her face opened into a beautiful smile. She always looked so wonderful when she smiled. 'Look after your father while I'm out. Make sure he doesn't get up to any mischief.' With that, and a flourish of scarf, handbag and hat, she was gone, pointedly ignoring her husband. Outside she hailed a passing taxi.

Timothy glanced back at his father.

'Timothy . . .' his father began, his voice trailing off.

'Yes, Daddy?'

For a troubling moment, Timothy thought his father didn't remember who he was. He had such a strange expression on his face, perplexed and despairing, that made him seem very old all of a sudden, an old man unsure of where he was. 'Have you seen that report that I . . . Oh, never mind, there it is.' His father picked up the report from where it had been left on his chair last night and retreated, without another word, into his study. Often, Timothy thought how one day his father really would be old, and one day after that he would die and there was nothing Timothy could do about it. He felt an uncanny, yearning sorrow for his father just then; it was hard to imagine a world without his father in his study, reading his reports. He often wondered what his father did in there, shut away for hours, or when he went off on business to those hot countries where the oil came from. Something had happened to his father on the last trip, but no one would tell them what. His mother would silence his questions with a sharp snap of her tongue. When he had come back, his father was different. Timothy didn't know why, but at night he had heard a sound as if his father was crying, a horrible, strangling sort of noise – but it couldn't be. He couldn't stand such a thought.

Harry vanished upstairs to play on the computer. Timothy considered joining him, but chose instead to go into the garden. Pulling on his trainers and coat, he unlocked the back door and went out, breathing in the cold, damp air. They had a small square of turf and gravel that his mother was always telling his father she wanted 'designed'. From this, a low iron gate opened into the communal gardens, which were as large as a small park and ran in a long strip behind all the houses on their street and the street next to it. Timothy opened the gate and stood at the edge of the lawn, shivering in the grey morning chill. A lone gardener was raking up leaves. Two fat squirrels chased each other up a tree. Following their movements, Timothy found himself scrutinising the high branches, even though they had shed their leaves and were too narrow for anyone to hide among anyway. All the same, he couldn't help looking.

Muffy was dozing in front of the television and, judging by her grumpy expression, was no more enthused by the idea of a walk around the chilly wet park than anyone else in the Dashwood household. Ignoring her plaintive expres-sion, Timothy roused the dog and together they went down to Veca's room. Veca was painting her toenails and listening to her iPod. She said she was meeting Marco, her German boyfriend, at Notting Hill Gate in half an hour. After some gentle prodding, Muffy simpered until Veca acquiesced and said 'Yes, all right, then.' They could all go for a short walk in Kensington Gardens.

They met Marco at the Tube station and set off together. Timothy walked ahead of the couple – partly because they could be so sickeningly soppy and he didn't want to listen to them getting gooey with each other – but also because he knew the Serpentine was quite far away and he wanted to make sure they got there. Muffy cheered up once she was out of the house and became quite excited by the other dogs in the park. Timothy let her off her lead and she ran round them in loping, gormless circles. The park had trapped an extra dose of morning gloom, a damp pall that sucked them in and shut out the rest of the world, like a little bit of the dream stranded on the waking shore. Veca and Marco fell behind, sharing a cigarette. Undaunted, Timothy pressed on, pretending not to hear their com-plaints about the cold. Now and then Muffy had to be discouraged from sniffing another dog or peeing against a tree, but the further in they went, the fewer people they seemed to encounter. Eventually they reached the Serpentine, a flat and grey expanse of water. The gloom was so thick that it was hard to see the other side – Timothy could just make out the darker streaks of distant trees and the white blobs of street lights, even though it was meant to be daytime. Ducks huddled together, heads buried under wings. Everything was very still – even the drone of traffic from the Bayswater Road sounded muted and far off.

Timothy breathed in deeply, tasting a little of the damp earth, letting the cold run into him. Here he was, just like in the dream. He wasn't sure what he had been expecting. Muffy was nearby, sniffing out some dog-trail or other. Perhaps it had been a mistake to come. The dream version, he seemed to remember, had been slightly different – the water had not been so still and flat, nor such a relentless, dull grey – and the park had been infinitely larger, a vast place where he could have hidden himself from the world and no one could have found him.

He was about to walk back to Veca and Marco when he saw another boy, about his age, crouching in the tall reeds by the edge of the water. 'Dashwood?' said the boy, 'Tim Dashwood?'

'Thornton?'

'I thought it was you.' Timothy felt a hardening inside. Thornton was part of Radley's gang. At school he *never* called him Tim, not like he had just then, quietly and cautiously: no, it was always just 'Timmy-wimmy,' like the others, flapping and twitching his arms. In fact, Thornton had never really spoken to him properly before.

'Yes,' said Timothy. 'It's me.'

'Yes.' Thornton scratched his hair and shifted from foot to foot.

'What are you doing here?' Normally Timothy would never have dared ask Thornton anything at all, but they seemed a long way from the rules of the classroom.

'I'm just . . .' Thornton made an empty gesture. 'With my parents, in the park, you know.' He shifted, not looking at Timothy. Thornton was a popular boy, good at sports and better still at taking the piss out of everyone else. It was a surprise to see him this way, all pale with harsh shadows under his eyes as if he'd been crying. His blond hair was messy and wet and his body looked somehow shrunken, as if he had withdrawn into himself. Even his clothes were dirty and rumpled, with mud splattered over his trousers. Timothy wondered if the boy had spent the night in the park, sitting by the water. Looking closer, Timothy was sure he was still wearing his school uniform under his coat.

'Are you okay?' he asked, but Thornton seemed to stare right through him, his empty blue eyes giving an answer, of sorts.

'I'm okay,' said Thornton.

'Okay. Well . . . I guess I'll see you then, Thornton.'

'Yeah. See you.'

Timothy glanced round one more time. He could see no sign of Thornton's parents – no sign of anyone at all. He called Muffy, who had been watching them both with great attention, and started back. Veca and Marco were under a tree, holding hands and talking intently about something. 'We can go home now,' he declared.

'Are you all right, Timmy?' Veca frowned.

'It's cold, that's all.'

As they started to walk away, Timothy allowed himself a final backward glance. Thornton was still standing by the water, as if he was waiting for someone.

Sunday

Just like that, Timothy was awake, his heart pounding: *Hurry* – they were in danger. He pulled open the window. *Hurry.* He was sure the boy would be there, sitting in the tree or standing on the lawn below. But no . . . nothing, not even a glimpse of his white kurta in the drab morning gloom.

Hurry.

Timothy closed the window and lay back down on his bed. Had he been dreaming? He was sure he could still hear the faint strain of his flute, playing so soft and melancholy somewhere far away.

Yesterday Mrs Dashwood had returned home in the late afternoon with several glitzy bags of shopping. She fluffed and huffed about, holding up skirts, scarves and a pair of 'darling' boots to Veca, who sat nursing a cup of cocoa and wearing her usual jeans and brown jumper. His father didn't come out of his study until it was time for the seven o'clock news and even then he didn't really speak to anyone. Of course, his mother wanted her husband to admire her new purchases or else get annoyed because she'd spent so much money, but his father wasn't playing. He just sat in his chair, *FT* spread over his knees, frowning at the television.

After dinner Mrs Dashwood declared she had an 'intolerable' headache and stretched out on the sofa. Muffy was confined to her bed in the laundry room and Timothy and Harry were sent upstairs early. They played their favourite computer game. Timothy was the insurgents, Harry the coalition forces. Thanks to a well-placed car bomb and an expert rocket attack on a torture camp, Timothy made it to the next level. Harry staged a worthy counter-offensive until one of his cruise missiles went awry, missing the rebel base and hitting a children's hospital instead. Then it was bedtime.

Still shaking off the dream, Timothy ventured downstairs. His father was already up and at the breakfast table with the paper. 'Be good to your mother today,' he said, loading his toast with orange marmalade. 'She's been having one of her migraines.'

Timothy's mother's migraines were rather like her headaches, but worse. When they had lived in the country she used to have them all the time and would lie very still in her bedroom, curtains closed tight against the light, complaining about the smallest noise anywhere in the house.

Only a little later, as his father tucked into his second plate of toast, did she come downstairs wrapped in her fluffy pink dressing gown, her eyes puffy and small. She peered at her family as if scrutinising specimens under a microscope.

'Mummy, can you help me with my homework?' asked Harry.

'Ask your father. I have to go out later.' She took a bottle of mineral water from the fridge.

'Daddy?

'We'll see. Daddy has homework to do as well, you know.'

It was hard for Timothy to know how seriously to take his mother's migraine. She ate some fruit and drank more water, disappeared upstairs for a shower and then reappeared in a long blue coat with a pink pashmina wrapped around her neck. She gave both boys a brief, intense hug, whispering 'Love you' in Timothy's ear before hurrying out. Their father had already locked himself in his study. The two brothers sat about together, vaguely bored. There was nothing fun on TV. Harry went to his room to do his homework. Veca was out with Marco. Muffy was restless, sniffing around the window and hall. Weekends were often like this, his mother off doing one thing, his father working and the rest of house feeling large and empty.

At lunchtime Timothy's father emerged to get some food and watch the news. 'Where's your mother?' he asked Timothy.

'She went out earlier.'

'Did she say where?'

Timothy shook his head.

His father sighed and sat down next to Timothy, mobile in one hand, black coffee in the other. He made a call on his phone.

Timothy listened as his father attempted to ask his mother how she was. He could tell by the pained expression on his father's face that things weren't going well. Abruptly, he put down his phone and swore under his breath. One hand ran across his face. His stubble looked particularly blue and rough this morning. He turned on the TV and they sat for a while watching in silence. The news had been bad yesterday and today it was even worse. Huge crowds filled a dusty street, chanting and shouting, firing guns in the air and waving flags as coffin after coffin, each adorned with flags and portraits, was carried aloft through the throng, bobbing like boats in a fearsome sea. The reporter wore a blue helmet and flak jacket and kept flinching at the shooting in the background. Grainy videotape showed a middle-aged American woman desperately pleading for her life. Men stood over her with Kalashnikovs and swords. A strange flag marked with a palm print hung on the wall. The commentator spoke about escalations and negotiations. There was a shot of the Prime Minister waving away questions. Timothy was used to these things.

'Daddy?'

'Yes, Tim?'

'What do you dream about when you sleep?'

'I don't know.' Daddy flinched. 'I'm too tired these days to dream anyway. I don't dream any more.' He gave a weak sort of smile. 'Why do you ask?'

'Oh . . . nothing.' There was a news story about football. 'Daddy?'

'Yes, Tim?'

'Sometimes, well . . .' Timothy paused. It could be quite difficult, trying to tell his father something. Usually his words would come out all wrong and it made him feel shy and awkward. Sometimes his father just ignored him, but he usually had his own idea about things, and whatever it was Timothy had tried to say would be engulfed by the answer. Still, he tried: 'Once, I had this dream about a boy.

I think he was from where we used to live. Soldiers had killed his family and wanted to kill him.'

His father looked at him as if he knew something but wasn't sure what to say. 'Well . . .' he began. 'We all have dreams a bit like that, sometimes. It's just a dream. Perhaps you should go and do some homework instead of watching the news.'

Timothy wanted to say something else but he didn't. He picked at a scab on his knee. The weather forecast promised rain. 'Daddy?'

'Yes, Timmy? What is it?'

'Nothing, Daddy . . . nothing.'

His father smiled: 'You're a good boy, Tim. Don't worry. You don't need to worry about these things. Everything will be all right, I promise. Your mother will be back soon. You *will* make an effort to be especially nice to her tonight, won't you?'

'Yes, Daddy.'

Timothy went and sat on his bed. He had a big soft toy crocodile, bright green with big yellow eyes and a silly expression. He lay back on his bed, hugging the toy. He had a little homework to do, but he had a feeling that it wasn't so important any more.

Monday

Timothy was glad when Edward arrived, taking his usual seat beside him in class. Traffic had been unusually light and Timothy had arrived at school much earlier than usual. It was never a good idea, he had learnt, to arrive at class before Mr Clarke. For some reason, Jason Radley was always early. With Peter, his older brother, they would hang around the back of the classroom, mimicking their father in his office – or how they imagined their father behaved – putting their feet on the table, chewing felt-tip cigars, bullshitting each other and randomly brutalising the other boys in class.

'Hello,' whispered Edward as he sat down.

'Hello.'

'Okay?'

'Fine. Yeah. You?'

'Fine. Did you do anything at the weekend?'

'No. Did you?'

'No.'

Mr Clarke came blustering into class. 'Sorry I'm late, boys,' he said, removing the register from his desk. He was wearing a pale grey suit that Timothy didn't remember seeing before.

He turned to Edward once more. 'Did you, you know . . . Did you dream about him?' he asked.

'Yes.' Edward looked down at his desk. 'Yes, a lot.'

'Gaylord!' someone shouted.

'Silence, boys.' Mr Clarke banged the register on his desk. It took another three bangs, each one louder than the last, before the class finally settled down. 'Radley, I said silence . . . Radley, did you hear what I said?'

'Sorry, sir, I didn't hear you, actually, sir, because you kept making such a noise with the register, sir, banging it like that.'

'Are you trying to piss me off, Radley?'

'Not at all sir, just explaining things to you—'

'Shut it, Radley.'

Timothy quelled his desire to ask Edward more questions and kept quiet. It was never a good idea to be caught talking by Mr Clarke, especially if you were generally thought of as a 'good student'. For some reason his sarcasm was always much more severe when he inflicted it on the good students. At times Timothy even wondered if the bullies and the teachers were in cahoots together, the various punishments they inflicted on the rest of the school signifiers of some wider, deeper power struggle.

Mr Clarke opened the register. There were many parts of the day that Timothy dreaded – many opportunities for him to be humiliated, abused and mocked. This was the first. He loathed the register: for some the mere mention of his name was enough to provoke the cruel temper of the class.

Mr Clarke started: 'Browning.'

'Sir.'

'Campbell.'

'Sir.'

'Caruthers.'

'Here sir.'

Now – his turn: 'Dashwood?'

'Here.'

The morning, so far, was merciful. No mocking laughter or cruel shrieks. When provoked, such a response would whip through the class like wildfire – *wishy-washy, Timmy-wimmy* – sweeping from one boy to the next, much too fast for Mr Clarke to stop. Mr Clarke usually ignored it anyway, content to let the boys carry out their own ordering of the social hierarchy. By the time he got to Pritchard, Radley and Saunders the malicious wave was usually broken, leaving Timothy to nurse his stung feelings.

Onward Clarke went, on through the register: 'Present, sir.' 'Sir.' 'Yes, sir.' 'Present, sir.'

Thornton's seat was empty. 'Thornton?' Mr Clark called his name a second time, in a slightly louder voice, as if Thornton was hiding under the floor.

'Sir, sir, Thornton's not here, sir,' called Radley. 'I think he's skiving, sir.'

'Thank you, Radley, I can see that.'

'Sir, he said he wasn't coming in Monday, sir, he told me, sir.'

'Thank you, Radley. Be quiet, please. Whitehead. Whitehead?'

'Sir!'

'Williams?'

'Sir, here, sir.'

Mr Clarke snapped shut the register. The bell for first period rang. Timothy glanced at Edward – they were seg-regated in different sets until the afternoon – and set off.

French first period and, as it was the last week of term, Mr Raul showed a video about the South of France. Timothy made doodles while the programme droned on. *Ici la plage.* He didn't want to go to the South of France. Weariness enveloped him. He thought of the news again, the young men fighting tanks and gunships with stones and rocket-propelled grenades.

A sharp knock at the door and Mr Walker, the deputy head, entered and whispered something to Mr Raul. The two left the classroom. The video went on but nobody paid attention. Both teachers returned and Mr Raul paused the video. Mr Walker stood at the front of the class and called out half a dozen names, Timothy's included. All the selected boys were from his class, 3-C. 'Pack up your books,' he declared, 'and follow me.'

With Mr Walker at the rear, the group were escorted back to their form room. Inside, Timothy saw the rest of his class, sitting at their desks and guarded by a prefect from the top year. Quickly, he took his usual seat beside Edward.

'Keep quiet, 3-C,' announced Mr Walker. 'If you have any prep, do your prep. If you don't have any prep, do some reading.'

'But Mr Walker, sir?'

'What is it, Radley? Don't you understand a simple instruction?'

'I thought we had maths next, sir.'

'Radley, shut it. Do some prep or read a book.'

'I don't have a book to read, sir, or any prep.'

'Perhaps I should set some extra work for you, then?' When Mr Walker said something, he meant it. Radley shut up. 'That goes double for the rest of you,' he added. 'Not a word, 3-C, I'm warning you now, not one word.'

A knock at the door and Reverend Fowler, the school

vicar, entered. Quiet words were exchanged with Mr Walker.

'Browning, take your bags and follow Reverend Fowler.'

Stephen Browning did as he was told.

Timothy watched the door close on the boy and turned back to his books. He didn't have much prep, just a few equations. Quietly, he started working through them, trying to take his mind off what was happening. He was sure he hadn't done anything wrong and he couldn't believe that their class, as a unit, had been so naughty that they deserved this collective confinement. But something strange was definitely happening and the uncertainty was perplexing. He glanced at Edward. Edward shrugged. He looked at Edward again and Edward moved his arm, tilting his book a fraction so that Timothy could see the answer to question three. Timothy had just finished question four when another knock announced the return of Reverend Fowler, alone.

'Campbell, Luke Campbell. Take your things and follow Reverend Fowler, please.'

Campbell went. It struck Timothy that they were being sent out in alphabetical order – Caruthers would be next and then it would be his, Timothy's turn. After such a thought it was impossible to concentrate on his equations: his nerves were suddenly on edge. Sure enough, a few minutes later Reverend Fowler returned for Caruthers. They were gone some time. Now, Caruthers had never liked Timothy much and he was a good friend of Thornton's. Timothy wrote *Thornton?* on the back of his rough book and turned it for Edward to see. Edward nodded and wrote in the margin, *He's gone.* Mr Walker approached their table. Instinctively, both boys returned to their equations, heads bowed studiously. The soles of Mr Walker's shoes made a squeaking noise as he paced back and forth. Timothy gazed at the next equation, but his mind was far away. Caruthers had been gone for about twenty minutes. Mr Walker stood by the window and seemed, in the pale watery light, like a papier-mâché man. The bell rang for the new period. One or two boys looked to Mr Walker, wondering if they were supposed to go, but he ignored them and remained turned to the world outside. A few minutes later the Reverend Fowler returned, once more alone. Timothy felt his anxiety deepen. What had happened to the other boys?

'Dashwood,' announced Mr Walker. 'Your turn. Follow the Reverend.'

Reverend Fowler's smile was thin and impersonal, like a letter from the bank. He was an old man who, if the rumours were true, had been at the school almost forty years. 'Come.' Despite his age, the Reverend swept down the corridors, black gown billowing behind him. Timothy followed, left, right, past the great hall and the dining hall with its familiar starchy smell and then upstairs to the headmaster's office. The Reverend knocked once and opened the door. Another thin-lipped smile and Timothy was ushered inside.

He had never before been to the headmaster's office and the room was much larger than he had imagined. At his end, near the door and by the window, was a modern desk with a swivel chair, computer and photocopier. The other side of the room was dominated by a grand dark-wood table around which sat Dr Scott – the headmaster – Mr Clarke, the lady detective from Friday's assembly and, right at the back, another older man. The walls were panelled in dark wood and hung with gilt-framed paintings of old men and a prominent portrait of the Queen. All the wood, not to mention the queasy feeling in his stomach, gave Timothy the impression of being in the bowels of an old ship, called before the captain on suspicion of mutiny.

'Sit down, Timothy,' said Dr Scott, gesturing towards a single plastic chair. Timothy took the seat, too over-whelmed in that moment to look anyone in the face. Reverend Fowler placed a hand on his shoulder. Perhaps the gesture was supposed to comfort him, he couldn't tell. A cold shiver crawled through his body. Hoping for some reassurance, Timothy glanced at his teacher, but Mr Clarke wouldn't meet his eye. The man at the back, half hidden in the gloom, made a loud slurping noise as he supped a cup of tea.

'Timothy,' began Dr Scott, 'this is Detective Sergeant Kennedy. She was at the school on Friday. You saw her, didn't you?'

'Yes, sir.'

'Hello, Timothy,' said the detective. She smiled but her smile didn't make Timothy feel any better either. 'Timothy, Mr Clarke tells me you're new to the school. Is that right?'

'Yes.'

'You joined this September.'

'Yes.'

'So this is your first term?'

'Yes.'

'Are you settling in? Are you making friends? Do you like it here?'

'Yes.'

'Good. Now, I just want to ask you a few questions about a boy in your class, William Thornton. Now, we are wor-ried about William. You see, his parents don't know where he is. They haven't seen him since Friday night. This means we now have two boys who have gone missing from school and as you can imagine this is causing us all some concern.'

DS Kennedy paused and glanced back at the strange man in the corner. He put down his cup and nodded at her. 'So, William is a friend of yours, isn't he?'

Timothy didn't say anything. He didn't know what to say. How could he tell them what it was really like? Again he looked to Mr Clarke, but still his teacher avoided him.

'Go on, boy,' said the headmaster. 'Don't be shy. Is William your friend?'

'No . . . no, sir, not much, really, I don't know him well at all.' Timothy looked at the floor and tried to resist the urge to bite his nails. He was sure that Mr Clarke would have already told them that Thornton was not his friend. They must know that much.

'I see. Well, has William – or any of his friends – have they said anything to you that might suggest where he could be? Did they talk about running away from home? Did William say he was unhappy? Anything like that.'

Timothy shook his head in one long 'no'. He felt the pressure of ten adult–teacher–police eyes scrutinising him and a prickly guilty flush began to brighten his cheeks. They would want to know that he had seen Thornton in the park and he knew he should tell them. He would be in trouble if he didn't say anything – or if he lied – and they found out. He knew it. There was no reason for him to be Thornton's secret-keeper anyway, and yet he felt reluctant to speak, as if to tell them about the encounter in the park – such as it was – would be to betray far more than he fully appreciated.

'Timothy,' Dr Scott spoke again, 'according to our records you are collected from school each day in a car by the au pair. I take it this is correct information.'

'Yes, it is, sir.'

'You don't walk or get the Tube or bus home? Not even once in a while?'

'No, sir. I'm not allowed to, sir.'

'Good.' Dr Scott dabbed his bald head with a handkerchief.

The policewoman wrote something in a notebook before continuing: 'And you've not seen anything out of the ordinary, or heard any other boys talking about any suspicious activity, have you?'

'No, sir, no, I haven't, sir.' Timothy felt himself blush all the more fiercely for calling the lady 'sir'. What an idiot! But there were no women teachers at Brompton Boys – apart from the nurse and the head librarian. Idiot! He blushed deeper still.

Dr Scott, Reverend Fowler and Mr Clarke exchanged the sort of knowing look that teachers were always giving to each other. The policewoman asked Timothy a few more questions but they weren't about anything important and were easy to answer anyway because he knew so little about Thornton. She asked a few questions about the other missing boy as well, but there was nothing for him to say, as he knew even less about Anderson. Then she produced a file with pages of photographs of men who, she said, were known to have kidnapped children before. She started going through the photographs, allowing Timothy a little time to study each page. The men just looked like men – there was nothing special about any of them. He knew the moment he saw the first page that they didn't have anything to do with what was going on. When DS Kennedy finished with the book she made another note and glanced again to the man at the back of the table. Timothy was aware that the man had been watching him throughout the interview; but because the room was quite gloomy and the man sat so still he hadn't really been able to register his presence yet, not properly.

Now the man began to speak. 'Timothy – look at me, will you, Timothy? That's better. Look me in the eye, if you please.' Timothy did as he was told. He looked at the man: there was a sense of ruin about him, his eyes like blue stars sunken into lizard slits and ringed with melancholy lines. With his pencil-thin moustache and surprisingly long and glossy hair, dark as freshly spilled ink and extravagantly curled, his countenance exuded the worn demeanour of a gargoyle or totem pole. But at the same time there was something charming about the detective. He projected a rough glamour, a sense of decadent mystery quite at odds with his profession. 'Have you seen William? Do you have any idea, any idea at all, why he might have run away? I don't want you to be frightened, Timothy, but I don't want you to lie, either. Boys sometimes get frightened, you know.'

Perhaps it was the man's voice – his commanding air, a superior tone that put the boy in mind of shabby chateaus or neglected monuments, of a great respectability run to seed. The man's suit was as black as his hair, while the collar of his tieless shirt was unbuttoned to expose a curl of twisting chest hair and emphasise the ever so slightly grotesque twitch of his Adam's apple: up and down it went, like a stone trapped in his throat. Unconsciously, Timothy felt himself touching his own. He knew his voice was about to break – the voices of several other boys in the class had already fallen – but he found it hard to imagine how he could accommodate such growth without choking. But he didn't really know why he was staring with such intensity at the policeman's throat. Perhaps because he felt sure that no adult, not even his father, had ever looked at him with such a concentrated degree of interest before. Then he noticed that the man kept his left hand in a glove.

To Timothy's astonishment the man made a pulling, twisting motion and, releasing a sigh as if he was putting down a heavy bag, he detached his hand in a single smooth motion. To the boy's further horror, he placed the prosthesis on the table before them and, with another, more profound sigh, scratched the stump with the fingers of his good hand. Unable not to look, Timothy saw how the arm tapered off just above the wrist to a fleshy point, encircled by a lattice of white scars. The man kept looking at Timothy as he did all this, as if daring him to react, challenging him to make some show of shock or horror at his disfigurement and so making it all the harder for the boy to maintain his composure. Despite himself, Timothy kept watching as the man scratched the stump with his nails, rubbing at it while he talked on. 'You said William was not a friend of yours. Is that correct?'

Timothy swallowed, nodding in agreement.

'And you are new to the year, a recent recruit to the school.' The man licked his lips. 'It's not always easy to make friends, Timothy, is it? Not when you join on your own, not when you're the new boy.'

'No, sir.'

'Your form teacher tells me the boys tease you sometimes.'

Timothy felt himself blush again, with shame this time, as if it was his fault that they teased him. He shrugged, trying to shake off the blush, trying to show it didn't matter what they did, he didn't care.

'They used to tease me too, when I was a boy,' the man continued. 'Boys do that. They can be very cruel sometimes, boys, even the best boys. Especially the best boys. Little savages they are, just waiting to take over. But even so, Timothy, this boy, William Thornton, you might hate him, you might think he's the biggest shit on the planet, I don't care.' The man sniffed – loudly. No one objected to his use of the word 'shit'. It was clear that the detective – he must have been that, Timothy decided – didn't care what anyone else thought. Briefly, the boy was reminded of a man in the Saudi compound, a journalist who Mummy said drank too much. He always had a red face, that man, like he'd been boiled in a pot of hot water; but then *that man* had certainly never spoken to Timothy.

'If Thornton is in danger, then all of you are in danger. Quite frankly, it is as simple as that. These are dangerous times and I know – yes – I am sure there is something else that you haven't told me yet. Please tell me, Timothy.' The gloved hand fitted back onto the man's arm with a click. He tugged the sleeve of his shirt over it. 'Come along now – I am waiting.'

'I . . . I think I saw him,' Timothy felt his face burning. He told himself again that he had no loyalty to Thornton. 'I did see him. In the park . . . on Saturday.'

'Which park?'

'Kensington Gardens. By the Serpentine.'

'What was he doing, Timothy?'

'He was . . . I don't know.' Timothy looked away. 'Just walking, I think, with his parents.'

'Did you see his parents?'

'No, I didn't actually see them.'

'Good. And what was Thornton doing?'

Timothy paused, choosing his words carefully. 'He walked past me. We saw each other and said hello, nothing else. I didn't really notice.'

'Who did you go to the park with?'

'My au pair, Veca, and her boyfriend.'

'Did they see William?'

'I don't think so, sir. They were by a tree, kissing each other.' Timothy blushed a little more.

'And how did William look?'

'Fine. I don't know. Fine. There wasn't anything wrong with him. At least, I don't think so.'

'He didn't seem out of sorts at all?'

'He seemed a little tired.'

'He looked tired?'

'I guess. I mean, sir, like he hadn't had much sleep. A bit pale.'

'A bit pale?'

'Yes, that's right, sir.'

'I see.' The man sat back. 'And what time was this?'

Timothy felt himself flush. 'I'm not sure. I think . . .' He swallowed. 'It was the morning. I think it was the middle of the morning.' His face felt hot and there was a bright white space in the middle of his thoughts.

'Eleven? That sort of time.'

Timothy nodded nervously. He didn't look up. He didn't want to see them all, watching him.

Thankfully, the man seemed satisfied, in a way. 'I can't think of anything else I want to ask this boy, not for the moment, at least.' He nodded at Dr Scott and then turned back to Timothy. 'Thank you, Timothy. I think I will need to speak to you again, before the end of term if I can. Okay?'

'That's fine, of course.' Dr Scott bowed his head ever so slightly at the man, 'No problem.'

'Come along, Timothy.'

The Reverend led him from the room. 'Now, that wasn't so bad, was it?' Another thin, empty smile. Timothy was taken to another classroom. Caruthers, Campbell and Browning sat at desks while three senior prefects stood guard over them, evidently relishing their power.

'Okay, Timothy,' said the Reverend, 'you've got to sit here and do some prep. Stay here until Mr Walker comes to fetch you. Keep quiet. Strictly no talking, understand?'

'Yes, sir.'

The Reverend walked away. Feeling the prefects watching him, Timothy found a table at the back of the classroom, furthest from the others. He wasn't going to do any more prep. Instead, he took out a library book. Some of the pages had been underlined in red biro. He read carefully.

The young men sat in a circle in the castle on the high mountain. The old man was speaking: 'In the kasbah they showed me the suffering, they showed me the conditions they had to live under while they were occupied by the French, the British, the Israelis, the Americans, the Russians . . . And they showed me what they had to do to get those people off their backs. The first thing they had to realise was that all of them were brothers: oppression made them brothers; exploitation made them brothers; degradation made them brothers; discrimination made them brothers; segregation made them brothers; humiliation made them brothers . . .' The audience, their eyes red from smoking hashish, nodded along to what the old man was saying. 'I read a story once where someone asked some group of people how many of them wanted freedom. They all put up their hands. There were three hundred in the room. Then the person said, "How many of you are ready to kill anybody who gets in your way for freedom?" About fifty put up their hand. And he told those fifty, "You stand over there." That left two hundred and fifty who wanted freedom, but weren't ready to kill for it. So he told the fifty, "You want freedom and you said you'd kill anybody who stood in your way. You see those two hundred and fifty? You get them first. Some of them are your own brothers and sisters and mothers and fathers. They are afraid to do what is necessary to get it and they'll stop you from doing it. Those are the first you must kill in the fight for your freedom."' The young men nodded. The hour was late: a cold, night wind blew against the castle walls, promising snow . . .

The class was detained throughout lunchtime until all the boys had been questioned. Threats of mass detention for Friday – the last day of term – ensured silence. Finally, the Reverend Fowler and Mr Walker re-entered the class accompanied by Andrew Wallace, last in the class alphabet. Mr Walker told them to keep what they had told the police to themselves and declared that Thornton's disappearance was not a suitable topic of gossip. The fact that he had gone missing had nothing to do with Thomas Anderson's disappearance. 'After all,' he added, 'you aren't even in the same year.' Then he went on for a bit about the need to 'stay alert' and 'be careful'. Timothy thought all his lines came from the police. The bell sounded for the post-lunch classes and they were released.

'You didn't tell them anything, did you?' Edward sidled up to Timothy in the corridor.

Timothy flushed for a moment, embarrassed at how the one-armed policeman had somehow made him talk. 'They asked a lot of questions, though.'

'Did they? They didn't ask me much at all.'

'Oh well. I don't know. That guy with the hand, though . . . who was he? He really freaked me out.'

Edward nodded. 'He made me feel kind of weird too.'

They split for separate classes – Edward was in the higher set for physics. A look passed between them before Edward turned off towards the new labs and Timothy went down to the old laboratory in the basement. He spent the rest of the afternoon pretending to work, quietly worrying that he'd given something away, but exactly what, or to whom, he couldn't really decide. He tried telling himself it was best if the police found Thornton, best for everyone: he knew this to be the case and yet, raging inside him like a vast sandstorm, the feeling was very different.

Finally, the school bell sounded the end of what had been a very long afternoon. Another letter was given out that explained the police had spoken to the boys as part of their 'routine investigation' and that any further questioning would only be conducted with parents present. The letter didn't mention any details – it didn't even give Thornton's name. Timothy threw it away as he exited the school. There was no point showing it to Mummy. She would only fret.

When they got back from school, Timothy was surprised to find his father already home. He sat in his chair, a cup of tea untouched on the table beside him. The queasy feeling of guilt that Timothy had felt after talking to the police had persisted and now the sight of his father, sitting there and waiting for him, made it hard not to think that he knew something was going on – as if they were all in it together, parents and teachers and police officers.

'Hi, Daddy.'

'Timothy. How are you? How was school? That bad?'

'They kept us in all lunchtime. They wanted to talk to us.'

'Why?'

'Oh, you know, this boy that went missing and stuff.' The boy felt a great reluctance to say any more, as if he had already given away more than he should have.

'Susan,' his father shouted, 'what's this about a boy who went missing?'

'I know,' his mother called from the kitchen. 'Isn't it awful?'

'But how?'

'He was on the Tube – can you imagine? Some parents.' She made an exasperated noise.

'I see.'

'They've got police at school talking to people,' she added.

'Gosh. Well. That must be exciting, mustn't it?' Timothy's father smiled, but it was a weak smile with no real feeling in it.

'Boys.' Their mother came through from the kitchen, her nails newly painted a shiny intense purple. 'Your father would like to talk to you.'

Mr Dashwood looked suddenly very weary, like a mere tracing of himself, his face leached of colour. For the first time Timothy noticed the grey in his father's hair. Then, not really looking at them and smiling this awkward, painful sort of smile, he started to speak. 'Now I don't want you to get worried – it hasn't been settled yet or anything – but I may need to go back to the Gulf, probably Saudi, maybe even Iraq. I might have to go quite soon – that was why I thought I ought to tell you.'

'Again?' asked Timothy.

'Will you have to go for long?' asked Harry.

'What about us? Are we coming with you?' Timothy added.

'Can we come too, Daddy? Can we?'

Timothy glanced at his little brother, surprised by his enthusiasm.

'No, I should think not. I'll be going alone. You've got schooling to do, and your Mummy to look after as well, of course. If I do go – and it's really not that clear yet – I shouldn't think it would be for long.'

'Maybe six months.' Mrs Dashwood's face shut tight.

'Probably not even that. And I'll be able to come back here quite often. At least once a month.'

'I wish we could come too,' Harry said again. 'It's so boring here.'

'Well.' Their father winced. 'It'll be pretty boring over there too. I'll just be working, you know.'

'Why are you going?' Harry added.

'It's complicated.'

'Why is it complicated?'

'Your father is tired,' snapped their mother. 'Don't pester him.'

'But why?'

'*Harry.*'

'It's all right.' Timothy saw the way their father looked at their mother. 'There has been a bit of a problem, in Iraq, you see. Our security was breached and, well, it's complicated . . .' An expression of strange distress darkened their father's face, like oil spreading from a ruptured pipeline. Something had happened: Timothy could sense it clearly, like a sort of undertow of the nerves, a jolting, downward pull. But he couldn't think what that 'something' was: there were only the images he saw on the news, the suicide bombs and assassinations, the soldiers like insects with their body armour and goggles, the great flat city shimmering in a hot afternoon haze. So close that sometimes he felt he could taste it . . . 'Now, why don't you both come here and give your father a hug.'

Obediently, they walked forward. Timothy felt their father's arms encircle them both and, embarrassed by this display, tried not to cringe too much. For a moment he felt the man's rough stubble on his own soft cheek and smelt that Daddish smell which only his father had. While Mr

Dashwood squeezed both the boys, Timothy lightly put his own arm, the one he could get free, around his father's shoulder. 'I love you both,' said their dad, although there was something about the way he said it that made Timothy wonder. Not that he doubted his father's love – it was just the overwhelming feeling he had that the man had something to do over there that was more important than all of them.

'Daddy,' he said, 'are you sure it won't be dangerous?'

'Of course not,' said Mr Dashwood.

'Don't be silly, Timothy,' said their mother.

'It's just that—'

'Everything will be fine. You mustn't worry about those things. Just concentrate on your school work and I'll be back in no time.'

'It's not even settled yet,' added their mother. 'Daddy might not even go at all. So don't start fretting about anything.'

Veca entered the room. 'Urgent call for Mr Dashwood,' she said.

Their father's face closed like a barrier. 'I'll take it in my study, thank you, Veca.' He was gone for most of the evening.

Tuesday

The next morning Mr Clarke skipped Thornton's name when he took the register. Sitting there, Timothy couldn't help but look at the missing boy's empty desk and chair, as if they held the clue to all that was wrong with the world. Unusually, Mr Walker conducted morning assembly. He gave a very long Bible reading about obeying authority. Timothy wasn't sure, but he thought Mr Walker was keeping an extra-close eye on his class, glancing at them every time he came to a particularly pertinent passage. All this business about God watching them made Timothy think about CCTV cameras, which he thought must be like the eyes of God, ever watchful: all the known world committed to tape, stored and secure and ready to be seen over and over again – God, CCTV cameras, all that and other things besides. They were being watched, that was certain, but the watcher didn't have anything to do with God.

The whole day was unhinged. First period, geography, and Jason Radley picked a huge fight with Mr Forbes, normally one of the most docile and amiable of masters.

A red-faced and outraged Mr Forbes was reduced to shouting, 'Get out, you little shit, get out of my sight,' while Radley, startled by the violence of his ejection, nonetheless maintained enough cool to delay his exit from the class, gesturing at Mr Forbes as he strolled out, each mocking twitch of his fingers coaxing further cries from the embattled teacher. Once Radley was gone a precarious, embarrassed silence filled the room, the atmosphere sharp as broken glass, the boys watching Mr Forbes with appalled delight as he struggled to compose himself.

The uneasiness persisted: in French, third period, Timothy was smartly upbraided for whispering to Edward. At lunchtime a fight erupted in the playground between two boys from his class – Austin Scatherby and Wilfred Rawls – a ferocious battle all the more extraordinary because both boys, being rather small and wimpish, were normally quiet and well behaved. They were nerds, awful at games and frequent victims of Radley's taunts – the very bottom of the Brompton Boys food chain. And yet there they were, swinging with fists and then writhing on the ground, two pairs of glasses knocked aside, Rawls gaining the upper hand, straddling his opponent and grappling with Scatherby's defensive hands, trying to punch his face. The growing circle of watching boys, thrilled by the escalating violence chanted, 'Fight, fight, fight,' and 'Smash him' and 'Break him, bust him down.' The mob was fifty strong before Mr Walker and two other teachers intervened, pulling the combatants apart. Blood streamed from Scatherby's nose and lip, while vivid red scratches marked Rawls's cheeks. A frenzied Rawls resisted the teachers, kicking and swearing as Dr Morgan and Mr Walker attempted to seize him. A burly senior prefect was required to pin back his arms and a brisk clip across the back of his ears was administered before the boy could be subdued. Glowering, pale and clearly shaken, he was marched swiftly away. Scatherby followed behind, tearfully nursing his wounds.

By mid-afternoon the grapevine reported that Rawls had been suspended until the start of next term, while Scatherby was last seen, his face in bandages, being driven home by his chauffeur in the family Jaguar. Radley loudly declared that if he'd known Rawls would get an early holiday just for beating up a 'poof' like Scatherby he would have done it himself.

At the end of school, as he packed his bag, Timothy was surprised to be approached by Stephen Murphy, one of Thornton's best friends. Murphy was a very popular boy: his father, they said, was a multi-millionaire, and Stephen looked old for his age – at least sixteen – but he was handsome anyway, with clear blue eyes, a regular, likeable face and thick black hair. Intelligent, confident and articulate, Murphy excelled with seemingly little effort in every subject. And he was vice-captain of the rugby team and captain of the cricket, which made him a virtual god by Brompton Boys standards. Timothy knew that Murphy lived in his neighbourhood: he'd seen him walking around Notting Hill Gate a couple of times – once with a very pretty blonde girl. The sight reminded Timothy how Murphy had claimed, several times, that not only did he have a girlfriend but that she let him 'touch her pussy'. The possibility that the pussy Murphy claimed to have touched belonged to the same girl that Timothy had seen was, perhaps, the most sickeningly jealous-making aspect of it all. Needless to say, a divinity like Murphy *never* spoke to a nonentity like Timothy.

It was therefore a surprise when Murphy came up to him. Timothy felt himself blush with a mixture of pleasure and fear. He was acutely aware that Edward was standing beside him, watching fiercely because Murphy never spoke to him either.

'Look—'

'What?' Timothy felt something take hold inside him.

'Don't think we don't know.' Murphy kept his voice low. His throat was pulsing and his fists were clenched: the boy was angry, very angry.

'Know what? What are you talking about?'

'You *know*. You can't lie to me.'

'I'm not lying.'

For an instant Murphy seemed astonished that Timothy had even spoken back to him. 'We know,' he said again. 'We know about Thornton, we *know*. Some of us aren't going to go that way. It won't be that easy. We have to take a stand. People like you. You think it's all a joke.' He put his face up close to Timothy. 'We know what you did. We're watching you. You don't realise how lucky you are.'

Timothy faltered, shocked by what Murphy was saying. Part of him wanted to laugh at the absurdity of it all and part of him just wanted to smash Murphy's face in.

There was more: 'There is going to be a fight, you know. A fight to the death. Don't think we don't know. Our way will win out. We are in the right. So watch your back, *Dashwood*. We'll get you sooner or later. Just you wait.'

That seemed to be it. Then, as Murphy stepped away,

the words just came to Timothy: 'Go fuck yourself, Murphy. You prick. What do I care about what you know?' He shoved past, bashing Murphy with his bag. A dozen equally astonished faces watched him leave the room. 3-C had never seen such a violation of the social order. Outside, Timothy felt his confidence evaporate and, fearing imminent reprisals – it was the end of school, after all – he ran to the sanctuary of the car.

'Sweetie! Hello! Give your mummy a kiss!' Timothy was astonished to find his mother waiting for him. 'You're not embarrassed to kiss your mother, are you?'

'Not here! Not at school!' He couldn't believe she could do this.

She sighed, started the engine and pulled out into the traffic. 'Well, I thought you'd be pleased to have me collect you from school for a change. I've got some crisps for you. Harry, give your brother some crisps.'

'Where's Veca?' he replied, glancing at his brother.

'I gave the poor girl the afternoon off. She's been working ever so hard and I missed my little boys. Oh, I'm so proud of you.'

'Mum – please!' Timothy sighed, taking the packet of smoky-bacon crisps that his brother offered.

'I'm your mother. I'm allowed to be proud of you. I'm always proud of you.'

As she spoke, they became snarled in traffic around South Kensington Tube. Still rocked by his reckless audacity after confronting Murphy like that, Timothy noticed several police vehicles parked around the station. Always fascinated by the police, he watched as they used dogs to check people's bags. A young Asian man, his hands bound, was being led into the back of a police van. Timothy wasn't sure – it wasn't really possible to be sure of such things, anyway – but he thought the man looked straight at him, his lips mouthing a word he couldn't decipher. Then the van's door closed, the lights changed and the Dashwood's car moved forwards, back into the ordinary push and shove of the city.

Wednesday

A new rumour swept through class. William Thornton, everybody was saying, had gone to meet his older brother. This brother, they said, worked for the government in Afghanistan. The story changed a little as it went round: some said Thornton's brother was a diplomat, others that he was a military spy, or else a security chief for an oil company, or 'maybe all three'. Anyway, what Thornton's brother did was not really the issue. Apparently – and this was coming from Thornton's best friends – his brother had gone missing a few weeks ago. He hadn't been kidnapped, but nobody knew where he was. Some even said he had gone to join the resistance and was hiding out in the mountains on the border with Pakistan, or even Iran: somewhere, anywhere, nobody knew. Now everyone was saying that William Thornton had gone to join him. Exciting, fantastic, preposterous – whatever this rumour meant, it did little to assuage the fact of Thornton's empty desk and chair, the conspicuous absence of the boy. He wasn't the only one away: Scatherby, Rawls and, much to Timothy's surprise and relief, Murphy were also absent from morning registration. Mr Clarke mumbled his way through the names. He was far from happy, three times shouting for silence as the rumour passed, whisper-whisper-whisper, from one boy to the next. Things, Timothy decided, were definitely changing.

Instead of going to assembly, Mr Walker came and addressed the class again. He told them not to talk about Thornton with other boys in the school and kept saying how they all 'understood' how 'distressing' and 'stressful' it was for them, but that they had to 'shut up', 'keep quiet', 'do as they were told', 'stop worrying' and then everything would be 'fine'. The furrows on his brow were deeper and more severe than before.

As they exited the class for first period, Edward whispered, 'I dreamt about him last night.'

'Really?'

'He said they were completely surrounded.'

'Surrounded?'

'By the enemy army. He said they were being bombed day and night. He said gunships attacked the hospital and snipers were shooting up ambulances. The streets were littered with corpses. They were running low on ammunition. They were fighting to the death. He showed me.'

'He *showed* you?'

'I saw the blood, splattered all over the wall, and bullet holes everywhere, and ruined buildings outside. They were shooting and we had to hide. I was pressed against the floor, my hands over my head. Warplanes were dropping chemical bombs filled with fire. The noise was tremendous. There was this smell, this burning-plastic smell. It was horrible.'

Timothy tried to work out whether his friend was telling the truth, or just trying to impress him. He'd never seen Edward look quite so serious and intense before, nor so pale, his dark and tired eyes floating like two rocks in the white sea of his face. 'Are you all right?' he asked as they entered the classroom for the next lesson.

Edward nodded, pulling books from his bag.

But halfway through the lesson Edward put up his hand and asked Dr Talbot, the geography teacher, if he could be excused. 'I do feel awfully ill and sick, sir,' he said.

Dr Talbot sent Edward to the nurse. An hour later, during double maths, Timothy, sitting by the window, saw Edward and his mother walking towards their car. His mother opened the front door and Edward got in. Timothy watched them drive away.

Timothy would see Edward again, but when he did everything would be different.

Timothy was in the toilets. He finished zipping his flies and washed his fingers in the sink. The door opened and both the Radley brothers came marching in, followed by Brown, a short, fat lout from Timothy's year, and Jones, a notorious pyromaniac from the year above. Jason Radley seized Timothy by the lapels of his blazer and shoved him against the sink. 'We know you started this,' he snarled. 'Even that wanker Morgan's gone now. Admit it. It's just you now. You and us.' He slammed Timothy against the sink a second time.

'Make him go away.' Peter Radley pressed his face so close that Timothy could smell cigarettes and see tiny bits of food caught between the boy's teeth. 'Just get that fucking boy out of my dreams.'

'Get off me,' Timothy gasped, too shaken to struggle properly. 'I don't know anything.'

'You were the first to start dreaming about him. You said so. You told us. You and that fuck Morgan.' Jason shook him.

'Just get him out of my head!' Peter yelled. Timothy squirmed, struggling to raise his hands to protect himself. Any second he expected them to start pummelling him.

'I can't,' he pleaded. 'I don't control him. It isn't up to me.'

'Fuck you!' Peter lunged forward and dragged Timothy from his brother's grasp. Timothy tried to twist away, but Peter seized one arm and, for a moment, the two grappled together. But Peter had two years' and several pounds' advantage over Timothy, using it to swing him round so that he stumbled backwards, hitting the wall, losing purchase and falling, one arm splashing into the tunnel of the urinal, his bottom banging against the piss-wet floor.

Timothy sprang up immediately.

'I said get off me.' He wasn't thinking – or rather, he was, but in a way that was different from before – and he pushed Peter, pushed him hard and with a strength that he didn't think he had. The older boy, not expecting such a sudden counter-attack, lost his balance, falling against a lavatory door. It was almost comic, really, the way the door swung open, Peter's expression shifting from rage to bafflement as his footing went and he tumbled down.

Timothy knew that, by rights, he was now about to die. The Radley brothers were fond of bog-washing boys, holding their heads in the toilet bowl and flush-flush-flushing until their victim was half-drowned. They also burnt boys with cigarette ends, dished out Chinese burns and black eyes, would even rob a victim of his trousers, throwing them onto a low roof or into a rubbish bin, leaving their prey aghast, half-naked and exposed in the playground to the mockery of all the others: they did all these things. And they did more, they did worse, they dished out such punishments to boys who hadn't even *done* anything. The Radley brothers punished boys just for existing. No one had ever pushed over a Radley. Suddenly weak-kneed, Timothy realised he was dead. His moment of defiance vanished and he braced himself for the first of many punches.

But something – he didn't know what – stopped Jason, froze him with his fists clenched. Jones was equally immobilised, his wet lips hanging open in something like awe. Brown, humbled, stood aside like a nightclub bouncer bowing before a premier league football star. Timothy walked past them. He walked down the corridor, he walked quickly, but he did not run and he did not look back. There was a pain at the base of his spine and in his left arm from where he'd hit the floor, and an embarrassing wetness on parts of his clothes, but still he walked. First he had faced down Murphy, now the Radley brothers. Exhilaration illuminated his world.

That evening, after dinner, Timothy was playing his favourite computer game, infamous for its graphic realism. A well-placed car bomb eliminated a squad of coalition troops. Soldiers, their skin blackened and bloody, lay strewn around the wreckage of their Humvee. Harry entered his bedroom. Normally Timothy would have chided him for barging in unannounced, but his brother's expression halted him.

'What?' He scowled, pausing the game.

'I need to tell you something.'

'What?'

'I didn't want to say in front of Mummy . . .' Harry glanced around the bedroom, as if someone else might be listening. His eyes, behind his glasses, were huge. 'I had such a funny dream last night . . . I dreamt about this boy.' He spoke in a whisper, drawing Timothy closer. 'He knows you. He says he's a friend of yours as well. I thought he was just my friend, but he's not. He's friends with all of us. He told me to tell you it's almost too late.' The words came out in a tumbling, nervous rush.

'Okay.' Timothy swallowed. He knew he should be surprised but somehow he wasn't. This was normal. He knew this. This was expected. Everyone was dreaming the boy. Even so, he asked: 'What did he look like?'

'Oh . . . he was a bit older than you. But he looked like us, except he was wearing a scarf on his head and his skin is, you know, darker than ours.'

'Where was he?'

'In the garden.'

'Outside, you mean?'

Harry nodded.

'You dreamt you were in the gardens?'

'I'm always dreaming about being in the gardens,' Harry replied, a hint of so-what entering his tone.

'This boy – you've dreamt about him before?'

Harry shrugged.

'Well – have you?'

'Sometimes, in my flying dreams. He's teaching me to fly on his magic carpet.'

'You're lying.' Timothy grabbed Harry by the arm and started to squeeze it.

'I'm not, I promise, Tim, I promise.'

'I'll hit you if you're lying. I'll give you a Chinese burn.'

'I'm not lying, honest I'm not.'

'What did he want me to do?'

'He said you'd know what to do.'

'Okay.' Timothy let his little brother go.

Harry looked as though he were going to leave. Then he turned round and said, 'Tim . . . do you think we will ever go back?'

'Where?'

'You know. Back there.'

'I don't know.' Catching the troubled expression on his brother's face, he added, 'Maybe – maybe we will.'

Later that night Timothy lay awake, sheets knotting and unknotting around his restless legs. His parents were arguing. The dispute had started in their bedroom and moved rapidly along the corridor, a procession of footsteps, his mother first, his father following. Now it was circulating, as far as he could make out, between the kitchen and the living room. It was hard to tell what they were arguing about. He heard his father saying, 'I have to' and 'I'm sorry, I can't help it.' It was easier to make out his mother's voice, shrill and high, but much harder to tell what she was saying. When she got angry Timothy was reminded of a Catherine wheel spinning out of control, bright sparks spraying everywhere but never lasting long. Things had quietened down a little already, but Timothy knew that the row would continue, in different ways, with his mother sulking or sobbing in that pitiful, despairing way she did, while his father explained and justified things. Back and forth, the low rumble of his father's voice and the pauses when he knew his mother would say something back. Sometimes the pauses were very long and he wondered what happened in those moments.

After a while someone came upstairs. From the lighter tread, Timothy was sure it was his mother. The steps hesitated, if only for a fraction, outside his door, but then he heard another squeak and the faint clunk further down the hall as his parents' bedroom door closed. Then, for a while, nothing, and then, after that, he thought he heard the front door close, but he wasn't sure. Maybe he slept a little. The quiet in the house was a vast thing, a mass of weighty silence broken only by the distant hiss of night traffic from Notting Hill Gate and the occasional wail of a siren – police cars, he imagined – racing to the tower blocks by the Westway. All of them, dreaming the boy, even Harry, even the Radley brothers, and how many other boys, at how many other schools? He wished the boy would come now and tell him what he should do. *He said you would know.*

Timothy slept – at least, it seemed to him that he slept. When he opened his eyes he was still in his room, lying in bed. A little while after– his bedside clock said three – he opened his curtains, letting in the rusty nightglow. In the gardens, in the tall tree that overlooked the house, up in a high branch, there, at last! There he was! The boy. Timothy waved. The boy waved back.

It was the end of Western civilisation. All the rottenness had finally risen to the surface. There was no more respect for decent middle-class Anglo-Saxon values because there were no longer any decent middle-class Anglo-Saxon values to respect. Fuck it. The whole shoddy game was up. 'I can't lie to you any more, son,' said the father, weeping. The boy saw his chance. Taking what money he could from his father, he packed a bag with everything he thought he might need, and off he went to join the Lost Boys.

The boy hated his old name and so, all the better to forget, he decided to call himself Shaka, after the great Zulu warrior. It was a good name. He'd been researching and planning the route all summer. Instructions had been left, here and there, by those who had already made the journey. Clues were easy to find, once he knew where to look: in the school library, under-lined in pulp novels about lost cities, alien invasions, moody detectives and corporate scandals; in obscure political tracts and papers on forgotten tribes and ancient rituals; in the graf-fiti daubed over abandoned buildings and alongside train tracks and Tube lines; there were blogs and web pages out there, full of information, although the government was getting wise, clos-ing down sites or blocking access. There were other places too, other sources of information, although much harder to find and even harder to crack. Rumours circulated about a call girl, an American, discreet and willing to indulge in the most unusual practices: she was said to know the best way of all. He spent futile hours searching for her card in phone boxes across central London. Time went on. Routes were drawn out in the back pages of exercise books, on napkins borrowed from coffee bars. Tips exchanged on Internet message boards. He was ready.

On the first day he burned his passport, his birth certificate, everything that said who he was, what he had done, what he owed. That was the most important part, so he'd learned . . .

First it was hard, travelling by night, sticking to backstreets and footpaths, never taking the easy road or the short way. On the outskirts of Dover he met a man who smuggled him across the Channel in the back of a truck and down through France in another. On the border with Spain another man, much older, mollusc-like lips twitching, promised he could stay the night if he could just touch him, he said. The old man lived in a richly decorated apartment in a vast, shabby mansion that stank of moths and dust. Sporting trophies and medals were displayed in tall glass cabinets. Dusty animal heads and African masks adorned the walls. 'I'm going to join the Lost Boys,' he shouted. The old man nodded. He had known all along. That was why he had approached the boy. They came to an understanding. The old man left him sleeping on the white, stained bed.

In the morning, on the bedside table, he found a book filled with old black and white photographs of more boys: naked skinny boys playing in the rubble of war-torn Naples and Berlin; dark-skinned nomad boys from the deserts of North Africa and Arabia, boys with swords and with snakes in wicker cases; Wild West boys from the American frontier, cocky with their Stetson hats and shiny stirrups; and he saw Native American boys with face paint, slave boys from the swamps of the South; warlike maroon boys from the mountains of Jamaica and Haiti; jungle boys from Mexico and the Amazon; mountain boys from the Himalayas, Buddhist-monk boys smiling benevolently; boys without places, names or tribes; posh boys from Eton and Harrow, as arrogant as warrior kings in their top hats and tails. So it went. The old man was gone.

Taking the book with him, the boy ventured outside into deserted streets darkened by long, sad shadows. Huge black birds circled high above. Political pamphlets, scattered by the wind, blew towards him. The names of anarchist and socialist groups – POUM, CNT, FAI, ANV, JSU – resurrected from the Spanish Civil War were scrawled on walls. Between their ancient slogans, handprints in blue and white. He touched his own palm to the wall. Yes, this was the way.

The boy began to forget who he had been. The Mummy–Daddy memories didn't hurt so much any more. He painted his *face with red dye and adorned his hair with feathers. He had visions: clouds became burning towers and fallen cities; he saw the Lords of War in their citadels of power; he saw a million people with their heads bowed; he saw the old man, hiding in a cave in the mountain. He walked for many days. Yes, this was the way.*

Thursday

Two minutes to seven. Veca's alarm clock jolted her from a vague dream about clouds made of ice cream. She sat up, yawning and shaking her head. Often she was quite bright in the morning, filled with energy and ready for the day, but the damp, chilly gloom of the English winter did wear her down. She missed the crisp, snowy cold of home: in London everything was blunted, sapped of colour, and sometimes she could quite easily imagine the whole city, even the entire island, slowly dissolving into the same grey mush. Still, the Christmas holidays were almost here, something she looked forward to almost as much as the boys did. Three weeks without having to get up quite so early, without having to face the morning traffic. Mrs Dashwood had even hinted that they might buy her a flight back home to Bratislava for a present. That would be nice. Hard to tell, though, with Mrs Dashwood: if Mr Dashwood had made the offer Veca knew she'd be able to count on it. On the rare occasions when he actually spoke to her he always did as he said, but with Mrs Dashwood things were normally a little more complicated. Any gift from her had a price, one way or another.

The air was colder than usual in her basement room and Veca shivered as she pulled on her clothes. She splashed water over her face and checked herself in the mirror, frowned at what might have been a spot and dithered for a moment over what to wear before settling on the same jeans and thick woollen jumper as she'd worn yesterday. Mr and Mrs Dashwood had been arguing late last night, which meant that Mrs Dashwood would almost certainly be in a bad mood. Veca knew that it was best, in such circumstances, to stay out of the woman's way unless she wanted to risk doing something, almost anything – not stacking the dishwasher correctly, leaving on too many lights, not tidying away her plate, flushing the loo, not flushing the loo – that might provoke her. Mrs Dashwood's tempers were as unpredictable as everything else: sometimes they were no more than an evil look or a stern reprimand, sometimes they were much worse. Mere threats could become severe punishments – privileges withheld, a free evening suspended, even insults, 'You stupid, stupid, *fat* girl, why did you do that?' Of course, when Mrs Dashwood went that far she would usually apologise later. Not always in the most direct way – she was not, after all, a woman for whom contrition came easily – but she would make some small sign: give Veca money for the cinema, put flowers or new toiletries in her room, small things like that. All the same, Veca did find such behaviour a bit much; it got to her after a while. The alternative was a moody Mrs Dashwood who moped around the house like a sulky adolescent, trying to get Veca to talk to her as if they were friends really. She would complain about Mr Dashwood and how he ignored her, or moan about the house or her children, so wicked and ungrateful, or her friends, so competitive – that sort of thing. As if she had it so hard.

No, Veca had a better idea. She decided, after taking the boys to school, that she would go out, maybe to the supermarket. They needed the usual staples – tea bags, toilet rolls, milk, fresh vegetables, olive oil, bread – but more importantly the trip would give her a chance to waste time, get a coffee, read a magazine, just be herself for a while. She'd be away from Mrs Dashwood all morning. Usually Mrs Dashwood went to the gym in the afternoon or, if she was really miserable, she might treat herself to a manicure or a facial or a shopping expedition with one of the friends she said she never saw. If she was lucky, Veca knew she could avoid Mrs Dashwood until home time, when other chores – like preparing dinner for the boys – would keep her busy.

Upstairs, Veca met Muffy, prowling about the hallway. 'What is it, Muffy?' she asked, rubbing the dog's head. Muffy sniffed and glowered at her, resuming her wary vigil by the front door. Veca had learnt that Mr and Mrs Dashwood's arguments often upset the animal, throwing it into confusion. Not that either of them gave the dog any attention. She went upstairs, for once knocking first on Harry's door. She wasn't sure why. She went up to the door and knocked smartly. 'Good morning, Harry!' She waited a moment before going inside. Harry was still in bed, half hidden by his duvet. For some reason his room was far messier than it had been at bedtime. The floor was littered with pictures torn from Mr Dashwood's news magazines and Harry's soft toys, usually heaped in a single pile on top of a trunk by the bed, must have had a midnight adventure. They were everywhere. 'Harry – what a mess! What have you done? Come on now, it's time for school.'

'Mmmgh.' Harry sat up, his hair a brown tangle, his eyes bleary and screwed up – like a little mole emerging from his hole.

'How are we this morning, Harry?'

'Sleepy.'

'Christmas soon – come on.' Veca yanked the curtains open, letting in what little light the grey morning would allow. 'Now, do you want me to help you get dressed, or can you manage?'

'I'll manage.'

'I've ironed you a fresh shirt. It's hanging in your wardrobe.' Veca smiled at Harry and closed his door, moving now to Timothy's room.

Knock-knock. In recent weeks it had become much harder to wake him up. Sometimes he was so deeply asleep that she had to go in and shake him awake. At other times she suspected he'd been up for hours – doing what, she had no idea. Once she'd thought she'd heard him talking to someone and had been sure she could hear a second boyish voice – two loud whispers together – but on going in she had simply found him asleep still and mumbling to himself from some muddy dream.

Veca knocked again, but much louder. Still no answer. 'Timothy,' she called through the door. 'Wake up, Timmy, I'm coming in.'

One-two-three, and in she went.

Timothy was in bed, lying on his front, hands under the pillow. 'Timmy, are you all right? Tim?' Veca leant over him. The room was surprisingly cold, as if his window had been left wide open all night.

The boy groaned and rolled over. His face was pale and puffy. 'I don't feel very well.'

'What is it?'

'I don't know.' He gave a weak cough. 'My head aches so much. I didn't sleep at all last night. I couldn't sleep.'

Veca touched his forehead. His skin felt clammy, a little sweaty, but not feverish. 'You don't think you can make school?'

He shook his head. 'Edward was ill yesterday. They sent him home in first period. I must have caught it from him.'

Veca clicked her tongue against her teeth the way she always did when unsure of something. 'I'll have to speak to your mother – are you sure you don't feel up to it?'

'Please, Veccy—' Timothy looked up, his eyes wet and haunted. 'I feel so bad.'

'Okay, okay, well, you better stay in bed.'

Sighing, she went downstairs. Harry was in the kitchen, fiddling with his bag. As she put Harry's cereal in a bowl, Veca said, 'Timmy is feeling ill this morning. He doesn't want to go to school. You feel okay, don't you?'

Harry gave her a funny, wary sort of look. 'Yeah, guess so.'

Tongue clicked against teeth again. A dilemma: should she go upstairs and disturb Mrs Dashwood, maybe even wake her up– and Mrs Dashwood didn't like to get up until the children had left – to tell her that Timothy was ill and didn't feel like going to school? She ventured upstairs and paused outside their bedroom. Veca hated going into that room, and she knew that Mrs Dashwood didn't like it much either. She hesitated, listening for any sign that the woman was up. She raised a hand to knock, and then quickly lowered it again. No, she couldn't do it. She decided to leave a note explaining that Timothy was ill in bed and that she had gone to the supermarket. She was sure Mrs Dashwood didn't need to go out this morning.

Anyway, Veca saw no reason why Timothy's mother

couldn't stay in and look after him for a bit. He was, after all, *her* son. It wasn't as if she had anything else to do. Veca often thought what a stupid, spoilt woman she was; she had no idea about real work, had never lived like her own mother did, back home. Mrs Dashwood had never had to carry shopping for an entire family all the way up to the sixth floor, had never had to wash the family dishes or scrub clothes with her own hands. Veca's mother's hands were wrinkled and scarred, her joints ached and her back was stiff. Not like Mrs Dashwood: her hands were a marvel, the most beautiful hands Veca had ever seen, softened with expensive lotions and creams, her nails like polished shells and her hair – good God – the first time Veca realised how much Mrs Dashwood actually spent at the hairdresser she could hardly believe it. Mrs Dashwood radiated health and beauty. It wouldn't hurt her so much to make breakfast for her child or bring him a cup of tea.

Veca was decided: she would leave a note, she would take Harry to school, she would drive to the supermarket and then get a coffee, read a magazine and forget all about the Dashwood family for a couple of hours.

Ten to eight. Harry finished spooning his cereal. 'Go and brush your teeth,' she ordered. 'We need to leave soon.' While Harry was upstairs, Veca made a quick cup of tea and wandered into the front room. Mr Dashwood must have left early for work. The briefcase and papers he had left on the sofa last night were gone. Normally, the sound of him leaving woke her a few minutes before the alarm. The argument he'd had with his wife had raged on very late last night and she wondered if he'd bothered going to bed at all.

She went to the window and brushed aside the curtain. For a minute she thought she saw a young gypsy boy, dark and scruffy, perched on the front garden wall. The curtain drifted back, briefly obscuring her view. She yanked it open again but the boy – if he had even been there at all – was gone. She shook her head. It was too early to start imagining things.

Lying in bed, Timothy heard the *clink* and *thunk* of the front door as Veca and Harry left. Listening very carefully, he could hear them getting into the car and the engine starting. Then they were gone. Quiet, again, in the house. Mummy must still be sleeping – although there was a chance that she was awake. His parents had a very large bedroom, with a huge separate bathroom and another room filled with racks and sliding-door wardrobes where Mummy kept all her clothes. It was hard to hear what went on in their room, but from their bedroom it was also hard to hear sounds elsewhere in the house. He could tell that Muffy was about, pacing downstairs and whimpering faintly. She knew what was going on. She was a clever dog.

Timothy kicked the sheets aside and got out of bed. It had been so easy pretending to Veca that he was ill. It was so easy making the old shapes, the ones they expected to see. He moved about his bedroom, touching one thing, touching another. He was free of it all, and how exciting it was to be free at last. He found some clothes and put them on. Downstairs, Muffy was scratching at the front door. Instead of greeting him with her usual friendly wagging tail, she crouched back, giving a low, suspicious growl. 'Shut up, dog,' he snapped and she fell silent. Pathetic brown eyes peered up and she slunk under the kitchen table. On top he found a note. *Dear Susan, Timothy says he is unwell and is resting in bed. I have shopping list and will go to*

the supermarket after taking Harry to school. Back lunchtime.
Veccy xxx.

Timothy tore the note into tiny pieces and dropped them in the bin. He picked up his school bag, upending it, letting all the textbooks tumble onto the kitchen floor. From the pile he collected a library book, pages underlined here and there in fierce red ink. He opened the cutlery drawer and took out the largest, sharpest knife in the kitchen. He placed it, along with the book, back in his school bag. He took one or two things to eat from the cupboard, adding them to the bag. Muffy was making a whimpering, grovelling noise. 'Shut up,' he said again. His mother had to stay asleep. For the last time he opened the front door. The damp morning air reminded him how much further he had to go. He smiled. He was other than what he had been.

THE TAPES

Arthur had never known such pain: a brittle laceration of the nerves, a corkscrew in his heart, gouging and twisting, a cancer-black hole of dread slowly spreading through each cell, a fist in his stomach, squeezing and pressing all day, all night. There could be no release, no let-up, no mercy. Shaken so violently, his world fractured. One small boy was all it took to upset the universe. No, he had never known that love could hurt so much, had never experienced a loss so complete or so consuming. Even to think was a torture, as if someone was playing a blowtorch across the exposed quiver of his brain: flickering nightmares – one image, then another, the cool formaldehyde smell of the morgue, the terrible sight of a white sheet over a small body. He saw himself saying, 'Yes, that's him, that's my son.' He saw himself walking away, his arms awfully empty, no little hand to take in his own.

At first, people were ever so kind.

'So kind of you,' Susan would say as she blinked away tears while on the phone to a consoling voice or received yet another delivery of cards and flowers. So many flowers came in the first few days that he could almost imagine Timothy had died. Bad news brought them out: old friends, colleagues and associates not seen for years. People who had heard about it through the bad-news grapevine, gossip and rumour spreading like ink in water. Others stumbled upon the story when it appeared in the *Evening Standard*. 'Mystery of the Brompton Boys,' a black and white Timothy beaming out, smaller pictures of the other boys who had also gone missing underneath. Each day brought more flowers, more phone calls, more invitations to chat. Arthur felt as though these sympathetic offerings were really charms or totems, ways in which others tried to ward off a disaster similar to that which had struck his family, as if Timothy's disappearance had revealed the precarious arbitrariness of their own lives. They saw what had happened, and they were afraid.

In the days immediately after the disappearance, Arthur had kept calm and controlled. As the house thronged with police officers and detectives, forensic experts and journalists, he kept a steady course. He had to. Someone had to be strong. Someone had to hold the family together.

Speaking kept him sane. He would deliver hectoring, incessant monologues to Susan, to her parents, to anyone who came to see them. 'They must find him, don't you think? They must. You don't just disappear. No one just disappears, do they? Impossible!' Pacing back and forth as he spoke, grasping the air for emphasis, an unbearable tension propelling him onwards. 'Someone must have seen him, they must have done – one of the neighbours, don't you think? Bloody fools. Jesus, you don't just disappear, do you? Not in London, not in the middle of the morning, not in this day and age. Impossible, surely? They must find him. They have the best officers on the case. They have a lot of experience. Someone will come forward. Someone knows what happened. Someone will tell the police. They always find them, sooner or later, don't they?' This way and that, his voice increasing in pitch and agitation, as if by sheer force of words alone he could conjure his son back home. He would work himself into a frenzy of indignation and anxiety while Susan sat in the corner, sometimes quietly weeping, sometimes silent and deathly pale, a faraway look in her eyes where his words couldn't reach.

Arthur remembered the long interviews with the police, giving statement after statement. They went over the facts so many times that he began to doubt himself, his wife, the au pair, everything about the fateful day. It was as if, rather than coming to some sense of certainty or coherence, a clear narrative of what must have happened when and why, the opposite occurred. That morning – had it really been the same as any other? He had left the house at six-thirty, a little earlier than usual. He was sure of that.

But why? He remembered how Susan had moved softly as he got out of bed, reaching for his arm and mumbling something. Did that gesture contain some other, hidden meaning? Had she been asking him not to go? And had his journey to work really been so routine? He remembered that traffic had been much lighter than usual, and on the radio the news reported another terrible bombing in Iraq, this story stirring other, darker memories. What constellation of order could be produced from such chaos? He had arrived at Canary Wharf earlier than normal, and for some reason had decided against going straight up to his office. Instead, he wandered away from the tower with a takeaway cappuccino. Why? He didn't usually drink coffee so early in the morning.

Arthur told this all to the police, and they dutifully noted everything down. But what help would such information be in finding Timothy? He didn't tell the police the thoughts he had that morning as he gazed towards the Millennium Dome shimmering in the morning gloom. Did it mean anything, the fact that in such moments he thought of his own boyhood, recalling the empty room where his brother once slept and the sound of other children in the street, the playful cry of young voices on a silvery summer evening . . . or the painful yearning he had felt for his own mother, dead for many years now. Only he knew the resemblance she bore to Timothy, the secret of generations mapped out in eyes, nose and lips. What did it mean? Could he tell the police this?

Instead, they had stuck to more prosaic matters. The police took their computers – the PC used by Timothy and Harry to play games, write their homework and message their friends, and Arthur's three laptops (two of them from work) – searching for cybernetic signs: encrypted files, child pornography, mysterious messages, plans or schemes, cracks and shadows in the façade of their family, virtual trails to a real boy. They accessed phone records and looked at bank statements, they spoke to friends and colleagues to confirm that Arthur and Susan and the au pair really had been where they said they were. They made sure he wasn't the one responsible. 'We need to eliminate you from our inquiries' – that was how they put it. They checked hospital records and social services in the search for past signs of abuse. They dug holes in the garden. They looked at things with special cameras. Men in white plastic suits put traces almost too small to see into clear bags. With a spatula they took scrapings of spittle from his tongue. They did the same to Susan, Harry and Veca. They would have questioned the dog had they known how to. 'We have nothing to hide,' Arthur told them. He hadn't cared what they did. He wanted to cooperate. There was nothing he wouldn't do, he told the police, if it could help them to find his son.

'People have been ever so kind,' said Susan, a weak smile floating like a mirage across her face, her manicured nails torn to shreds with worry.

All this Arthur remembered now as he sat alone in his office, high above the world. Those endless nights, ragged with sleeplessness, driven to some far edge of emotion, when he would press his hands to the glass and stare into the darkness. His warm palm left a mark on the cold window and he would stare at the pattern, trying to catch some portent of his destiny in the imprint of fading whorls. The memories came in a rush: sitting in Harry's bedroom with his wife, the two of them stroking their child, touching his hair and his face, unable to let go, to leave him even for an instant. During those first awful days, Susan took to sleeping in the same bed as the boy. 'My darling,' she would whisper as she stroked his hair. 'My most precious little one.'

Harry seemed to enjoy the deluge of attention, the au pair banished to the basement, his parents jostling to perform rituals of bedtime and breakfast, bath-running and story-reading. Had they been trying to make up for past negligence, for working too hard, for worrying about other things? Arthur wondered. Perhaps they had been, even if it didn't feel that way. He remembered trying to talk to Harry one night. 'Don't be frightened,' Arthur had said, not really knowing what to say or how he could reassure the boy when there was no reassurance, not anywhere. Maybe he was just trying to make himself feel better. Still, he couldn't forget what Harry had said in return. 'Timmy is okay. He just had to go away. We all have to go away.' He remembered the look in Harry's eyes as he spoke – a look he had never seen before: haunted and sad and something else, something he didn't quite know how to describe. A sorrowful, deep sort of certainty.

Then there was the senior detective in charge of the case, Captain York, a striking-looking man with glossy black hair and an artificial hand. The Captain had a habit when speaking about delicate subjects of scratching the lattice of white scars around the wrist of his damaged limb. Arthur often wondered what had caused such an injury, but never quite dared to ask. Despite his unorthodox appearance, however, the Captain inspired him with confidence. York reminded Arthur of a gentleman pirate or a cavalier, the sort of romantic character found in a children's story. He projected an air of weary experience, speaking fluently, his long sentences full of multiple sub-clauses and phrases such as 'balance of probability', 'determined and undetermined outcomes', 'emotional causality'. As he spoke, his fingers would rub the join of flesh and plastic. Timothy's case was described as 'exceptional' and 'abnormal' but, he added, this gave cause for 'comfort'. If nothing else, Arthur was reassured by the education and values they clearly shared. It was clear to him that the Captain was no ordinary policeman.

Nonetheless, it was difficult for Arthur to accept much of what was said. York explained that all the available evidence suggested Timothy had left the house deliberately. There was no sign that anyone else had entered the property to take him. The absence of a ransom demand made kidnapping an unlikely explanation. The police had determined that a few of his possessions were missing: his school bag, a set of clothes and his favourite trainers. But the real question, according to the Captain, was how far Timothy's disappearance was connected with others from the school. 'There are probable and improbable coincidences,' York said, sipping his Earl Grey. 'I would call this one of the latter. If we find just one of the boys, we will find them all.'

Some things Arthur found hard to contemplate. Could Timothy really have chosen to run away? It seemed so improbable. For reasons he found difficult to understand, he wanted desperately to believe that someone had kidnapped his son: a bad person, an enemy. He saw the logic, the perverse symmetry. They would have done so to try and hurt him. He was important, he made a lot of money, he represented powerful interests. It made sense to him that someone would do this. He gave the police the names of everyone he could think of who might have a grievance against him – but the list was not very long, nor, he had to admit, very convincing. Of course, other enemies existed, but they had no names he could provide.

As for the alternative: if it really was the case that Timothy had run away of his own free will . . . well, what then? Was it an elaborate game, a cruel trick that the boys were playing against them? Arthur could see no reason for such behaviour. As a father, he was certain he had given his son everything he could possibly have wanted. It was incomprehensible that Timothy, still so young, still so innocent, could reject it all.

'Everybody has been terribly kind.' His poor wife. Her suffering was unbearable to behold, the comfort he could give so pitiful. Never before had Arthur felt so inadequate, so far from what she needed. Like a porcelain statue flung to the ground, her delicate beauty revealed a mesh of fractures and cracks. With tender words and caring caresses he tried to hold her together, but there was little he could do. Bereft of her beloved boy and beyond her husband's care, she slipped from his grasp. She grew weak with stress, the deep hollows and shadows of her face testament to her suffering. The family doctor upped her medication, adding antidepressants to tranquillisers and sleeping pills.

'We've interviewed a number of known paedophiles in the area,' Captain York told him, sipping his tea. 'We're checking up on their statements. But to be honest, I'm afraid we don't really have any strong suspects. In my experience, and this is the truth, their victims are usually much younger than your son. There are other lines of inquiry we are following. I'll keep you informed, of course.'

And so the days passed by, endless, empty and awful. Visits from the police became less frequent. Computers were returned, holes in the garden filled in and items of Timothy's clothing brought back, neatly pressed and folded, as if from the dry-cleaners. Still there was no sign, not a clue, not a hint of brightness to break the dark.

At night Arthur slept fitfully in an armchair in front of Sky News, or slumped over his desk, the price of oil flickering across his face. Snatched moments of oblivion. Sometimes, in the midnight memory of past and present, he dreamt of boys: not of Timothy particularly, simply boys, lost boys – Europeans and Asians, Africans and Americans – boys with steely eyes and ink-smudged features, boys with magic carpets and pirate costumes, boys with painted faces and Red Indian headdresses. Boys who saw his sorrow, and who did not care. He dreamt that they waited on the outskirts of great cities and in the green depths of the jungle. These dreams could have been timeless, could have continued for ever: but always he would awake, the image of them lingering in his mind, waiting under the tree in the park, in the empty places, unforgiving and relentless. Consciousness brought realisation, a bitter, crushing feeling he couldn't even grace with the word despair.

One morning Captain York came in a car and took Arthur to the police station. They sat in a windowless room, surrounded by monitor screens. 'We'd like you to take a look at this,' the Captain explained, massaging his wrist. He showed Arthur a sequence of grainy CCTV footage: a small group of teenage boys hanging around a bus stop. 'Notting Hill Gate,' the Captain said, 'Look at the time. It was around then that we think it most likely Timothy left your house. What do you think?'

Arthur could see five boys, one of whom looked slightly smaller and younger than the others. He scrutinised this boy first. The kid wore a white baseball cap, and his face was never clearly visible. Arthur didn't think Timothy had ever worn a cap like that before. They stopped and paused the footage. They increased the magnification. It was so hard to tell. None of the other boys seemed familiar, but Arthur had no real idea what Timothy's friends looked like anyway – it wasn't as if they ever came to the house. The group wore ordinary clothes, jeans, trainers and dark jackets, and there was nothing particularly unusual or memorable about any of them. 'I don't know,' he said.

The sequence was six minutes long. They watched it over and over again. Arthur admired the orderliness of the boys. Four minutes into the footage they stood aside, politely letting people off a bus. The boys waited a little longer. He saw no sign of coercion in their body language, had no sense that they were engaged in anything unusual.

The conclusion came with the arrival of a bus headed for Oxford Street. They were the first inside. Seconds later, the bus pulled out of the frame. 'We're still trying to track down the footage from the camera inside that bus,' the Captain explained.

The second sequence was from an eastbound Central Line platform. Amid the waiting people, York pointed to a boy, about Timothy's age and height, conspicuously alone, his back to the camera. He was carrying a large rucksack, another item that Arthur was sure didn't belong to his son. The footage did not last long, and the Captain slowed it down, frame by frame. 'We never get a clear shot of his face, I'm afraid.' Arthur wanted to be certain, but, looking at these flickering pictures, he sensed nothing. He found it impossible to believe that the boy on the screen could have been Timothy. They had never let him go alone into the Tube. That couldn't be his son he saw, so calm and confident on the platform. Seventy seconds later a train arrived and the platform was briefly swamped with departing passengers. The last image of the boy was of him getting on board, the doors sliding shut, the train moving away. 'I suppose you're also trying to find the footage from that train,' Arthur said.

Days turned into weeks. 'People disappear every day,' said Captain York. 'More of them than you'd imagine. A loving mother pops out to the corner shop and never comes back. A teenager walks across town to visit a friend and never arrives. People leave for work in the morning and are never seen again.'

Never. There was something rather ominous about the appearance of this word in the Captain's speech.

'Sometimes they want to vanish, start a new life somewhere. Who knows what goes on in the human heart?'

York shrugged. 'Clues are one thing, but we rarely know the truth.'

Arthur remembered pacing his and Susan's bedroom after the Captain had left. 'What does he mean, no clues, no leads, nothing? How can this be? How can he talk about resources like that? They have to find him. Our little boy. How can this be?' A red tide of rage: he remembered ripping a mirror from the bedroom wall and flinging it to the floor, the way the breaking glass matched his anger. With shame, he remembered yanking clothes from the wardrobe, pulling out his own Savile Row suits and Susan's designer dressers before storming downstairs, an incoherent voice screaming in his head, vaguely aware of his wife calling out in a vain attempt to calm his anger, and then moving into the kitchen, pulling plates and cups from the cupboard and smashing them against the granite work surface, throwing another at the window and watching china shatter glass. Why was he doing this? He remembered Susan imploring him to stop, and he remembered knocking her hands away and grabbing her by the arm and throwing her onto the floor. With shame, he recalled the way she was sprawled across the broken ceramics, hiding her face in her hands, and he remembered Veca rushing in to whisk Harry from the room. He remembered finding himself in the garden, his rage spent, mud on his hands and knees, grovelling in the dirt.

None of this was easy.

Arthur kept busy. He had to stay strong. Someone had to. Waves of despair washed over him, worse than anything before. He arranged an interview with a sympathetic journalist who promised to publicise the case. But when the story appeared he couldn't even bear to read it, nor look at the accompanying picture of his family, taken shortly after their return to England. The story grew a life of its own. For a few days journalists and photographers lingered outside the house, intermittently ringing the doorbell. Arthur said things to them – he couldn't remember what. Other parents whose children had gone missing from school held a press conference. Perhaps he should have attended but it all seemed too much to bear – all that public weeping and pleading. What he read in the papers seemed to have no relation to the great tumult in the private reaches of his heart.

He set up a web page with a picture of Timothy and details of his disappearance. He sent thousands of e-mails. He received a reply from someone who said a criminal gang in Brighton was holding his son. He passed the details on to the police. An address was raided – nothing was found. 'You will get hoaxers,' sighed York. 'People who seek to profit from your misery, exploit your vulnera-bility. Just pass anything you get on to us.'

Arthur received a message from someone who said a boy matching Timothy's description was living at a house in Dagenham. Without telling anyone, he drove to the address, a scruffy council house in a depressing cul-de-sac. He had never been to this part of London before, and the shabby streets and vast industrial sheds seemed a million miles from Kensington. He sat for a long time in his car, watching the house and wondering what to do. After a couple of hours another vehicle pulled up and a boy of about Timothy's age and height got out, followed by a woman. But the boy was not Timothy and the woman was clearly his mother.

Arthur got further e-mails reporting sightings. Someone wrote that they had seen a group of young English boys, dressed as Berbers, roaming about the Djemaa-el-Fna in

Marrakesh. Another claimed that someone matching Timothy's description had been squatting in an abandoned flat in their building in Hackney before disappearing one evening with a larger group of youths. Reports came of sightings in a gypsy camp in Cornwall, on a train heading across the Ukraine, in the Spanish quarter of Naples and the Armenian district of Jerusalem. Dutifully, Arthur forwarded each message to the police. He didn't know what to think. He received an e-mail from someone who had been to Thailand on holiday and claimed to have seen a group of English boys running wild on the beaches of a remote island. Timothy seemed to be nowhere and yet everywhere. Then, after a while, these e-mails stopped.

From the computer, Arthur turned to the city beyond. Despair gave him a restless, nervy energy and so, come nightfall, he took to the streets. He began to see his neighbourhood with new eyes. When they first moved to Notting Hill, the exclusive boutiques and hip art galleries, the fashionable restaurants and organic grocers, the rows of glazed white houses and the gleaming, luxury cars made it seem the rightful place to live. Only now did such flamboyant wealth strike him as feverish, a deranged and monstrous delusion, a gaudy bubble about to burst. How stupid he had been to believe that such displays of privilege could ever keep them safe.

In these moments, he would think of the other places where his work had taken him. He remembered the dust and grime of Kabul, the crowds of desperate men and the women sheathed in dirty blue burkas; or Dubai, the armies of migrant labourers sheltering from the midday sun in the shadow of empty towers. But most of all he thought of Baghdad, that city of blast walls and barricades, with its frightening traffic jams and low-flying helicopters.

Cushioned in luxury limousines or armoured jeeps, Arthur had never quite made the connection before, between those places and his home. He had never quite seen it, the dusty road leading to the stucco mansion.

Distress made the city unfamiliar. He would trail through the sweat and grit of the West End, past crowded theatres and boisterous pubs filled with drunken office workers. In their faces he saw no joy, only desperation and denial. Through the canyons of the City he stumbled, the after-hours area deserted save for street sweepers and garbage collectors. Insomnia pushed him further, through Shoreditch, Whitechapel and Stepney, past the curry houses and Bollywood video stores, the mosques and warehouse conversions. After evening prayers the streets would fill with young men, unfamiliar and disenchanted. On street corners and outside fast-food restaurants they would linger, as if waiting for some great event to unfold. He found it almost impossible to imagine his son in a place like this, their little boy, alone in such a world, and after all they had done to try and protect him.

Once, after midnight, a gang of youths, no more than sixteen or seventeen years old, confronted Arthur on a quiet street. Hoods, baseball caps and scarves hid their faces, whilst garish yellow chains and pendants hung across jackets and tops emblazoned with images of dead hip-hop stars. He stood passive as rough hands pushed and shoved him. None of this mattered. He felt as though he were made of water, as if their fists could pass right through him. He made no move to resist as they took his wallet and his phone. 'Get outta here man, get the fuck away,' they shouted at him, as if his indifference intimidated them. But he felt no fear. These boys couldn't do anything to him. He started to laugh. 'Oh, you boys,' he said. 'You poor boys.' A fist struck his face, but that didn't matter. 'You poor boys,' he said again, walking away.

One night Arthur found himself outside a church, a splendid Gothic structure, whose spire reached high over Notting Hill. He had never really thought about the building before, never thought about going inside. The doors were locked anyway. Seated on a bench outside, he tried to find the words. *Dear God, dear Lord, if you are there, if you do exist, if you do care about us, please bring my son back to us. He's just a little boy, dear Lord . . . He doesn't mean anyone any harm. Why did you spare me, God, only to take him? I'm the wicked man. I'm the sinner, the liar. Take me, God, not him.* He had never felt God's presence – not even in the dark room, with death whispering in his ear. No power to take away his fear. Not then and not now. He remembered the hood, the ropes tight around his arms, the heat of that place.

Nothing, I said nothing, I told them nothing.

Nothing.

A light rain started to fall. Arthur lifted his face up to the sky. The rain fell and he was alone.

A few days after Arthur decided to return to work, the CEO, Sir Charles, summoned him to a private meeting. Facing him across a long black table Sir Charles said, 'I take it the police have had no luck.'

'I need to keep busy,' he told his boss, 'I can't sit at home waiting any longer.'

Sir Charles spoke quietly. 'I know someone – a private detective – name of Rupert Errol Buxton. A very unusual man. He has what we might call a special talent, a gift, if you like, for finding people, children in particular. Some claim he has psychic powers. I'm not sure about that. Nonetheless, his intuitive abilities are remarkable.' Sir Charles went on in a gentle, confidential tone. He told Arthur that some years ago his niece had disappeared. She'd been fifteen and she had run away with a much older man she had been seeing secretly. It took a week, he said, for the detective to track her down. 'Her boyfriend was associated with all sorts of dangerous people – heroin addicts, benefit cheats, prostitutes, God only knows what. You wouldn't believe it. As far as I'm concerned, Errol Buxton pretty much saved her life. I appreciate the circumstances are different, but nonetheless, I thought he might be able to help you. Would you like my secretary to give you the number?' A faint smile crossed Sir Charles's lips as Arthur expressed his immense gratitude.

And so the next stage started, a process bringing him to this moment, sitting alone in his office, a shoebox full of tapes on the table in front of him.

Arthur told his secretary to cancel his appointments and block any calls. Then he pulled both sets of blinds, closing off the world. He didn't want to see his secretary at her desk, bathed in the blue throb of her screen, and he didn't want her to see him. For a while he didn't move – he simply stared at the box of tapes. Then he began taking them out, one by one, spreading them over his desk.

Buxton had made no real effort to catalogue the tapes. A few almost illegible dates and times were scrawled in biro on the faded and peeling labels. Arthur did his best to arrange them in some sort of meaningful order. He sighed and yawned, running a hand over his face. Sometimes the very walls of his office seemed to melt with fatigue. He had taken a great risk in getting hold of these tapes. Indeed, he was far from certain that he had them all. They – whoever they were – had left him as much as they wanted him to find. The tapes, and those cards, the prostitute with the gas mask and fairy wings. *Have you been a bad boy?*

If there was a path to follow, a journey to make, this was where it started. He had to know how much Buxton had found out. The information on those tapes was his, he had paid for it and he had suffered for it. Now, at last, he might find some answers.

He took the first tape to hand, inserted it in the machine and pressed 'play'.

Long pause . . . loud tape hiss . . . faint noises in the background. Someone starts talking. He recognises Buxton's voice.

– Time is . . . a quarter to midnight, on the eleventh . . . right . . . yes . . . Thoughts on the Dashwood case. All the evidence, such as there is, makes it quite clear to me that the boy must have run away of his own free will. I have to agree with the police in that I'm confident this is not a kidnapping or anything of that nature. Unfortunately, the case is far more complex. Certainly Tim's disappearance fits the pattern established by other boys from his school. The fact that his friend Edward vanished in similar circumstances only a few hours later is overwhelmingly suggestive of a direct connection. From what I can tell, all of the boys appear to have chosen to run away. And we have no idea where they might have gone . . . and no idea why. The fact that none of the boys in question have so far been found, and the lack of any circumstantial or supporting evidence leads one to conclude that, well . . . It does seem increasingly likely that the boys have been following a pre-arranged plan. I suspect they must have run away with the intention of meeting each other again . . . But the lack of e-mails, text messages, letters, notes . . . [*Buxton sighs*] . . . it's almost not right to refer to this as a running-away. Vanishing. That might be the more apposite term. But such a word . . . well . . . there are implications that none of us want to consider.

Arthur leans over his desk, listening carefully. He can feel the perspiration running down his back, despite the fierce air-conditioning in the office.

– In front of me, a photograph of Timothy Dashwood, a school portrait, taken a few months ago. He looks quite the English schoolboy, fresh-faced and rosy-cheeked, with a quiff of soft, light brown hair, a gentle chin and sensual lips . . . There is something about those eyes, an artistic intelligence, I think. The innocent are so alert. [*Pause*] He does look a little young, perhaps, as he is nearly thirteen. His parents tell me that his voice hasn't broken yet. Now . . . there is something about the way he sits, like he's flinching from the camera, as if he's slightly intimidated by it . . . but then he knows . . . he seems to know something. It's like . . . hmmm . . . how can I put this? He seems, almost, to recoil from himself, from that uniform he's wearing. He knows he has to be here, but he doesn't want to be. [*Another rummaging sound*] His mother, Susan Dashwood . . . she called him a sensitive boy and she said it with a considerable amount of pride. Like her little boy might just manage not to grow up like any other man . . . [*Pause*] Okay. So, he's a dreamy type, I gather. The real question: what impulse was he acting on? Why did he decide to turn his back on his comfortable life? What are we dealing with here? [*Pause*] It could be that we're just confronted with a more involved, protracted, organised form of adolescent rebellion . . . Or . . . perhaps, as York has suggested, this could be something much more extreme, a sort of schoolboy terrorism, a rejection of reality itself? His disappearance seems to be one of many . . . part of a pandemic of vanishing. Where have they all got to? Are we dealing with a conspiracy here? A coherent plan executed with great success? And if this is a conspiracy, who is behind it? Someone must be in charge. Of course, the possibility remains that this has been something more spontaneous, but still . . . So many questions . . .

Impatient, Arthur rewinds the tape. He remembers his first meeting with the man. Buxton had a small, neat office above an estate agent in Clapham. The walls, as far as Arthur could recall, were hung with framed certificates, commendations, letters from grateful clients and pictures of the detective smiling alongside reunited families. Buxton had sat behind a white IKEA desk, regarding Arthur with interest, a single pile of papers in a neat pile to one side, a laptop, its screen down, on the other. The man had a sharp, intelligent face, his pointed nose and chin and the furrows on his brow suggesting a deep, penetrative concentration. He was a little younger than Arthur had expected – in his early forties at most – but nonetheless projected an air of quiet certainty. He let Arthur speak, and sat, listening carefully, never inter- rupting, simply nodding now and again and watching him with intense blue eyes. His expression seemed neither sympathetic nor surprised, as though this was all quite rou- tine. 'I've been following your case,' he'd said, 'and the other disappearances from your son's school. I'm confident I can help you.' Remembering those words, Arthur stopped rewind- ing the tape and presses 'play'. Again, Buxton is speaking.

– Mrs Dashwood greets me, she is—

Arthur stops, winds the tape back a little, then continues.

– New client, Arthur Dashwood. I'm already familiar with

the basic details of the case. Captain York has consulted me about it several times before. The police have drawn a blank, as usual . . . [*sigh*] Either that, or there are things I've not been told. Anyway, I'm at their house bang on four, as arranged. They live in a grand villa in one of the most desirable streets in Notting Hill, usual West London chic, sugar-white stucco, flower boxes, perfectly clipped topiary, a phalanx of BMWs and Porsches and Range Rovers up and down the street. The au pair lets me in, directs me into the front room and mumbles something about wanting a drink. She is about twenty-one years old, maybe a little older, not unattractive, but rather plump and maternal . . . She scurries off and leaves me in the lounge alone for some time. First impressions. Well, all the clutter startled me, the bouquet of dead flowers on the dining table, the stack of old newspapers beside the sofa. They read the *Guardian*, *The Times* and the *Financial Times*, as well as the London freebies. Plastic bags from the supermarket, a takeaway pizza box, a dirty teacup on a side table, incongruous among silver-framed pictures of smiling relations. Timothy Dashwood on the beach with his parents, three smiles squinted against the sun. Christmas tinsel still hangs around the bay window, perhaps the most pathetic thing of all. Small details, minor disorders by most standards . . . but in these houses, with these sort of people . . . it's significant. It's not the way it should be. I know these people. They keep their houses smart and slick as a company credit card and their families turned out as accomplished and efficient as a squad of management consultants . . . There has been a disturbance in this house, an explosion of emotion, but it's like it has all been caught inside, trapped, as if they shut the windows and locked the doors the moment it came out – and then kept it here, stifling them all. [*Pause*]

Mrs Dashwood greets me, she is profuse, apologetic for the delay, her words come out in fits and starts and yet it seems like a single great rush. She is quite beautiful, tall and slim, with a mane of golden-brown hair and a full smile that she keeps flashing at me like a lighthouse warning a ship off the rocks. It won't do any good. I can see rocks everywhere. [*Pause*] She tells me her husband is on his way back from work and apologises again and tells me that she has just come off the phone from talking to him . . . I tell her it's okay. I don't tell her that I know how embarrassed she feels, to have reached this point, this despair. To actually have called on someone like me . . . So now here I am, the miracle worker, the last-resort man, the child detective. I dream the lost children . . . [*Pause*] I conduct the preliminary interview, as routine. Throughout, she scrutinises me as carefully as I watch her. I know she isn't quite sure how she should behave with me . . . am I staff or somehow her equal? She's hiring me, of course, but I know she hasn't quite accepted just what it is that I've come to do. [*Long pause – a sighing noise – something being picked up, put down again*] Again, I have to say she is quite a beautiful woman, although I can see how much of a strain recent events must have been for her. Anyway, her beauty is part of her front, a performance intended to disarm me. At first glance, she radiates the same wealthy glow as her house, but it doesn't take long before she slips and her pain starts to show. As she talks, she stares at a spot on the wall behind my head and I can't help feeling this strange disconnect, as if her words and her voice and her being don't quite match up, as though everything is at cross purposes . . . almost as if I'm watching a badly dubbed movie, an actor who has lost faith in her role. While she talks on this large dog slouches over and slumps by her feet and looks at me with empty, sad eyes. [*Pause*] I tell her I'm taping everything and that this is a condition of my employment and that Mr Dashwood agreed my terms by phone. She nods automatically as I tell this to her and, well, it's obvious to me that she has no idea really what she should say or how she should react. Until her son went missing such things were never part of her life. She frets about her husband coming back but I tell her it's okay, it doesn't matter, I've started already. These first impressions are very important. I tell her, as gently as I can, that I need to see everything and know everything, that I want her to open up the innermost secrets of her family to me. This is what I need, this is the only way I can help her. She understands, I think, but it is hard for her. It is hard for everyone when we first meet. But losing the child is always harder . . . [*Pause*] I tell her little about my methods, I explain they can seem rather unconventional, but that I'm not the police, I'm not *like* the police, that's the point. And my methods work. I think she understands, I think she might even believe me. She doesn't flinch, anyway, when I ask for a few photographs of Timothy, a couple of items of his clothing, unwashed, if possible. I tell her I also need to see his room. [*He coughs and clears his throat*] We go upstairs, to the first floor. She leads me to his door. I ask her where the other bedrooms are and she points to his brother's room, the first door in the corridor, and then their room, further down and facing the road. I wonder what they have in the other rooms, upstairs, because a house this size should have five or six in total, but I haven't time to look now. I ask her to leave me alone and I go inside. [*Pause*] Sometimes, when this happens, when I go in the child's room, everything becomes much clearer . . . [*He sighs*] Like the Young case when I could feel, right away, the girl's misery . . . or the Morris case – then, the moment I entered the bedroom I knew the poor lad was dead. It was like descending into a mausoleum, that bedroom . . . I have my gift, as they say, but it offers no comfort. [*Pause*] What comfort indeed? [*Pause*] This time it's much harder. It's all very, very opaque, like a curtain has passed over my mind, shutting off certain things . . . a sort of haze . . . like water suddenly filled with ink. The swirling is suggestive, but everything keeps changing. Nothing is clear. [*Pause*] For a start, the room has been cleaned and tidied since Timothy vanished. I know the police have searched the house from top to bottom and confiscated certain items and I'm pretty sure, at least from what York told me, that they didn't find anything of great use. But as a result many traces have been lost, not least because it has been a while now and the emotions, although they linger like a stain or an echo, in the end they fade. Anyway, it's quite a large room, with a single bed in the corner, a bookshelf and wardrobe opposite, a small desk by the window. He has a nice view over the communal gardens. [*Another pause, longer than before*] So I pace around, touching the bed and the coats in the wardrobe. I squeeze each item, running them through my hands, hoping for a sense of something . . . but they are all so dry. There is so little left, so little residue. The rest of the house was richer. Then I lie on the bed, keeping my feet on the floor and try to think what it was like for him, in his room. It was growing dark outside so I turned out the lights and lay down again, watching the shadows. Then . . . as I'm sitting there . . . it slowly occurs to me. This boy was trying to be someone else, and he did a pretty good job too, I think, of fooling his parents. His room is the almost perfect copy of what a middle-class thirteen-year-old boy's room would look like. But it's a put-up job, a confidence trick. The posters on the walls – a Ferrari, a rap star, a map of the world, a space shuttle – the thin shelf of books, the Harry Potter, the Philip Pullman – it's all too normal, too generic . . . even the model sports car in a box, the selection of pop and rock CDs, the computer games. There's no edge, no hint of resistance. [*Pause*] An everyboy. [*Pause*] He's fooling us. [*Pause*] This is who he wants us to think he is. [*Pause*] But this isn't him, this isn't Timothy at all. [*Pause*] I try and collapse the boundaries of his world and imagine sitting in this room, each evening, with my prep and the view of the gardens below, the faint noises from downstairs, the toilet across the corridor. I am a new boy. The new boy at the new school. Why would I want to run away? Bullying? Loneliness? The yearning to be somewhere else, a desire to escape overwhelming all else? To escape every-thing, most of all myself? A hatred of the world and all that is in it? [*Pause*] His school books are piled, quite neatly, on his desk. I flick through them, looking at his messy, rather spidery handwriting. He seems to get good marks though, As and Bs in his history and English. The gruesome sketch on the back of another exercise book is the first thing that comes close to surprising me. A masked man raises a samurai sword above the head of another man, blindfolded and kneeling beneath him. Despite the cartoonish details and the garish colours, there is something quite uncanny about the sketch. A ritual decapitation . . . like one of those horror videos on the news. This boy has an eye for the blood-thirsty details. [*Pause*] Mrs Dashwood brings me Timothy's rugby top which she tells me hasn't been washed. She didn't have the heart, she said, and I wondered what that meant. Perhaps she didn't think he would ever need it again. I was sitting on Timothy's bed when she came in and after giving me the shirt she sort of stared at me for a moment. I could tell it made her feel uncomfortable, the sight of me on the bed of her missing son, holding his clothes. I wanted her to go away and leave me alone. I needed to press my face into the top and inhale what remains of the boy, suck up the last of his smells, the lingering atoms of skin and hair. [*Pause*] Instead, I followed Mrs Dashwood into the kitchen. The au pair made me a cup of tea. She kept her gaze on the floor the whole time. I wondered if she was the sort to lurk just outside the room, listening as I explained to Mrs Dashwood that I would have to speak to everyone in the house. Instead I gave Mrs Dashwood the usual spiel about understanding how difficult all this was for her. She stood and nodded and tilted her face towards me and demurred. The way she tilted her face . . . the nakedness in that expression . . . sporting her vulnerability like a bruise, a stigma. She has very clear skin, bright and pale, but she was also showing me the fresh lines around her eyes and mouth, the shroud of anxiety, the fret and sleeplessness surrounding her. She was trying to show me she had nothing to hide. I couldn't tell whether I believed her or not. Her son, certainly, he was hiding enough.

Arthur stops the tape.

The description of his wife stings him, the awareness of her pain. What happened should have made them closer. But it seems as if the strain has been too much to bear. Or perhaps Timothy's disappearance has simply exposed the faults in their relationship. He has read that the parents of children who die often split up afterwards, as if their relationship can go no further without their offspring. He has always thought how sad that is, that the love which made the child can also die with the child. But he also knows that for quite a while the situation with his wife has not been ideal. Most of the time work has kept him too busy to think about it, but what good would thinking about it have done

115

anyway? Saudi Arabia had been a terrible strain, his job was stressful, the places he had to go to, the danger she felt he was in. It wasn't always so easy to open up. Still, his love for her has endured, a weight around his heart.

With a sigh, he reaches for the next tape.

– All in all, I think we lived in the Gulf for about eight years in total. [*There she was, his wife, chattering away*] Our second boy, Harry, he was actually born in the American hospital in Dubai. At first we were in the UAE, but then Arthur was posted to Saudi so that was where we ended up spending most of our time. It was a little unusual at first, especially if like me one so loved the green of England . . . but the compounds were very comfortable – luxurious, in fact . . . it was rather like living in a big resort hotel. Everything was paid for by the company, everything was taken care of. There really wasn't anything to do.

– Did you get bored?

– Not really . . . well, sometimes, but Arthur was home a great deal at first and we met lots of lovely new people. There was a great sense of community, a lot of socialising. The company encouraged everybody to make friends, not that there was anything else one could do, really, if you see what I mean. There was nowhere else to go . . . of course, some people did go a bit stir crazy and there were the inevitable affairs and suchlike . . . [*Pause*] I suppose the men without wives were worse, or those whose family were back home. They would drink a lot . . . that sort of thing. We didn't. Well. [*She sighs*] There were quite distinct groups, you see, largely divided on national lines, the French and the Dutch and the Germans and the Russians all tended to stick to themselves a little more. The British . . . we mingled a bit, mainly with the Americans

and Australians, South Africans too. Most of my friends
were like me – wives with small children and all our husbands worked for the same company. We'd meet for coffee,
take classes together in Islamic culture, basic Arabic, that
sort of thing . . . It helped with the staff, if you could speak
a few words. Or we'd just go to the gym or relax by the
pool. It was pleasant, I suppose. The days would just flow
past. At least to start with, before the trouble. It was like
sleepwalking, really. I worked out a great deal at the gym,
kept thin, had a splendid tan. What else was there to do? It
was just this sort of endless pleasant cycle, you know, gym,
beauty spa, television, planning the next social occasion.
All very pleasant, but all the same, rather empty . . . [*Pause*]

– Of course.

– Like I said, it was fine. But it was hard to go out and
leave the compound, Saudi Arabia being such a strict country, so *different* from our own. We didn't have much contact
with the real country – no contact, to be honest. I had to
wear a veil when I went out and . . . but there was nowhere
to go to, anyway. We had all the shops we needed in the
compound. Outside was . . . I never felt very comfortable.
The men. So many men out there. I always felt like they
were staring at me. Of course, they could tell you were a
Westerner. It was obvious, really.

[*Another pause. Someone shuffles*]

– So what happened?

– It was only after the attacks began to escalate. [*A sharp
intake of breath. The thought of what she might say to Buxton
makes him suddenly uneasy, as if there are secrets between them
he had never before recognised.*] There had always been threats,
you see, but then things got much worse very quickly. As I
keep saying, we never went outside much anyway, out of
the compound . . . the company certainly didn't encourage

it . . . but then suddenly there was this great threat, all this danger which had always been so vague before and unspecified, now it was real, and still, everything stayed more or less the same . . . That was what was so frightening, because it all seemed so unreal. We would get these daily e-mails from the head of security informing us if the threat warning was high or very high or moderate . . . and giving 'tips' . . . it was always full of 'security tips' . . . gosh, you know, like how to tell if your staff were behaving suspiciously or what to do if someone rammed your vehicle . . . I couldn't bear it, really, I hardly ever used to read them. [*Pause*] Then a compound a few miles away from us was attacked. That was when it really hit home. [*Pause*] It was an awful attack. A colleague of Arthur's was killed. It was terrible, appalling. They . . . Well . . . It was said that his body was tied to a car and dragged around the streets. No one ever found out if the rumour was true. [*A longer pause*] A lot of people were killed in the attack. They killed the Westerners. All the Muslims they let go. And then of course Saudi soldiers stormed the compound and more people were killed in the shoot-out. It was horrible. We'd been to that compound for dinner, Arthur and I. I'd been there. And then there it was, on the news, all shot up . . . broken glass, pools of blood . . . Afterwards, everything seemed so much more frightening. [*Pause*] Some of the men in the compound had firearms training. Carrying guns was allowed . . . Arthur bought a pistol which he kept locked in a box in the bedside drawer. It terrified me, that thing, just the sight of it. God, I hated him for doing that . . . really . . .

That pistol. She was right: a lot of men had bought guns after the compound attack and the head of security had organised basic firearms training. Susan had shunned him after he'd purchased the weapon, terrified that he'd have an accident. Even after he agreed to keep it locked in a box the gun had been a sore point, something they never spoke about. All the same, despite his wife's pressure, there was something undeniably thrilling about owning a gun. Sometimes, when he knew she was asleep, he used to unlock the box and take out the gun. He enjoyed its weight in his hand, the lethal brilliance of the design. Loading a full clip and flipping off the safety catch, he used to step into the warm night, the presence of the weapon sharpening his senses, filling him with a nervy adrenalin surge. Outside, he would stand for a moment or two, pointing at imaginary targets in the darkness. Such childish behaviour. Susan was right, ultimately. It was a stupid thing to do. They didn't need a gun.

– And there were lots of new guards around the compound, people we didn't recognise. Of course there were rumours that it was the staff and guards at the other compound who had helped the terrorists to get in. I never knew if this was true or not, how could I? But it was difficult to trust anyone, and there were so many staff, you see, maids and cooks and drivers and guards and pool attendants and compound managers and gardeners, all these people. Of course we always had excellent relations with our staff, always . . . but some people had terrible rows. And there were . . . stories. More rumours. I just didn't know who to trust, you see. They had a faith we lacked. I began to wonder if, secretly, they all hated us. [*Another pause. Susan clears her throat*] It was awfully difficult to know what was going on and with the children, as you can imagine . . . I didn't want them to get upset or worried. Timmy, of course, he was always so sensitive to the smallest change, it was like he knew what was going on without anyone telling him. [*Pause*] Then things just got worse, someone was kidnapped – no one I knew – just an oil worker, an American, kidnapped from outside the hotel where he lived . . . it underscored the dangers . . . They executed him on the Internet, chopped his head off. Awful. I still remember his wife on television, pleading for his life. Poor woman . . . The atmosphere was so horrible. A lot of my friends left. Their husbands stayed on. It became an issue, between Arthur and me, what we should do. I didn't want to stay – I was desperate to leave, in fact, desperate to get back to England. But Arthur was always saying how safe we were . . . well, I didn't care how safe we were supposed to be or how slim the odds of an attack were . . . the last compound was just like ours and anyway, I knew it couldn't happen back in England, no matter what. We wouldn't need to keep a pistol in the house, for goodness' sake! I thought I was going mad with worry. I didn't want to stay but I didn't want to go back to England alone, leaving Arthur out there. Each day he left for the office or to visit a refinery or a pipeline and he'd go off in this bulletproof car with all these guards and I'd have nothing to do except sit about the villa or watch television or go swimming or try and play with the children, worrying all the time what might happen. All day I would be watching people, watching the man cleaning the pool or weeding the garden, the man who polished the cars in the car park or who put my shopping in a bag in the compound super-market, watching them, thinking they could be anyone, *anyone*, a terrorist, a fanatic, anything, I just didn't know, I couldn't tell. And they would *look* at me. I can't describe it. I felt so guilty when they looked at me, as if I'd done some-thing, as if we were somehow to blame for what was happening. And in a way we were, that was the thing, that was what I couldn't get out of my head. Of course Arthur never agreed with me about this. We couldn't even speak about it, but I had the feeling that I – that we – that we deserved what was happening to us. We deserved it. It was like some sort of punishment . . . I . . . it's hard to explain. I felt we were being punished for being Westerners, you know, but in a way that was right. We should be punished. We should. It was . . . it is our fault.

A long pause. Arthur considers his wife's words. 'Our fault.' Maybe she was right. Maybe this was their punishment.

– I had a small breakdown when we finally got back to England, I admit. It was the stress . . . I stayed *compos mentis* while we were out there – I had to keep it together, for the children and for Arthur as much as for myself. I know the situation put him under a great deal of stress as well and I had to try and support him . . . [*Pause*] I don't know how good I was at doing that . . . [*Sigh*] But back home . . . we had this big house in Sussex far from anyone and it was all so strange and we were safe, safe at last and it should have been a relief but it wasn't and I still didn't feel safe and I wasn't used to it, having to do things myself again – cooking, cleaning, all those things – and Arthur was working harder than ever and the children were disorientated and missed their friends and I missed my friends and Arthur was away all the time. He had to keep going back to those places. I would worry so much when he was gone. It was like I went into some kind of a trance . . . [*Pause*] I'd drift about the house, checking the news every hour or so just trying to make sure nothing bad had happened. I had so many fears . . . I felt hemmed in by them all, suffocated. It could be a plane crash, a bomb, a hijacking or a kidnapping . . . suicide attacks, chemical weapons, anything. The whole world felt like a monstrous camp, with half of us dreaming and the other half full of hate, and death never more than a breath away, whether we knew it or not. [*Another long pause*] But when he was home nothing I ever did seemed to be right or to please him or to be as good as it should be. I used to ask myself what I was doing there, in that house, with him and those children . . . I wasn't myself, I didn't feel like I belonged to myself . . . it was like . . . [*Pause*] I don't know . . . like a stranger had occupied my body and it was all I could do to sit by and watch. The feeling passed, of course. They always do. The doctors said it was delayed shock. I'd suppressed all my fears, you see, when we were over there, to such a degree that it wasn't until we were safe and I could relax that I was able to express them. Well. That was what happened. I didn't say I was the strongest woman. I just love my children and my husband, you see. I love them.

– I understand. [*Pause*] There is more, isn't there, Mrs Dashwood?

Arthur recognises that tone. It was true, what Sir Charles had said – Buxton *was* gifted – he had a way of getting one to discuss issues one would rather keep hidden. It was as if he could sense the secret unspoken thing just below the surface of what was said, the thing you had to hide when presenting yourself to others. Carefully and delicately, he would draw it out with searching looks and gentle words, like a fisherman reeling a prize catch from the ocean. He made you trust him, that was what he did: he made you *want* to tell him such things.

– Yes. [*Arthur can feel Susan's desire to speak, the need to unburden herself emanating from the low-fi hiss of the tape*].
   – Yes?

122

– It's silly, I don't . . .

– Please, Mrs Dashwood. We all want to find your son.

– Yes, but you're a detective, not a psychiatrist . . . or a priest.

[*Buxton laughs*] – Well, sometimes I have to have a little of that, too.

– I suppose I've never told anyone this. [*Arthur sits forward, immediately curious. His wife has an ability to find meaning in the things he would overlook, a habit that used to beguile him but now, more often than not, leaves him feeling dismayed and confused.*] I had such dreams in that house. I've never had dreams like that before. When Arthur was away, such vivid dreams! I . . . this is very hard for me to explain, I hope you understand.

– Just do your best, Mrs Dashwood.

– I dreamt about this young man. He would come to my window – in my dream, when I was asleep. He would wake me up, in my dream . . . He was an Arab boy, dressed traditionally, like a character from *1001 Nights*! Most of all I remember his smile. A charming smile! He had such divine little pearly teeth . . . and, well . . . [*Pause*] For some reason I used to wake up from those dreams terribly . . . excited. I can't explain it. It was like being a teenager again, which was about the last time I dreamt of boys, I can tell you that for sure. I would just wake up in such a state, all confused and flustered. All day I'd have this funny itchy sort of feeling, like the boy was outside somewhere, sitting in the trees or clambering over the roof of the house, stupid, I know . . . [*she laughs, quick and brittle, like a twig about to snap*] but sometimes I would even go into the garden, not really looking for him, exactly, you understand, it wasn't like I was looking for him . . . how could I? That would be ridiculous, wouldn't it? But still, I'd go outside . . . [*She trails off*]. I'm not making any sense at all, am I?

– Please, don't worry, Mrs Dashwood. This boy you used to dream about, did he remind you of anyone?

– I really don't . . . I'm not sure . . . I'm not even sure if I should be telling you this . . .

– That's okay.

[*Pause*]

– I'm sorry, can we stop? I think . . . I need . . . I need to think about this . . . I need to be getting on, you know. I'm sorry. It's just . . .

– It's okay . . .

[*A few more words are said, but they are rendered inaudible by the poor quality of the tape. Moments later, it ends.*]

Arthur sits for a moment, shaken by these disclosures. How odd it feels to overhear his wife talking to a stranger in this way, as though he has been eavesdropping outside her door or following her down the street. He selects another tape.

– So tell me a little more about Timothy. What is he like?

– Nice. Quite a sweet boy. A bit shy. But always very polite to me, not like some of the children I have looked after. Timothy was never like that. [*Veca, talking quickly*] He was moody, though, like his mother. He could brood on things, like she does, and it could be hard to know what he was thinking. He like her in lots of ways, more than you might realise. There were . . . some things, always going on in his head. He had deep thoughts. I don't think he like school much. He was, how you say it? Picked up?

– Picked on? Bullied?

– Yes, bullied. I could tell. He never would say anything, but I see it, I know by the way he look some mornings, when I take him to school. So pale. I think he was frightened. I would feel so bad sometime, driving him to school. [*Pause*] I know the family used to live in another country and he was trying to settle into the new place. He shy and I sorry for him, because his parents always so busy with things . . . I knew he wouldn't tell them what was wrong. I also think they not even notice. [*His face colours as he hears her words. It's not like that, he wants to shout at the tape player, she's wrong, she doesn't know anything.*] He never had any friends home to visit and he never go out with anyone. Only imaginary friends.

– What do you mean by that?

– Pretend friends. You know, in head. Timmy talk to them, in room or garden. I'd overhear him, talking to himself. He was embarrass if he thought you hear him. He didn't like anyone to know. He knew he was too old to be doing it.

Arthur listens as Buxton gently questions Veca about this behaviour. She tells him about overhearing Timothy whispering to himself late at night in his bedroom, or else in a quiet part of the communal gardens. Talking to the trees, she says, and always stopping the moment he saw you. Arthur doesn't want to admit it, but he can't deny what she is saying. He also remembers hearing the quick whisper of his son's voice coming from his bedroom when he should have been asleep. Whenever he went in to check, the boy would cease immediately, usually pretending to be sleeping, hiding under his duvet. Arthur rarely bothered to say anything to him, assuming it was enough just to peer in. Sometimes he would go a little further, unable to resist briefly touching his son's head to whisper a tender 'good night'. He knew Timothy resented such intrusions, but that was normal, he thought, a common sign that his boy was growing up, making a claim for some privacy.

*

– What was it like, this talking to himself?

   – It was . . . I don't know . . . like half a conversation. Like he was talking to a friend, but the friend wasn't talking back.

   – A fluent conversation, is that what you mean?

   – Fluent, sir? I don't know word?

   – Like the way we're speaking now.

   – I'm not sure I understand, sir . . .

Impatient, Arthur fast-forwards the tape. He has given little thought to Veca and how she must have felt about what happened. In the end, he decided to let the girl go. Not that it was really fair – she wasn't to blame for what had happened – but then it didn't seem fair to keep her on either. He presses 'play' again. Veca is still talking.

– To be honest, I wasn't sure he was ill. Holidays only one day away and I think probably he just pretending. But what would it matter! I felt sorry for him. He said he was ill and I knew he not like school. His mother should see him. I know I should have woke her up. Perhaps if I done that, everything now different . . . I not know. She could get so cross if I woke her.

   – What is she like, Mrs Dashwood?

   – Moody! She could be very . . . what is the word? Sulky. Sulky and prickly. Sometimes she could be a total bitch. She would say Veca you do this, you do that – make tea, cook dinner, go shops, do it this way, all the time! Officially, okay, I am only meant to work seven until seven with Sunday and two afternoons free a week. That's what agency said, with contract. But Mrs Dashwood could be very sneaky woman. She be like, Veca could you do just this one little thing for me, can I borrow you for one tiny second, please? Sometimes I stay in my room because that was only way she wouldn't bother me. She never went to my room. And I didn't much like going to her bedroom, not even for cleaning. It make me feel uncomfortable, especially to disturb her if she is sleeping. She doesn't like that. I thought I would get in trouble. She relies on me to do all the things with the boys . . .

– You mustn't blame yourself, Veca. It's not your fault. The boy tricked you. He ran away.

– That is what I try and think too, it is just that . . . [*Her voice cracks and he can see her, weeping quietly, dabbing her eyes*] I just wish I make him get up and go to school . . . [*A pause, a noise outside, rustles on the tape*]

– What's that?

– What? [*More noises, indistinct, but familiar, in a way he can't place*] Oh, that. [*Pause*] [*The noise again, rustling, like a ball of paper being crumpled and uncrumpled over and over.*] I think it's those rough boys again, we get them all the time, these wild boys . . . I don't know where they come from. Always making trouble.

– Never mind.

More noises obscure the voices while the rustling continues and Arthur thinks, yes, this sound is something he too has heard, late at night, in those shadowed moments when he turns from the computer, a space in his thoughts, a fearful rustling in other places.

– Often I would hear Mr Dashwood walking about the house late at night. I would hear the ceiling creaking above my room as he pace about.

– Would he often do this?

– Mmm, sometimes . . . Since Timothy went missing, a lot more. They don't even talk so much, Mr and Mrs Dashwood, not now. At first, for a bit, but now I don't know . . . Often, though, I find him up late at night. If I need the toilet or a drink, my room is in basement, you see, so I must go upstairs and walk through kitchen. Sometimes Mr Dashwood in his study, working on computer. Once or twice I find him sitting in kitchen, not doing anything. Staring at nothing. [*Noises incomprehensible*] One time, before this happen, we had this little talk. It was very late but we were talking and it was a quite nice talk, you know? I feeling sorry for him, I think this poor man lonely. It's like . . . you know . . . He has this lovely house . . . but he lonely. His wife mean to him and he work all time and cannot sleep. Sad, you not think? [*Pause*] So we talk a bit and I feel awkward. Normally, Mr Dashwood ignore me and leave Mrs Dashwood to tell me what to do. But now he's asking me question about my home and what my family does, sort of things Mrs Dashwood never ask. I don't think she care about who I am at all.

Arthur remembered this conversation, only a couple of weeks before Timothy's vanishing. He'd had a nightmare about Baghdad again, and had been sitting in the kitchen wondering if he could go back to sleep when Veca came up. It was true, what she said, he rarely gave her any thought. Managing her was his wife's job. He had enough people to manage. He had never really considered what she thought of him or his wife. It seemed irrelevant. The boys seemed to like her, and that was all he really cared about. Again, he found himself wondering how much his own behaviour had made what had happened possible. The tape continued, Veca talking about his family and her life in England, while Buxton probed the circumstances behind the disappearance. By now Arthur was more than familiar with the details of what had happened: how Veca had dithered for a little while in Knightsbridge after dropping Harry off at his preparatory school, how she went on to the huge Tesco in Earl's Court to do the shopping that his wife had requested. He knew what she had told the police, he had read her statements, been asked to corroborate certain details. The difference, after hearing her voice, was in the details: the subversive little ways she had found to waste time, to fill up the morning – getting a coffee in the supermarket café, reading a magazine – the small postponements before she knew she had to get back to the house, everything behind that terrible, cold morning.

– I got back to the house before lunchtime [*she went on*] and when I went in, everything so quiet. Then I am thinking something not quite okay. It was this funny feeling . . . Mrs Dashwood was not there, but I knew she often went out. But I expected to see Timmy. I thought he would be playing computer. He like to play computer, especially if his parents not there to tell him to stop. So I think, okay, maybe she take him out with her. Only the dog was home, and she was upset, barking at me when I come in and running round me. I thought Muffy just being silly, but she knew Timmy was gone. I remember putting things away, doing little tidying jobs in the kitchen because Mrs Dashwood not like any mess and I was thinking I should go up and check on Timothy. Maybe he still sleeping, I think. But I kept putting it off, I not so sure why.

Arthur knew this. He had been in a meeting when the calls came in. His secretary had entered the room, and he remembered the funny expression on her face. She was probably just worried about his reaction – after all, she knew she was not supposed to disturb him in such meetings unless it was an emergency. He had been meeting with representatives of the Bahrainian oil ministry. Thinking back now, it was impossible to recall anything at all from the fateful meeting. But he remembered his secretary coming in, the way she whispered that his wife was on the phone and that it was urgent.

– And when you couldn't find Timothy in his room, what did you do then?
    – Right away I phoned Mrs Dashwood. I thought she must have taken him with her.
    – But her phone was switched off, is that correct?

Of course it was. His wife had no idea Timothy hadn't gone to school. Finding the house empty when she got up, she had assumed Veca had taken the boys to school as normal. Timothy only had a narrow window of escape – no more than half an hour. How could he have got so far in such little time?

– Yes, she was at gym. So I leave her message asking if she got my note. I felt a bit round the wrong way, you know, but I couldn't put my finger on it. What was I supposed to think happen? The idea that Timmy would run away was not in my mind. Why would he? It make no sense. It still make no sense and I tell the police this and everything. Mrs Dashwood phoned me back and she say what note and so I say I leave a note about Timmy being ill in bed, and again, she say what note? I can't forget the way of her voice, you know, as she say that. So I say I left note on kitchen table, where she would see it. But she keep saying to me, what note? I was walking around, looking under things, in case the note fallen on floor. We were looking for a missing note when it Timmy who is missing! [*She makes a hissing noise*] And so I said is Timmy with you and she said she thought I take Timmy to school. She said she not see Timmy when she got up. Then I notice his favourite trainers are not where he leave them always and then, in the corner, by Muffy's bed, I saw this big pile of his school books, pens, all these things dumped in big pile. Oh God. It was worst feeling. I go all over house, calling Timmy, telling myself that nothing happened and I was being silly. I went into garden too, calling Timmy in case he out there. But he not there, no one was out there. Then I start feeling very much scared.

Arthur keeps listening. He remembers going to answer the phone, finding Susan scarcely coherent, saying something about how Timothy wasn't at home and he wasn't at school and they didn't know where he was. Her voice sounded like a sheet of glass breaking apart, and her words felt like a shard of ice pressed against his spine. From the moment he took that call, everything was different. Veca continued, her narrative broken by occasional sobs, her distress painfully apparent, talking about how the police were called and what they did. For a couple of days she was a prime suspect. Arthur had even floated the theory to Captain York that she had arranged to have his son kidnapped by an East European gang, to be sold into slavery or some similar, unspeakable horror. But her story had checked out. The poor girl didn't know any gangsters. Indeed, listening to her voice, the way her English – normally so coherent – broke up as she tried to articulate her feelings, Arthur was in no doubt about her innocence. He found himself feeling sorry for her. He wanted to hate her, blame her negligence for what had happened: but it wasn't her fault. She wasn't the negligent one.

– All the colour gone from his face now. [*She was talking about him again*]. Sometime he shout lots, at Susan or people on phone. But most of the time he just make cups of coffee and eat biscuits. He not look at me any more. He hardly ever seems to sleep. It's just awful. And Mrs Dashwood . . . she is worse.

Arthur stops the tape. He gets up and paces once round his office. He sits down again, rubbing bloodshot eyes. He tries not to remember the expression on his wife's face when he rushed home after her phone call. 'He's gone,' she'd said, standing in the doorway, solemn as a statue in a graveyard. 'Our Timmy, he's not here any more.'

Quickly, he puts another tape in the machine.

– . . . Shortly before we returned to England, I started having the strangest – how can I put this? [*Susan, this time sounding more measured and thoughtful, her voice thankfully without the heightened, brittle emotion of the previous tape*] Visions . . . hallucinations, I'm not sure how I'd describe it. I think, to be honest with you, these things I thought I was seeing were just a reflection of my state of mind at the time. As I said, I was ever so anxious.

– Yes.

– And so you see . . . oh dear, I'm not making much sense, am I?

– That's quite all right Mrs Dashwood. You just tell it to me in your own way. Tell me whatever you feel like.

– Thank you. [*Another pause. Arthur is surprised by how relaxed she sounds. It has been a long time, he thinks, since she spoke to him in this way.*] Well, the situation was, as I said, rather tense, and I started imagining – well seeing, really – but imagining, these other children. I kept thinking they were Saudi boys – it was only boys – running around the compound. They were dressed traditionally in long white thawbs, and they were . . . well, they didn't seem very old, the

132

same sort of ages as Timothy and Harry. [*Another pause*] The trouble is, I mean, the way I'm saying it suggests I *saw* them, like I can see you now. But I didn't. [*She sighs with frustration*] I'm not explaining this very well. [*Buxton says something in return, but his voice is muffled slightly*] It was more the case that I heard them, or glimpsed them, out of the corner of my eye, always disappearing round a corner, or just sort of glimpsed, in the distance as it were . . . but hazy, rather like a mirage. [*She gives a hollow little laugh*] I must sound rather crazy, I know. [*Another pause*]

– So how could you be sure how old they were?

– I beg your pardon?

– Well, you said they were the same age as your children. But then you also said that you never really got a clear view of these Saudi children.

– Yes, okay, I understand what you're getting at. It's just . . . I can't. Oh dear. I can't really give you a very clear answer, I'm afraid. I'm awfully sorry. It was more like a feeling. I can't be certain about anything.

– That's quite all right. Feelings are very important. We actually know far more than we realise. We just need to let our feelings guide us more. Anyway, I'm digressing. I'm fascinated by what you have to say. Continue, please.

– Okay, well, these boys . . . yes, well, anyway, one day Timothy said something to me. It was something like, 'Mummy, where have all the Arab boys come from?' I didn't know what to make of it. It stopped me dead in my tracks when he said that. Because I'd been sort of seeing them, but at the same time I couldn't have been. But then he said this and—

– Can you remember what you said in return?

– I asked him what he meant. He'd said he'd seen some Saudi boys outside yesterday, and he thought they wanted to play. Then he looked at me and he asked me if he could go and play with them.

– So how did you respond to this suggestion?

– I guess I thought that . . . which is to say, I mean, it was possible that they were the children of some of our Saudi workers. Anyway, I said that he could, but that he must come and introduce them first, so I could ask their parents.

– And did he agree with your idea?

– In all honesty, as far as I can remember he just looked a little disappointed and went back to whatever he was doing. He never mentioned the subject again. This was only a month or so before we went back to England. He knew we were going back.

Hearing his wife's words, Arthur feels a strange chill that has nothing to do with the air-conditioning. There are so many connections – he understands this now – so many possibilities, so many shadowed links between imagination and reality that his mind whirls, at once giddy and terrified.

– Was there anything else unusual about your time in the compound? Anything at all?

– I have been thinking about this – as you told me to. There was something which I forgot. It connects with everything, really. Actually, I can't believe I didn't tell you about this earlier. [*At once, Arthur is certain he knows what she is referring to*] Shortly before we came back home, a child went missing in the compound. It was . . . let me remember, one of the American children, a boy.

Arthur remembers what happened. He vaguely knew the father, an executive in the company. The boy was thirteen years old, a blond, cheerful lad who was friendly with

Timothy. They didn't find out until quite late in the evening, when they received a phone call from compound security, raising the alarm. Leaving Susan to watch the boys, Arthur had spent part of the night with other parents, staff and security guards, searching the compound, looking under vehicles and checking bushes and storerooms. Rumours spread, suggesting the boy had been kidnapped, smuggled from the compound in a service vehicle by an extremist group. Arthur didn't speak to the boy's father that night, but he did remember the man's face, ashen with worry while he was deep in conversation with Saudi security men. He remembered thanking God it was another boy missing, and not one of his own.

– Early in the morning, apparently, the boy just turned up outside the gates. I never saw him – I mean, he came back, and the emergency was over, but I never saw him again. I can't even remember the boy's name.

Kagan, Arthur thinks to himself, Robert Kagan. As far as he knew, no one was ever able to understand what had happened to the boy that night. He returned dirty and a little tired, but unharmed in any way. Compound security and a psychiatrist spent a long time interviewing him, trying to find out where he'd been and what had happened. As far as Arthur was aware, Robert had not been forthcoming with any answers and the exact circumstances of what had happened remained a mystery. Grainy CCTV footage apparently showed him, with two other unidentified boys, using a rope to scale the compound wall. Arthur had never seen this footage, and it didn't seem to explain how they were able to avoid the barbed wire and electric fencing. The compound was rigged with motion-sensitive equipment designed to respond to the slightest disturbance. Stray dogs, birds, even enthusiastically struck baseballs frequently set the sensors off, so he had never understood how three adolescent boys and a rope could have evaded detection. Despite the happy resolution of the crisis, he remembered seeing Robert's father in the compound café. Rather than expressing relief, the man was shaking his head and saying something about how his son 'wasn't quite the same any more'.

[*Susan continues*] – I said before that I had strange dreams when we moved back to England. I think I should have said the dreams started earlier. [*She hesitates again, a mannerism familiar to Arthur. She would often pause this way when worried about embarrassing herself*] They started before then, these dreams about the Arab boy. A long time before. [*Her voice lifts a little, as if the memory of these dreams delights her still*] I was having them in Saudi. Almost every night.

– Dreams about an Arab boy. Is that correct?

– Oh, yes . . . and he had such brilliant pearly-white teeth. Such a divine little boy, like my Timothy might have been, if he was born over there . . . [*She trails off, a sadness deepening her tone*]

– Can you remember much about these dreams? Any specific details?

Impatient, Arthur fast-forwards the tape. Buxton's approach can be quite infuriating. He can't see the relevance of Susan's weird dreams to their case. Throughout their marriage, as long as he can remember, she's been having strange dreams of one sort or another. Such speculative mumbo-jumbo is not helpful. He starts the tape again.

– . . . Husband and I went through a difficult patch about thirteen years ago, before any of the children were born.

We'd been married for four years and we were trying for children. It took us a little while. At the time I was terribly worried that Arthur was going off me, you know, that he didn't love me as much as he used to or didn't find me as attractive as he once had. I think I thought . . . well, I'm not sure really what I thought. He wasn't having an affair or anything like that, I could tell that much, I was sure. [*Pause*] Anyway, I became pregnant and I was awfully happy. I thought that meant the relationship was saved. [*Pause*] I thought that meant everything would be okay. [*Pause*] Then, five months into the pregnancy, I miscarried. Arthur was away on business. I woke up in the night and I knew something was wrong . . . When I turned on the light, the sheets were covered in blood. [*Pause*] Oh, it was awful. [*Pause*] An ambulance took me to hospital. It took ages to contact Arthur because he was in Texas . . . It was all over before I could even speak to him. I wanted him to come back home as soon as he could. The baby – a boy – I called him David, although it was too late for any of that. [*Pause*] But I wanted what was left, the body if you could call it that. I told the hospital I wanted it. In the end they just gave me the ashes. Arthur was still in Texas and they sent me home, but not with my baby . . . just this horrible plastic box with the ashes of this five-month thing that hadn't even quite become a human being yet. I remember . . . God, it was so awful . . . I felt as though my insides had been turned inside out, as if I'd been scraped clean by something cold and hard and merciless. I remember walking through Kensington Gardens and I was just sort of crying and as I walked I emptied all the ashes into the wind. It was the middle of winter and it was raining and the ashes were just kind of gone. God. Such a horrid thing. It was like emptying a Hoover bag – a quick plume of dust and then nothing. That was David. I never told Arthur that I'd named him. I never told Arthur what I had done. [*Pause*] I said the hospital had taken it away and that was all. He was home the next day – he was home as quick as he could come. I remember him crying on my lap and saying how sorry he was. I didn't know why he was so sorry. I thought our marriage was dead and he wouldn't want me now. I was like a polluted lake, a dirty river. Death was inside me. I thought it was over . . .

Arthur stops the tape. For a while he sits, seeming to stare at nothing. Some time passes before he feels able to press 'play' again.

– When I was recovering from the miscarriage I first began having these dreams. That was when . . . I'm sorry . . . it gets confused in my head. I'm not making sense, am I?

– Let me get this right. You are saying that these dreams didn't start in Saudi? You are saying they started much earlier, after your miscarriage?

– I think so. I think that was when the dreams started. But I think they stopped, for a long time. With the visions – if you can call them that. I think being in Saudi made the dreams start again – these dreams, I mean. [*Pause*]

– Can you go on? You were telling me how you felt after the hospital. I'm sorry, I understand this must distress you.

– It does . . . but . . . it's okay. [*She breathes in deeply*] After it happened, I sort of went into this depression. I was still in a lot of pain although the doctors said it was all psycho-somatic . . . there wasn't really anything wrong with me, they said, not physically. But I felt sick, sick deep inside, as if all my blood had turned into tar. They gave me some sleeping pills and some other pills . . . I don't really remember what they were supposed to do . . . anyway . . . Arthur was being awfully kind to me, but he was at work all day. He had to go. The company hadn't been very happy that he'd had to come back from Texas to see me, so it wasn't like he could stay home nursing me. He always has to work. It's just the way it is . . . [*Pause*] There wasn't much he could do for me anyway . . . [*Pause*] Arthur was out at the office all day and I just sat about in the flat . . . I don't really remember what I did. Hours seemed to blend together, morning and afternoon, night and day, I hardly noticed . . . it was as if I'd sit down, in the morning, with my tea, and before I knew it, before I'd done anything, it would be almost dark out. [*Pause*] Everything felt so flat and grey and empty. He was terribly kind to me, Arthur, and kept saying things to me that were supposed to be a comfort . . . you know, how it didn't matter, all that sort of thing. But he didn't understand. Not really. It was like he was somewhere else, on the other side, talking to me from somewhere far away . . . even when he tried to put his arms around me it was like, I don't know, like I'd been put behind ice. A wall made of ice. [*Pause*] But I didn't want him to touch me. I couldn't stand it. I didn't want anyone to touch me. [*Pause*] I knew it hurt him when I moved out of the bedroom, I knew he would find it cruel. I knew this . . . but all the same, what he felt, it didn't seem to matter. In the end he slept on the sofa and made me take back the bed. He can be very stubborn, my husband, stubborn but very sweet. Each evening he just kept on asking me what was wrong and, oh, I don't know, I must have driven him half crazy. People only have so much kindness and understanding inside, don't they? [*Pause*] He would cook dinner . . . run me a bath . . . he did all these nice things but I just wanted to be left alone. I wanted to disappear, melt away, just vanish into the sky . . . anything. [*Pause*] I don't know. [*Pause*] I was silly, I was silly I know and I was awfully cruel to poor Arthur because he was suffering too. It was our child that we had lost, even though I felt so much that it – that he, I mean he, my David, had been all mine. [*Pause*] One day, when Arthur was out at work, the boy came back to me. I thought he was David, grown up a few years. He was David and at the same time he wasn't David. He was what David might have become, and he was all the thousands of other boys as well, all the boys who were denied any real chance of life, all the ones cut off too soon, betrayed and poisoned by us. [*The sudden violence in her voice, the shift from wistful recollection to passion surprises him*]

– Us? You had a miscarriage. No one was to blame. It happens.

– It happens. Well, yes, I suppose that's what a man would say. Whatever terrible thing it is, oh well, say the men, it happens. [*Pause*] I'm sorry. I'm being rude, I don't mean to . . .

– That's quite all right Mrs Dashwood.

– No, I apologise, I'm just being silly. The past gets all messed up in my head sometimes and, oh dear, I am sorry . . .

– Can I get you a tissue?

– I have one, really, don't worry. In the dreams he would . . . well. It's hard to explain. But he said . . . [*Pause*] He said one day you will have another little boy or little girl and then I'll come and I'll take them away with me. He wanted someone to play with, that's all. [*Pause*] It's hard, growing old, but it was harder still, not growing up at all. But I turned away from him. I had dreams like this, you see, these sorts of dreams, for a little while. [*He can see her, quite clearly, dabbing at her eyes and nose*] Funny, the things you remember, isn't it? [*Pause*] Eventually, I started to feel better and stopped taking the pills. I let Arthur back into bed with me. [*Pause*] But it was like a miracle.

– What do you mean?

– I was pregnant again. We'd hardly made love . . . but there it was. Although I was awfully worried I might miscarry . . . it all went fine and I [*Pause*] . . . I had Timothy and I started to forget all these silly things. [*Pause*] When Timothy was six months old Arthur had to go to Saudi Arabia – that was the first time. He went for two months. I was alone with the child. But I was quite happy – he was such a good baby – I had what I wanted. My lovely little boy. Sometimes, though, I would hear him, gurgling away to himself, and I would go upstairs and the bedroom window would be open, even though I'd be sure it had been closed before and he'd be lying in bed, bright-eyed and wide awake and then I'd remember something I was supposed to have forgotten. [*Pause*] I don't know what I mean . . . [*Pause*] I just didn't realise he would be taken from me, too, just like the first. I thought I would be allowed to have him for longer, you see, for much longer than this . . .

Another pause. After a few minutes Arthur fast-forwards the tape, but the rest seems blank, just an empty hiss and that faint rustling sound. Arthur gets up and moves around the office. He peers behind the blind and looks out at the expanse of the city. Is Timothy out there, he wonders, running wild among the hazy city lights? He rubs at his eyes as waves of exhaustion press down upon on him and then, with a sigh, returns to his desk. Another tape goes into the machine.

– I would like to thank you both for agreeing to speak with me. I appreciate it. I'm sure I needn't tell you, but I'm certain that if we can find Timothy, or at least gain some insight into his disappearance, then we will also be closer to finding out where Edward has gone.

– That was what we thought.

– We want to help in any way we can.

Arthur recognises the voices of Linda and Clive Morgan, Edward's parents. He sits forward, attentive and pensive. Edward had disappeared on the same morning as Timothy.

– Okay, so we know that the police have been unable to find any definite connections, but the police believe, and I agree with them, that these disappearances must be connected. It's impossible to conclude otherwise. We need to try and find out why this has happened. [*Buxton clears his throat*] So, perhaps we could start with you telling me a bit more about what happened on the morning when Edward went missing?

Back in Saudi, in the closed world of the compound, Arthur had known all his son's friends. But since their return to London, Timothy's schoolmates had become no more than names. He had never met any of them. All he had ever seen of Edward was the picture printed in the paper, and a couple of portraits in the Morgans' home. All showed a serious, rather young-looking boy with glasses and a thick mop of tawny blond hair. Was he also 'pretending', Arthur wondered, recalling Buxton's opinion of his son? Had their children duped them all? He had met the Morgans a couple of times previously, at school-related social occasions which Susan had pressured him to attend. He knew that Clive Morgan worked for the Foreign Office and the family had been living in India. Like Timothy, Edward was a new boy, alienated and vulnerable after years spent abroad. He had no idea whether these parallels offered any meaningful clues about what had happened. Different possibilities fluttered through Arthur's mind. He could only hope that Buxton had made better sense of the situation.

– He told me he felt ill and didn't want to go to school, [*Linda continues*] I thought he was just being silly, so I sent him off. Then, at about ten thirty, I had a call from the school office. They said Edward was sick and needed to go home. At first I was a little annoyed. I thought he might be able to manipulate them, but he wasn't getting the better of me. But when I came to collect him, I do admit, he was rather pale.

– This was a couple of days before the end of term?

– That's correct. It was Wednesday. The reason I mention it is that . . . well, it's all part of the odd behaviour that started before the actual . . . [*She hesitates, unable to finish her sentence. Susan was the same, reluctant to let words like 'disappeared', 'missing' or 'vanished' pass her lips, as if to speak so directly was to confirm something she still could not accept*]

– Could you tell me a little more about this behaviour? He didn't return to school, did he?

– No, there was something wrong with Edward. He spent a lot of time in bed. But I did catch him wandering about the apartment on a number of occasions, in a strange state, rather as though he was sleepwalking.

– His sleeping was disrupted ever since we came back from India. [*Clive cuts in*] I think it was all part of the trouble he had adjusting to life back here. He would have these terrible nightmares.

– Yes, they were awful, quite upsetting really. He would be screaming like . . .

– They were so violent. He actually managed to rip his bed sheets.

– Did he ever tell you the content of these dreams? [*The discussion is muffled by the poor quality of the tape. A few inconclusive words filter through before Linda resumes her narrative. Her voice comes across much clearer than before, as if she is sitting closer to the tape recorder*]

– I'd ask him what he was doing and he'd look at me in this rather confused way, as if he couldn't remember who I was. I'd end up leading him back to bed. His nightmares were one thing, but this was quite different. I'd never seen him behave this way before.

– Did you call a doctor?

– Perhaps we should have . . . but he didn't seem to have any physical symptoms to suggest anything was really wrong. No fever or sore throat, nothing like that. He just looked very pale and seemed listless, irritable. I thought he was overtired, exhausted by the end of term. He's at that age, you know how it is.

– Was there anything else about his behaviour? Anything at all unusual?

– No, well . . . [*Clive whispers something to his wife that the tape fails to pick up*] There is another thing [*she continues*]. The night before he . . . before he disappeared [*her voice wavers*] we caught him trying to get out of the apartment.

– How do you mean?

– He was struggling with the front door. We heard him rattling the chain. It was late, after one. We'd gone to bed, but I hadn't fallen asleep. Again, he seemed to be in some sort of trance. I don't know . . . it's rather hard to explain. He was very pale, and his eyes were all red. He really didn't look himself. Even the way he stood wasn't right. He was sort of hunched, like this, you see, and with his hands raised in this funny way. The whole experience was quite uncanny. Edward was looking at me, but at the same time

I don't think he could see me. It was like he was seeing something else. I asked him what he was doing and he muttered a few words in this funny sort of high-pitched voice . . . it was most curious. How can I put it? What he was saying didn't make much sense, I'm afraid. He wasn't speaking English.

– That's right, [*adds Clive*] I actually thought he was speaking Hindi. That was what it sounded like to me. He learnt a few phrases when we were over there.

– Let me get this right. You think he spoke to you in Hindi?

– Just a few words. [*Linda starts*] It's not impossible, is it? I used to speak French fluently and sometimes I have dreams in which everyone is speaking French . . .

– There is something you must understand about my son. [*Clive cuts in again*] Edward was fascinated with India. He loved living there. He was terribly upset when my posting ended and we had to come back home. I call it home – but India was as much home for Edward as England. He's spent about a third of his life there. He used to speak to the driver and the gardener in Hindi, you know, 'How are you today?' – that sort of thing. Our gardener had a son the same age as Edward who used to help out around the house. Krishna. Lovely lad. Edward was always very curious about him. He was always asking questions like where did they live, why didn't Krishna have to go to school. Sometimes they used to play together. We didn't like to encourage such informality, but at the same time it was rather sweet.

– Interesting. Very interesting. [*A long pause. Arthur senses that Buxton is trying to think something through*] Okay, that's great. I might come back to that in a minute – thank you, Mr Morgan. If I may return to you, Mrs Morgan. You said you found Edward trying to get out of the flat and in some sort of trance. Is that correct?

– Yes. I put him back to bed. He resisted, actually, when I laid him down, kicking the sheets and mumbling under his breath.

– In Hindi?

– I couldn't tell. In that funny sort of voice again. It rather gave me the creeps. But I sat with him for a bit until he quietened down and went back to sleep.

– I see. And how many times did this behaviour occur?

– Just a couple. On the whole he seemed perfectly fine. Tired and a little moody, that's all. Not so different from normal, really . . .

– And what was he doing when he wasn't in bed?

– Playing that bloody game. [*She tuts her disapproval*] What's it called – the one they're all obsessed with?

– *Insurgency* [*Clive adds*]

– That's it. Oh, it's dreadful. All the boys are mad for it.

Susan too hated that game. Arthur remembers how annoyed she was after he bought it for the boys. At first he wasn't sure what all the fuss was about. After all, he thought *Insurgency* was just a computer game, the sort of bloodthirsty if essentially harmless entertainment enjoyed by most boys. Arthur knew he would have wanted the game himself, when he was Timothy's age. However, *Insurgency* was an unusually realistic and brutal game. Players could fight on either side – for the 'Coalition', a large, Western-style army with modern technology, or the 'Insurgents', a ragtag and ill-equipped but seemingly endless force of guerrilla soldiers. The scenarios took place in an unnamed country, in flat yellow deserts or high brown mountains, in small mudbrick villages or in the streets of a vast concrete city filled with checkpoints and faintly sinister monuments. Ostensibly a strategy game, whichever side one was on things got nasty.

If you fought for the Coalition support was invariably undermined by collateral damage and troop deaths. As the Insurgents proved immune to laser-guided bombs and attack helicopters, players were forced to adopt more extreme measures – summary executions and torture camps. The Insurgents were no better: unconcerned with civilian or their own casualties, they used suicide bombers and improvised explosives to terrorise the Coalition. Arthur had seen expansion packs for the game that added proxy armies, local militias, foreign mercenaries and fanatical groups that could be deployed by either side. The most controversial aspect of the game, other than the frighteningly realistic graphics and real-time play, was the gruesome corpse-count tracker that always ran along the bottom of the screen – three columns, one each for Coalition, Insurgents and civilians. The number of civilian deaths always outnumbered the rest.

Since the disappearance, Arthur had started to play *Insurgency* himself. Sitting at the computer, as Timothy had done, using the same controls, he could imagine they were a little closer. Like his son, he chose to be an insurgent rather than side with the technologically superior Coalition. He wasn't sure why – it just felt right. The game turned out to be far more challenging than he had expected. His first few attempts had ended disastrously, his men annihilated by air strikes. Success was dependent on ruthlessness: it was necessary to hide in civilian areas, to plant bombs in markets and traffic jams, to attack schools and hospitals, to take hostages, to use the most brutal methods imaginable. There seemed no limit to the scenarios presented by the game. Some nights, when the pain of what had happened was unbearable, Arthur found a strange distraction in stalking the streets of a nameless Third World city, coordinating car bombings and assassinations. In the intensity of the battle he was able to forget himself, the weight of recent weeks peeling away to give a sensation close to release.

On the tape, Linda continued to relate Edward's disappearance to Buxton. Arthur was familiar with the details. When news about Edward reached them, Susan, briefly transported from her grief, had decided they should visit. On a dark, chilly afternoon some days later they had sat in the Morgans' rather formal front room, offering what little comfort they could. Where Susan's grief was dramatic, at times all-consuming, a tempest of sorrow, Linda was much more modest. She wept softly as she spoke, her voice quiet and low, as if a single stone of sadness had lodged in her throat. As she talked, she dabbed her eyes with a handkerchief, apologising for her tears with self-deprecating little smiles, as if to say 'It's all right, don't worry about me, I'll manage.'

Listening to her, Arthur had thought how much worse it must be for them, as Edward was their only child. Linda told how Edward had complained of a headache and said that she had popped out to the pharmacy to get some paracetamol. She almost never left her son alone, she explained, but their building was so secure, and he was a sensible boy. She never imagined anything could happen. Gone for only half an hour, she returned to find the door of the apartment ajar. Inside, she could find no sign of Edward. Her immediate thought was that he had lapsed into another trance and, disorientated, had somehow wandered out. Arthur found this hypothesis questionable. The Morgans lived on the fifth floor of a plush mansion block, and a porter sat guarding the entrance hall. It struck him as most unlikely that anyone could have wandered out of the building unseen, without knowing exactly what they were doing.

After the visit, Susan kept asking him: why had Edward vanished at the same time and on the same day as Timothy? What did it mean? Part of her wanted desperately to believe that the boys had run away together, that it was all part of an elaborate plan. She found comfort in such a thought. Arthur was less optimistic. For him, Edward's vanishing made kidnapping all the more likely. He knew what it was like. He had enemies and Clive, working at the Foreign Office, must have enemies too. Most of the pupils at Brompton came from wealthy, influential families. He imagined that the same gang had kidnapped them all, luring them away with e-mail messages or other, more subtle forms of persuasion that the police had yet to discover.

– Let me just check this. [*On the tape, Buxton fiddles with some papers*] Let me see, it says that CCTV footage from a camera in the corridor shows Edward leaving the apartment at 1.37, a few hours after we think Timothy had vanished. He is wearing white trainers, khaki trousers and a black hooded top. None of the cameras in the stairwell detected him, so we can assume he took the lift to the basement car park. Indeed, we have a few seconds of footage, according to the police, which show him in the basement. We presume. Then what? There is a barrier to the car park entrance, isn't there? But I guess anyone could walk under that?

– That's right. [*Clive affirms*] The barrier is unmanned.

– And so our last sighting comes eight minutes later, from a traffic camera at the junction of Old Brompton Road and Cromwell Road. And that's it?

– Yes, the police showed us that footage. [*Clive again*] I'm sure it was him. But that's the astonishing thing. Thousands of police cameras all over this bloody city and still a boy can disappear . . . it's as if the earth just swallowed him up. I find it unbelievable.

Clive's exasperation and despair reminds Arthur of his own feelings. How could it be? How could someone just disappear like that? The facts seem to confound reality itself, the rules of the world, the standards and the values and the expectations they relied on. It couldn't be. Arthur gets up from his desk and paces to and fro around the office. The tape continues, silent, for a couple of minutes, just a low dead hiss, then a break. Buxton resumes talking.

– Okay, a few thoughts about the Morgan case. Certainly, I don't think the boys have been kidnapped. I've worked on those sorts of cases before. This is something quite different. I think they are alive, yes, and I think there's no doubt the disappearances are related. First, we have a number of alarming parallels with Timothy, not least due to the time and method by which both boys seem to have vanished. However, the lack of any circumstantial evidence . . . it's infuriating. There should be some sort of indication that this was something they planned together. But we've found nothing in their school books, computers, phones, no evidence of an arrangement, nothing at all. [*Under his breath Buxton mumbles something that Arthur cannot make out*] Unless they kept everything entirely verbal, precisely to avoid leaving any clues . . . not a wholly implausible possibility. However, there are other, deeper similarities which interest me more. [*Another, longer pause during which Buxton seems to be shuffling around in his room*] A number of interesting issues raised by Edward's father, I have to say. Clive Morgan . . . hmm . . . he has something of the benevolent colonial about him, with his pink shirt and khaki slacks,

his upper-crust accent just oozing genial affability. A pater-
nalist. He's a good fifteen years older than his wife, closer
to sixty, I would think, than fifty. Hmm . . . yes . . . I can see
him, sitting in his diplomatic bungalow, enjoying a gin and
tonic in the late-afternoon sunshine, a half-read copy of the
Bhagavad Gita by his side. I get the feeling he's the sort of
man whose curiosity only takes him so far. [*A short, bitter
laugh escapes Buxton's lips*] I wonder if he ever made a
connection between his life and the world around him,
between the green trees and spacious mansions of the
diplomatic quarter and the great slums and shanties of the
city? Did he ever consider, whilst enjoying his hot water
and his air-conditioning and his electricity supply, the millions of others out there? No, no – I don't think he ever
saw that far. Edward saw much more than his father did.
Understood far more, in his way. [*Another long pause and
Arthur begins to wonder if Buxton has finished his ruminations.
Then the detective resumes talking*] Looking through Edward's
school books and other items certainly seems to confirm
what his parents told me about his fascination with India.
I see that we have an essay about Gandhi and the end of
British rule which received three House points from the
history teacher. A very good mark, I gather. What else? A
lurid felt-pen drawing of Kali standing on a pile of bloody
corpses. Many of the bodies are wearing business suits. A
Western-looking city is burning in the background . . .
[*Buxton shuffles something*] A report by one Reverend Fowler,
the school vicar, expressing concern after Edward claimed to
be a follower of Shiva during an RE lesson and said he
wanted to become a sadhu when he grew up. He has a whole
scrapbook filled with pictures of these Indian holy men with
their saffron robes and ash-covered bodies. I can see why this
must have upset your typical Church of England vicar. Edward

has pictures of sadhus with long dreadlocks and shaggy beards, some of them smoking hashish through huge pipes or else engaged in various acts of physical mortification – perched on poles, standing on one leg – that sort of thing. One even seems to be buried head first in the ground. [*More shuffling sounds*] When I spoke to his parents they were a little embarrassed about it. Clive tried to dismiss such an interest as nothing more than adolescent foolishness. I'm not so sure . . . [*Another long pause*] Clive then told me a slightly rambling anecdote about an encounter the family had at a chai house outside Delhi. He said there was a very poor Indian family squatting across the road, itinerant tribal people, probably Dalits, he said, the lowest-caste Indians. Talked about their jet-black skin and the bright saris worn by the women, although he also claimed not to have paid them any attention . . . Well. [*Buxton pauses, drawing breath*] Then he told me how they were all stretching their legs, having some tea, that sort of thing, when he realised that Edward wasn't with him. At that moment, he said their driver saw Edward on the other side of the road, talking to these Indians. Clive told me he called Edward to come away. He said there was an Indian boy in the group, possibly Edward's age, although Clive wasn't very clear about this detail. Poverty makes it hard to guess someone's age, I suppose. He said the two seemed to exchange what he rather vaguely calls a 'look' before Edward came back to them. The sort of 'look' people who know each other would give. I can't quite convey Clive's awkwardness as he related this anecdote to me. He didn't really seem to know what he was saying. He stated that Edward denied it later, in the car, and claimed to have just been looking at them. [*Another pause*] I don't know. Perhaps we are grasping at straws here . . . What can I make of these connections – Edward from India, Timothy with his time in Saudi? Of the two boys from Brompton who first disappeared – Anderson and Thornton – I can't find any evidence of a similar situation, but then I've not had the same access . . . So many children have disappeared now, they can't all have this fascination with foreign places. [*A rummaging noise distorts the voice on the tape*] I'm trying to understand whether what we have fits previous patterns. Normally, in group disappearances of this nature we have a leader somewhere, a charismatic authority figure. A persuader. Certainly, that was the case with the Kingsbridge suicides back in ninety-six, or the Stornoway commune. But this could be an event of a wholly different order. The circumstances are much more mysterious, the boys involved are younger and the numbers greater . . . [*Another pause*] One does wonder, however . . . elsewhere in the world, such cases are less unusual. I have . . . [*The tape wobbles, distorting Buxton's voice again for a moment or two*] According to one report commissioned by the Pentagon, the psychology of the abandoned child is of particular concern for military planners and strategists. Intelligence experts believe slum children could act as a secret weapon of anti-state forces. The report cites the vast numbers of dispossessed young people in the Third World as a potential cause of global instability. From Lagos and Port-au-Prince to Kinshasa and Kabul, the problem is only getting worse. On the one hand, we move towards ever greater control – a global panopticon. And yet, on the other, we see numerous situations that defy such measures. I wonder . . . [*Another pause*] I think it's time I had a discussion with York. [*The tape ends*]

Arthur thinks about what he has heard Buxton say. The detective's words raise memories of all the cities he has travelled to in the course of his work. Arthur thinks of all the boy children he would see by the side of the road, hawking goods or simply waiting and watching. So many young eyes, so many boys, watching him drive past in his air-conditioned SUV or limousine. All the contradictions of the modern age: the glittering skyscraper hotels where he would sleep in a soft bed, high above the sprawling shanty towns. Most of all, he thinks of Baghdad, the crowd of boys who came after the explosion, standing amid the smoke and the fire, their eyes filled with a serious sort of excitement. Watching and remembering, all those children running past, impervious to the peril, and then the hands that came out of the darkness, hands to take him away. With a dreadful shudder, he selects another tape.

Arthur's own voice greets him.

– I've compiled a list . . . The police have it as well. Potential enemies . . . anyone at all that I can think of who might have reason to kidnap my son. I represent certain powerful interests . . . There are many people who might want to harm the organisation I work for and they might try and do it through me, or through my family. Now, I want you to look—

Arthur stops the tape, takes it out, inserts a fresh one.

A dull tape hiss . . . he fast-forwards the tape . . . more hiss . . . again he fast-forwards it . . . still nothing.

Impatient, he yanks it out and inserts another.

– Attempted to interview Harry Dashwood today. [*Buxton's voice again*] I can't say the meeting was a great success. Harry is nine years old and he has the same dark brown hair and serious expression as his father. Mrs Dashwood tells me he has changed since Timothy's disappearance, becoming much quieter and more withdrawn. Under the circumstances, such behaviour is to be expected. Before the interview, Mrs Dashwood showed me a number of drawings she had found in his room. She said that Harry was never particularly interested in drawing before Timothy disappeared, but she tells me that now he spends hours obsessively working at a picture. She showed me a sequence of four pictures, each one on a separate A4 sheet. She thought these were particularly significant. I could see why. With each picture, the execution is quite crude, bright felt-tip pen and black ink with cartoonish two-dimensional figures. Harry's clearly not a natural artist – but the pictures do have a compulsive, obsessive quality to them. The first shows four figures clad in black suits – rather like ninjas, I suppose – sitting on the roof of a house. The house is a typical box with a triangle roof and pointy chimney, divided into four rooms, two up and two down. Two children are sleeping in one of the upstairs rooms whilst a couple – presumably a mother and a father – are sleeping in the other. The second picture repeats the scene, but now one of the black-suited figures has entered the children's bedroom and is talking to the children. The other three remain on the roof. In the third picture, all of the black figures are back on the roof, and one of the children is with them. The other child – and I assume he is meant to represent Harry – remains in his bedroom, looking out of the window with a rather forlorn expression on his face. [*Pause*] Interestingly, one of the adults is also up – it looks like the father, and he's in a downstairs room watching something on the TV or a computer . . . I can't quite tell. [*Pause*] The background – left blank in the other pictures – has also been coloured in an intense red colour, suggesting flames or a most spectacular sunset. [*Pause*] However, it's the last picture that is the most alarming. Again, we have the same house, more or less . . .

but the chimney leans as if it's about to topple and the windows are wonky, with jagged shapes clearly meant to depict broken glass. Other lines suggest crumbling plaster or missing bricks. There are no children in this house. We have two bodies – one male, one female – hanging from a bare tree outside the house. I assume they are meant to represent the mother and father from the previous drawings. When I say hanging . . . they have ropes around their necks and blood is vividly shown coming out of wounds on their bodies, suggesting stab wounds or something similar. The tree itself resembles a tangle of black wire. The sky is full of M shapes, which I think are meant to be circling birds, although there are so many that the overall effect is quite demented, and adds to the impression of menace that characterises this picture. [*Pause*] It is the sort of drawing I might expect a traumatised child to make, but nonetheless . . . [*Buxton's voice trails off for a moment. He seems to be rummaging through his notes*] I tried asking Mrs Dashwood what she made of this picture, but she deflected my question. She wanted to know what I thought. I said *I* thought Harry was interpreting the trauma of Timothy's disappearance as a sort of death of his family. I suspect he has picked up on the tensions between his parents. The picture might even represent a way of punishing his parents – imaginatively, of course. Unconsciously, I am sure he blames them for Timothy's disappearance. I told her it was a coping strategy. However, I'm not entirely sure I believe that. It seems too easy an explanation. I wonder if something else isn't going on here. [*Pause*] Okay, so I started the interview by showing Harry the pictures and asking him what they meant. He was very evasive. I asked him if the two children in the pictures were Timothy and himself. Again, it was hard to get a direct answer. Mrs Dashwood was present throughout, and

I could feel her anxiety growing as Harry resisted my questions. There is something quite volatile about the boy, a sort of force within him. Despite his apparent lethargy and his withdrawal from the world, the boy is like an overflowing container, he's . . . how can I put this? There is something within him, waiting to spill out. Certainly, his self-control did not last long during the interview. [*Another, longer pause*]. Eventually, I got somewhere. Harry said that Timothy wanted to go away. I have it written down exactly. He said 'the other boy told him to' and that this boy was 'friends' with Timothy. Unfortunately, that was about as far as I could get. I tried pointing to the ninja figures in the drawing and asking him if they were supposed to be the 'other boy' but he wouldn't answer. The most he would say was that they were 'just drawings'. I couldn't tell if he didn't understand what I was asking him or if he was simply pretending not to. I've not met many children who have been so difficult to interpret. [*Pause*] Next, I asked him if he would consider drawing the boy he was talking about for me, but he said he couldn't. He wouldn't even touch the pen and paper we had for him. Mrs Dashwood tried to coax a response out of him as well, but he wouldn't budge. Harry said that I was a 'grown-up' and so I was 'stupid' and 'couldn't understand' what he meant. I changed tack slightly and tried asking him why he thought Timothy had gone – in fact, I used the words 'run away'. I wanted to see if these words would influence his responses at all – if he agreed with this interpretation of events or if he saw things differently. In a very low voice, quite different to the strident tone he had been using with me earlier, he said, and I quote from my notes: 'You won't ever find Timothy. You'll only find him when he comes back. But it's too late now. When he does come back, he'll be different. Everything will be different.' That was what he said. 'Everything will be different.' He looked me in the eye as he said this – the first time he made eye contact throughout the whole interview. I felt as if . . . either he was trying to provoke me, playing a trick of some kind or . . . I don't know. The way he said it . . . Quite remarkable words for a nine-year-old. Indeed, it's hard to associate these words with the child. After that, the interview didn't go so well. Harry became progressively more aggressive and hostile. With Mrs Dashwood increasingly discomforted by her child's manner, I decided to terminate proceedings. It wouldn't do to distress the child further. [*Pause*] So what conclusions can I draw? Perhaps Harry feels that Timothy gets more attention in his absence than he ever did when he was here. If anything, he seems a little jealous of Timothy's disappearance. And envious. He acts as though he is privy to some privileged information about his brother, but I'm not sure if that isn't just a pretence, a strategy designed to focus attention on himself. It seems more than possible that he could have invented a scenario to try and cope with what has happened. At the same time, the pictures I saw were quite unusual . . . I can't rule out the possibility of a conspiracy of some sort. Fact is, the number of disappearances continues to increase. Only the police know how many and these motifs in the drawings – the dark, masked figures, the sense of threat, the mood of adolescent terrorism, the rejection of everything – none of these themes are invalidated by what I've seen. We have reason to be very concerned.

Arthur stopped the tape. There was no way he could deny the change that had taken place in his youngest son. A shadow had fallen over the boy. Harry had sunk into himself. Squirrelled away in his bedroom for hours at a time, he filled sheet after sheet of paper with these strange, disturbing drawings. The ninja figure Buxton had seen was a familiar character, often brandishing nunchucks and throwing stars, but there were others. Harry often drew a boyish figure in a green suit in the tops of a tree, playing a pipe. When Arthur first saw this figure he complimented Harry on his creation, encouraged that his son had turned away from other, more morbid themes. 'That's nice,' he'd said, 'I like this picture.'

'He plays his pipe and all the boys run away,' Harry had said in a low, flat voice.

'Like the Pied Piper, you mean?' Arthur had replied and then, when Harry didn't answer (the boy had continued drawing, adding leaves and branches to the tree, filling the sky with squiggly bird shapes), he continued, 'So where do the children go?'

'They go to fight.'

'Fight? Where?'

'In the war.' More and more squiggles filled the sky.

'What war? There's no war, Harry?'

'Yes, there is. The war is here.'

'But there's no war here, Harry,' he'd answered, confused and troubled by the relentless intensity of his son's behaviour.

'Yes, there is,' the boy had said, his pen working faster and faster. 'Yes, there is.'

Many of the scenes Harry drew seemed to come straight from *Insurgency*, as if to punish his mother for banning him from playing the game. He drew cartoons of insect-like soldiers in battle armour and helmets moving through ruins, or standing over bloody corpses. Sometimes the elements seemed mixed up – drawings of soldiers wearing fairy wings would appear, or ninjas playing the flute in a tree, or soldiers sitting on the roof of a house, or half-ninja, half-solder composites. They referred Harry to a psychiatrist who prescribed a variety of medications and gave regular – if largely futile – counselling sessions. The medications made Harry puffy and lethargic, dimming his anger and casting him into a sluggish twilight world. He didn't draw so much, didn't do so much of anything, in fact, but would simply stare listlessly into space for hours at a time, indifferent to any attempt at distraction or amusement.

Still, all this had been a while ago now. Harry didn't live with them any more. Arthur and Susan had decided it would be better if he went to stay with her parents on the south coast for a few months. Since Arthur had let Veca go, Susan's ability to manage the boy was failing. Arthur's in-laws were doting and capable grandparents, and with fewer disappearances outside London it seemed safer to leave him with them. They had driven down and spent a couple of days by the beach. The change seemed to do Harry and Susan good, the two of them spending relaxed hours on the beach, building sand castles and exploring rock pools. Despite these encouraging signs, the open sky and the disconcerting cries of the circling seagulls had left Arthur feeling disorientated and anxious. The weather was very still, the sea ominously flat, as if all the wind had been sucked from the world. Unable to shake the feeling that Timothy might try and return home, only to find the house empty, he had paced about, restless and tearful. His in-laws had trod carefully around him, but behind their solicitude he sensed an undefined suspicion, as if they blamed him in some obscure way for what had happened.

Leaving Harry behind had been difficult, and as Arthur drove back to London the fear that he might never see his son again had been almost overwhelming. He'd driven as fast as possible, frightening Susan by recklessly overtaking everyone on the motorway, pushing the Range Rover as fast as it would go. He couldn't allow himself to stop and think. He had to banish the burning, yearning feeling that filled his heart, his eyes and his mind. Without Harry, the house was horribly empty, the pair of them left even more adrift than before. Arthur spent longer hours at work. He seemed to have so little left to hold Susan to him any more. He managed to speak to Harry most days, even as their telephone conversations grew shorter and more formulaic. The feeling that everything had been planned in advance was increasingly difficult to deny. He grew afraid not to call at the pre-arranged time, in case nobody was waiting to answer, in case that house was empty and Harry too had gone. He couldn't help thinking that was what the boy really wanted, that all their love would make no difference and he was simply biding his time, waiting for the right moment.

For a moment Arthur looks at the surveillance camera in the corner of the room, wondering if anyone is watching at this precise second. Then he selects another tape.

– After Timothy disappeared, how did things change at the Dashwoods'?

– Well, sir, everything changed . . . [*Veca again. She sighs before replying*] I not like it at all. For a couple of weeks the police were here every day, even a police lady staying with the family . . . WPC Douglas . . . she slept in one of the spare bedrooms upstairs. The police lady, she just spent time helping me make tea for everybody. She keep saying we must be strong and positive. I felt she watching me all the time. [*Pause*] Mrs Dashwood hardly leave her room. Detectives speak to her up there . . . that one in charge, with only one arm, he was always going up, interviewing her for

161

hours. I not like that man. He make me feel creepy all over. I would bring them cups of tea . . . I had to knock and leave it outside the door. I don't know what they spoke about. I know he drank a lot of Earl Grey tea, no milk. [*Pause*] When Mrs Dashwood did come downstairs, she seem lost in thoughts. All the things that normally she get me to do she forget, like she just stop seeing me. I just had to mind Harry most of the time.

– Okay. And Harry, how was he?

– Mmm . . . for a few days they not let me near him. I was – what you say? Suspected. But then, after the police lady left house and things get more quiet, I start to look after him again. No one tell me to, exactly, but Mr Dashwood was back at the office and Mrs Dashwood in her bedroom so . . . [*Pause*] But Harry changed, different. He very calm, but in a way that not seem right to me.

– Calm?

– Yes. They say it was shock . . . he was, what is the word? Turned in to himself?

– Withdrawn, do you mean?

– Withdrawn. Yes. I think so. He started seeing this, you know, special doctor, but it stopped.

– He attacked the psychiatrist. That was what I've been told.

– He bit him, sir. Bit his hand.

– Yes. I heard about that. And what do you think? Is he suffering from shock?

– I can't say, sir . . .

– I know you're not an expert, Veca, but you do know Harry. I just want your opinion.

Another long pause. Again, Arthur felt a pang of guilt for having letting the girl go. He supposed she had gone back to Slovakia. In many ways, she was just another victim in all this.

– He is withdrawn, yes. Maybe it is shock. It must be terrible for him. But he seem very calm. He would just make these cartoon drawings of soldiers, things like that.

   – Did he ever speak to you about what happened?

   – Mmm. Only a little. Once, really. [*Pause*] It was bedtime and I was in his room, saying goodnight. I feel I should say something, so I try telling him he shouldn't worry and soon the police find Timothy and catch whoever took him away. And . . . he looked at me so funny, as if he not believe a word I am saying. I could tell he thought I was talking rubbish . . . As if I was the child and he was the grown-up and he was just letting me have some silly idea about everything being okay. Then he said to me . . . I can't quite remember the words exactly, but he said something how Timothy wasn't coming back, but that it was okay . . . like he was the one trying to reassure me. [*Pause*] Like I was the child. [*Pause*] Then he said everything would be different anyway.

   – Different?

   – That's the word he used. Yes, sir.

Arthur sits forward, beads of sweat appearing on his forehead.

   – Do you think he knows something?

   – [*Pause*] Maybe Timothy said something to him, you know, with these other boys from school missing also . . . Maybe they talk about it, the disappearances, maybe they have plan to run away, I don't know . . . [*Veca trails off, her thoughts overwhelmed by what has happened*]

Buxton asks her a few more questions about Arthur and his wife. Veca talks about the bad atmosphere in the house, the silence at night. She says she doesn't think Arthur and Susan are sleeping in the same bed any more. She talks about finding him slumped in front of the television, or the sound of his footsteps, late at night, pacing to and fro. She talks about hearing the door slam, also late at night, and wondering where he is going. Arthur listens to this with a sense of distance, as if she is talking about someone else. She doesn't know, he thinks, she can't possibly know.

– Is there anything else, [*Buxton asks*] anything particularly strange or unusual? You can tell me. Don't be shy!

– There was one strange thing, I suppose . . . But really, I don't think it's so important.

– Go on, Veca, please. Everything is important.

– Okay, well . . . it was . . . [*She falters, and Arthur can sense her reluctance, as if this is something that does not easily fit into words*] I couldn't sleep, I remember, it was very late, about three a.m. I go upstairs for water and I see back door into garden wide open. And I am thinking this is not right, because I shut it before I go to bed.

– Shut it? Or locked it?

– Yes! Locked it with the key, top and bottom. Always I do this. So I was a bit worried. I put on coat and go outside.

– Why didn't you just lock the door and go back to bed?

– I . . . I don't really know why, sir. I just did. I had a feeling, you see . . .

– Okay. So what happened?

– Well, the back garden is very small and I could see that the gate into communal gardens was open also.

– Is it normally locked? [*Pause*]

– I'm not sure. I don't think so. There's no need. [*Pause*] Thing is, sir, I had the strangest feeling. It was such a bright night, sir, so clear, with a full moon and very cold. I went into the garden and there, in the middle, I see Harry. [*Pause*] He was wearing his pyjamas and just standing there . . . His head was tilted back and his arms open, like this . . .

– I see.

– I go to him and see he is still sleeping.

– He was sleepwalking?

– I think so. I don't know.

– So he had managed to unlock the back door and walk into the garden in his sleep?

– He not recognise me. He was there but . . .

– What did you do?

– I take his hand, like this, very gentle, and I take him back into the house. He not wake up. He was so freezing cold and his eyes were closed and his mouth was open. He was breathing in a funny way, like . . . [*She makes a muffled gasping noise*]

– You put him back to bed?

– Yes. But it difficult, because his body got so heavy.

– I see. Well, they say sleepwalking can be a sign of distress.

– There was something else though, sir . . . I not sure how to say it. You know, sir, how it is sometime you see something, or think you see something but you not understand what it is you see and so you sort of forget about it? I mean, maybe it was, you know, just imaginings. Everything was more like a dream, to find Harry in garden . . . I think I am being silly.

– Don't worry, Veca. Like I said, you can tell me. It doesn't matter.

In the pause that follows, Arthur senses that Veca is trying to work something out for herself before speaking.

– As I was leading Harry back to the house I had one last look at the garden and . . . I thought I saw . . . [*Pause*] I know it doesn't make sense . . . [*Pause*] I was very tired and it was late. [*Pause*] I just thought I could see, under the tall trees and hidden by the bushes . . . well . . . more boys. People. I don't know. Standing there. That's all. [*Pause*]

– Really? Fascinating. [*Pause*] How many people, or children, how many did you think you could see?

– I don't know. Lots, I think. But I only looked once. It was just a glance, you know? I was imagining things. That was what I think. I take Harry and I go to house and not think about it again. I lock back door and not look outside any more. I was imagining things.

– Yes, you must have been.

– The garden couldn't have been full of children . . .

– Of course not. What did you do next?

– Nothing. I just put Harry back to bed. He was muttering strange things, but he stay sleepy.

– Did you look into the garden again?

– Only from Harry's window. It was empty, of course it was! I didn't really see anything anyway. It was, you know, trick of light, trick of imagination. Maybe I was sleepwalking too [*Veca gives a nervous little laugh*]

– Okay. Thank you again, Veca. You've been very helpful.

– I try, sir. I only wish I could know something for sure.

– So do we all, Veca, so do we all.

Arthur stops the tape. For a moment, he feels his head spinning. He thinks he can remember them – the children under the trees, the rain falling like tears – images uncertain as the memory of a dream. Children, faces hidden by masks and scarves, bodies swathed in dark sheets. He shakes his head. He remembers the boys he saw in Baghdad: the way they seemed to stand on every corner, as if waiting for him to sweep past in his convoy. He remembers the pitter-patter of little feet scampering down a hotel corridor in the sleepless depths of the night. He gets up and takes a drink of water. Determined now, he takes the next tape. He must keep going, he thinks, he must press on.

– It's just gone four a.m. and I'd better get this down before I get too tired . . . I had a tip-off earlier, from Captain York. There's just been a big raid, looking for children. It has all been quite extraordinary. [*Arthur hears the nervous excitement in Buxton's voice, a breathless quality, as if he is pacing as he talks, back and forth around his office*] I met York in the East End, near an old council estate. He was in an expansive mood, unusually candid concerning the more outré elements of this crisis. Seems disappearances have reached epidemic proportions over the last few weeks. He told me the Home Office reckons over a thousand kids have gone AWOL . . . The situation seems to be spreading out of London, hitting the plusher corners of the provinces . . . children reported missing from places like Tunbridge Wells and Reigate, Winchester and Virginia Water, Sevenoaks and Beaconsfield . . . The overwhelming majority are boys, usually around eleven, twelve, thirteen years old, boys on the cusp of puberty . . . although some are as young as seven . . . and others are older . . . York told me the disappearance of the youngest children has been the most baffling. Kids vanishing from bedrooms in the dead of night, nothing else missing but their pyjamas and dressing gowns . . . The true extent of the problem is being kept from the public to stop a nationwide panic. [*Buxton pauses for a moment, coughing*] The target of the raid was a condemned block awaiting demolition. York said they'd had the place under surveillance for several days, following a tip-off from builders on the site. Wrecking balls and bulldozers had already pounded most of the estate to dust, but as many as two hundred children were estimated to be living in the remaining block. York was upbeat. He said the authorities have started locating a lot more of these children than before. From what they can tell, the children appear to be hiding in groups of varying sizes, gathering in desolate parts of the city, abandoned factories, disused warehouses, old churches, forgotten corners of outer suburbs . . . they seem to be waiting, hoarding basic supplies, as if preparing to go somewhere. He said the children are taken to secure areas for disinfection and interrogation before being returned to their families. Disinfection. That's the word he used. He called it a 'virus', the disappearances, the running away – he said they'd been infected. He clearly relishes his curative role. [*The sound becomes distorted, a nasty twist and hiss of static*] . . . the riot squad went in. The first unit encountered stiff resistance and it was hard to tell what was going on for a few minutes. There was a small explosion that brought down the ceiling in one of the apartments onto the first unit. A second unit assaulted the block from the other side, I think, entering the second floor. I'm not sure. We had reports from officers that an entire floor was soaked in petrol. Then there was another explosion, and from outside I saw flames coming out of broken windows and rushing up the building. It was quite something. Back-up squads and tactical teams went in next, followed by firemen and paramedics. The police took some casualties, but no fatalities, thank goodness. I only hope they weren't too rough with them . . . No matter how savage they seem, they are still children, after all. Still . . . no one likes it when the people you are supposed to be saving fight back. [*He sighs*] Reports came through that children were fleeing the building from all sides – dozens and dozens of children, escaping down stairwells, jumping from first- and second-floor windows. I must say, it was frustrating, having to wait behind the lines with the gaggle of social workers and child psychologists, trauma therapists and counsellors. Everyone seems to have their own theory about what's happening and why . . . What is it they say? It's an expression of the id in revolt against the superego, or else the consequences of an over-pressured education and an ever-diminishing sphere of childhood innocence, or a symptom of a more generalised collective cultural anxiety, a reaction to globalisation and multiculturalism, a spontaneous cult of alienation induced by the collapse of the nuclear family, an attempt to forge a situational solidarity with the oppressed Third World masses, even just the result of too much exposure to violent computer games and Internet porn . . . I guess I'm still trying to keep an open mind . . . [*Pause*] The fire brigade extinguished the blaze and the area was declared secure . . . By now the first of the children were being gathered together outside on the forecourt of a warehouse opposite. Floodlights shone over three dozen boys, maybe more, all of them sitting cross-legged on the floor, hands on their heads. It was like looking at assembly time in some delinquent school. On their faces I saw a mixture of expressions – fear, bewilderment, some weeping, others looking very lost and confused . . . but others . . . they didn't flinch at all . . . they seemed defiant and angry . . . [*Pause*] So many fierce eyes regarding me with real hatred and disgust . . . it was quite chilling . . . [*Pause*] I could almost imagine them, tearing me limb from limb with their bare, grubby hands and picked nails . . . The air simmered with a sort of hot anger. I took out some of the pictures I have of Timothy Dashwood, but even if he was among them it was impossible to reconcile this picture I have – the schoolboy neat with his tie and clean shirt – and these wild-looking fellows. All the time I was looking at them I had to keep telling myself they're children, middle-class kids from good homes and the best schools . . . but they seem more like animals . . . I don't know what will come out of this . . . [*More distortion, as if a radio is being tuned in and out. Radio-static flicker*] Once the area was secure we were allowed in. Apartments had been knocked together, creating a single interlocking structure. In the torchlight I followed York through rooms filled with rubbish . . . plastic bags crammed with rotten scraps of food . . . areas that smelt like a toilet. . . everywhere this animal stink, this thick dormitory fug . . . I think we came next to living quarters, with mattresses on the floor, sleeping bags, a few pieces of old furniture, a kitchen, a dirty bathroom . . . scattered candles, Christmas lights strung across ceilings . . . that smell again . . . here and there the walls were covered in strange writing . . . much of the script looks like . . . I'm not sure . . . Arabic or Persian, Urdu, attempts at Egyptian hieroglyphics or Mayan pictograms . . . delirious characters . . . and, hanging on the walls, flags for countries that I've never seen before . . . inky palm prints, pictures of unfamiliar buildings . . . a castle high in the mountains, a maze-like city in the desert, photographs of masked fighters, terrorists, crude drawings of the Prime Minister, the Queen, the President . . . world leaders and infamous terrorists mingled with Batman and characters from comic books and computer games . . . in some their hands are tied and they wear orange prison suits . . . in others . . . [*He pauses*] it's hard to describe properly. Hard to remember – there was so much weird stuff in there . . . I saw walls plastered with pictures culled from magazines, photographs from the recent wars . . . American soldiers with wraparound sunglasses, dead civilians . . . corpses laid out in a yard . . . bloody streets . . . York said his men had found weaponry in the basement – home-made swords, spears and pikes, primitive pistols, customised shotguns, hand grenades and nail bombs . . . It was a relief to get back outside, really, away from that evil smell. I spent some time watching as the boys were searched and their hands were tied with cord. Social workers in fluorescent jackets videotaped everything. I guess the police were anxious to avoid accusations of abuse and costly lawsuits from irate middle-class parents. Almost all the boys were white, Anglo-Saxon. The ones I heard gave fake names in their prim English accents. They were all calling themselves Abdullah or Ahmed, Krishna and Shiva, Huey and Castro, Lao Tse, Kutulooho, all sorts of strange foreign-sounding names that I can't repeat . . . the police were writing it all down, anyway . . . Wait, I'd better . . . [*A shuffling sound and the tape stops*]

Arthur mutters something to himself, frustrated. A few tapes remain. He picks up one, looks at it, puts it down and takes another. Puts it into the machine and presses 'play'.

– Thanks for taking the time to talk to me, Mr Dashwood, I appreciate you have a very busy schedule and— [*He stops the tape. He thinks there is no need to hear this. He knows what he said. And yet. His voice. It feels surprisingly good to hear himself speak, at last, after all the others. His point of view. He sits for a moment, then he presses 'play'*] None of this has been easy for you.

– This is my son . . . I want to be clear, you understand? I will do anything I can to get him back. I've compiled a list, see here, all these names – you've heard of some of these people, perhaps? The police have it as well. Potential enemies, people I might have crossed, might have given cause to dislike me, and others. You'll see. It includes anyone at all that I can think of who might have reason to kidnap my son. I represent certain powerful interests. How shall I put this? Regardless of myself, there are many people who might want to harm the organisation I work for, and they might try and do it through me, or through my family. Now, I want you to look through this list and see if any of the names match with your information. [*Yes, the old kidnapping argument again, he was still flogging that dead horse. Of course, Buxton wasn't buying it for a moment.*]

– I appreciate you doing this for me, Mr Dashwood, but I don't really work that way.

– Yes, but . . .

– Thing is, I really don't think your son has been kidnapped.

– Yes, I know what you think. You think he's run away with his friends. You think this is all some big conspiracy.

– I'm not sure if I'd use that word.

– Why not?

– If you don't mind, my point is that all the evidence, the little we have, suggests your son planned his flight, his escape, whatever we call it. You must see that.

– No, I don't. I disagree. I think someone took him. Someone took them all.

– But we've had no ransom note, no demands for money or information, nothing that we would expect from the sort of kidnapping you're talking about, Mr Dashwood, sir. I think we need to stretch our minds a little more, please, if you'll allow me?

– But how do we . . . [*Pause*] I'm just not sure. [*That rustling noise again*]

*

Arthur tries to remember when, exactly, this interview occurred. Two months ago? Or three? And where were they? Sitting in his office, in the same seat? Or were they at home? He is surprised how hard it is to remember, even as he hears himself talking on and on.

– I would like you to tell me a little more about yourself, Mr Dashwood, and your own childhood. What was it like?
   – What do you mean?
   – Your childhood . . . I want to know a bit more about you, the real you . . .

For some reason he struggles to answer these questions. There are many things he doesn't want to think about, doesn't know how to put into words. It is better to stay focused, keep his eyes on the surface and move forwards. Sometimes it is better to say nothing, nothing at all.

– I had a perfectly normal childhood, I suppose. Happy enough.
   – And?
   He hears himself sigh with exasperation.
   – I don't see what you expect me to say? [*Pause*]
   – Well, I was wondering if you might tell me a little about your brother Phillip?
   – I don't [*Pause*] I don't have a brother. [*Pause*] What I mean is . . . I haven't seen him since I was about eight. [*Pause*] Look. He didn't disappear, if that's what you're trying to get at. It was nothing like that. His foster-parents adopted him. My parents went through a difficult patch [*Pause*] and we were placed with foster families. Different ones. I was very young at the time. I don't remember it. I never think about it. How do you know this? [*Pause*] I suppose this is what I'm paying

you for. [*Pause*] Well, what can I say? His foster family adopted him and I never saw him again. My parents never mentioned him. We forgot all about him. It might sound horrible, but it was for the best. And I have forgotten him. I have no interest in seeing him again. I was very young at the time, you understand? I hardly remember it.

– You never wanted to try and find him?

– Why should I? [*Pause*] What would be the point? [*Pause*] He was my brother, so what? [*Pause*] I don't believe there is necessarily anything special or magical about families or siblings or any of that. Who is your brother or your sister, in the end, or your parents? You don't choose them, why do they matter so much? They don't have to matter. They're just the people you're born with, born into. I don't know why he stayed with his foster family, I have no idea, really I don't . . . They were always loving and kind to me, my parents. [*Pause*] Always. [*Pause*] I can't imagine how hurt they must have been by it . . . I'm sure . . .

Was that true? Was that the way it happened? Arthur thought he could remember his parents taking the toys from his brother's room, small things at first – a toy car, a pair of trainers, a school book – and burning them each evening in the garden, as the sun went down. Each day, another item burnt, until there was nothing left in his brother's bedroom except a bare bed, an empty wardrobe, a chair in the corner. Soon even these items were destroyed as well, everything, even the pictures in the photo albums, just ash in the grass. The brother that never was. Was that really the way? Sometimes he still had dreams, with Phillip in the garden with the other children, the moonlight white on their skin. But whenever he went to look, the lawn was always empty and no one was ever there. Arthur shook his head. Strange, the memories came in these moments . . .

– And your parents, what happened to them?

– I assume you know. You seem to have done some research.

– Divorced.

– Yes. They divorced. And they're both dead now, anyway. You know this, of course, don't you? This doesn't have anything to do with Timothy and quite frankly I resent this line of questioning. [*On the tape, a phone starts ringing*] Oh, who the hell is it? Oh right, look, stop that tape, I need to speak to this person. Hello, Mr Rashid, one moment, please. I told you to turn that recorder off. You must excuse me, please, if you wouldn't mind, please leave the room.

[*Tape stops*]

[*Starts again*]

– Okay, shall we try a slightly different tack?

– As you wish.

– I can see that you've worked in a lot of quite exotic places. Did you enjoy working in the Gulf?

– 'Enjoy?' I don't think that's quite the right word.

– Oh? Why not?

– It was hard work, demanding, it carried with it a great deal of responsibility, a lot of stress and many challenges. This upsurge in militancy and terrorism never helps. It *was* stressful . . . for all sorts of reasons. Being there took a toll on my family and I didn't enjoy that. [*Pause*] My wife . . . It's been very hard for Susan, you see, living in the compound. She didn't take to it all that well. Maybe she's told you about it already? [*Pause*] She's . . . well, I tend to think that she's terribly English and she needs to be able to just pop out to the shops or go for a stroll around the park. She needs rain. The heat dried her out. And, as you can imagine, all the vague threats and dangers, they didn't help. It was bad enough for her, stuck in the middle of a country where you can't really go out on your own as a woman and then to be thinking as well that you are surrounded by these strange people and some of them might actually want to kill you, kill us all, for no reason that you understand but just because of who you are. [*Pause*] For myself, I was never worried. [*Pause*]

– For your family?

– Sometimes. Sometimes I was worried. It wasn't exactly the nicest of places to be. They weren't always the nicest of circumstances. The situation was stressful, but the risks, the real risks were minimal, I was sure.

– So why did you move back to England?

– I felt it was better for everyone, especially Susan. The stress, the place, the climate, everything got to her. Quite frankly, she didn't have much to do over there but sit in the compound working herself up by worrying over this and that. It wasn't healthy. And I felt it would be more suitable for the boys, better for them, to be back in their own culture.

– A Western nation, you mean?

– No, that's not really what I was thinking about. Our contact with actual Saudi society was so minimal anyway. It was more . . . oh . . . you see, the compound had a good school, an excellent school, in fact, with much, much better facilities and technology than the schools back home. But it was American-run, the teachers were all Americans, it followed the American syllabus. [*Pause*] I never liked that.

– So you moved back to England?

– Yes, yes, we did. It was a bit chaotic for a while, I had

to keep going back to the Gulf and I was in two minds at the time, I didn't know if the company might require me to spend longer over there – I was still travelling back frequently and I couldn't decide whether I wanted my family to be with me or not.

– But you decided to stay here, in the end?

– You could say that. The company decided, finally, they wound up the main Saudi operation and transferred proceedings back to the London HQ. Now I don't travel nearly as much as I used to. [*Pause*] Most of my work is done from my desk.

– I see. [*Inaudible*] How did you feel, going to work in those places, alone, without your family?

[*Pause*]

– To be honest with you, I loved it, on the whole. I got to see a lot of places – Baghdad, Kabul, Riyadh, Jeddah, Dubai, Damascus, Khartoum, Baku, Beijing, Jakarta . . . the names alone are rather wonderful, don't you think? [*Pause*] When I was a small boy I always wanted to be an explorer . . . Perhaps I became the next best thing, or the nearest you can get to it these days . . . It was very exciting, getting sent to negotiate multimillion-dollar contracts, supervising the construction of new pipelines and refineries. The world craves oil, needs oil, and my job is to ensure it keeps flowing, as much oil as possible. Oil for all. [*Pause*] Well, for us, anyway. [*Pause*] It made me feel pretty important, travelling in armoured cars and helicopters, being protected by bodyguards, it was all something of a schoolboy fantasy. And I'd thought I was born too late to know what it was like to have an empire. [*Arthur laughs*] Of course, some places are much more exciting than others. [*Pause*] You want to know? Of course you do. [*Better to say nothing, and yet he talked. Buxton had that gift, Arthur saw it now, to provoke confidences and confessions: even if one didn't want to talk, still, one would talk. That clever, sly way he had of looking at you. There he was, on the tape, despite everything, talking to the man]* Take Baghdad, for instance. Now, that's one place I won't forget. [*Pause*] I remember . . . [*Pause*] I was there a few weeks after we took the city. The insurgency was getting started but this was before all the real horrors were unleashed. Bad things were happening, but it was still considered relatively safe. I wouldn't go back now. Anyway, they put me in a hotel in the Green Zone, the Al-Rashid. They said it was very secure and [*Pause*] on the whole, I felt safe. Later it was struck by rockets, but then . . . [*Pause*] Anyway, I remember . . . no, that's right [*Inaudible*] There was a blackout the first night I was there . . . actually, there was a power cut every single night, but for some reason it took a few minutes longer than usual before the hotel's back-up generator kicked in. The air-conditioning stopped and as it was so hot I went onto my balcony. We weren't supposed to, in case of snipers, but I didn't think about that. The room was on the twelfth floor, and I could see right across the city. For a time it was quiet, then there was gunfire. I could see tracers, red and green, arcs of bullets rising from darkened swathes of the city. All night it was like that, on and off, the crack and ripple of distant shots, the drone of circling Apaches, chopping and slicing the sky. At one point, very late, I saw explosions, five in total, orange flashes on the horizon, the dull booms drifting across and rattling the windows. [*Pause*] I felt such a surge of excitement and power. It was . . . I can't describe it. [*Pause*]

Yes indeed, Arthur remembers those nights and days. He will never forget them. Even now, listening to his own dry voice recounting those moments he feels it – a quickening of the heart, a sharpness in his throat. With the dread and the horror, an almost overwhelming exhilaration.

– I hardly slept the whole time I was in Baghdad, [*he continues*] I couldn't. [*Pause*] I didn't need to. [*Pause*] The first night I sat up on the balcony until dawn, enjoying a grandstand view of the fighting. I could feel it, in the air itself, a sort of seething. It was like . . . you could sense forces colliding, ideas producing a new reality. [*Inaudible*]

During the first few days, the view from the balcony was the most that Arthur got to see of the real Iraq. They stayed in the Green Zone, meeting officials from the Coalition Provisional Authority in Saddam's palace. He remembered the incongruity of it all – these ad hoc offices and meeting rooms in gaudy, ceremonial settings. The terrible bad taste of a tyrant. The people he met were dapper young men, fresh-faced and glowing with that peculiar American optimism. Even before it happened, he'd been sceptical of their assurances about services being restored, about how many millions of barrels of oil would soon be flowing and how democracy and stability were just around the corner. It was hard to talk to anyone who wasn't a Republican and a Christian, who wasn't charged with a sense of righteous purpose that seemed utterly disconnected from anything else. He remembered the signs for Bible-study groups and prayer meetings, the way pork was served for every meal in the canteen or how the officials he spoke to seemed to see the country as a tabula rasa on which they could impose their fantastic ideas. He had enough experience of the region to question all these notions. And every night, unable to sleep, he would listen to the faint crackle of gunfire, the thud of mortars.

*

– You see . . . well, you see there was . . . [*Pause*] Something happened. [*Pause*] On the fourth day there was a bomb in the street. We were . . . [*Pause*] We'd had a meeting at another hotel, outside the Green Zone. We were rushing through the traffic in a convoy of armoured jeeps. The whole city was so strange . . . the colours, all grey, dullish reds and browns, dirty whites. Concrete and dust and intense hot sunshine. The air strikes had been remarkably precise, that was one thing I noticed. One would see the old government buildings, concrete ziggurats and citadels split apart by cruise missiles, and you could see the places that the mobs had looted, these bedraggled, ruined buildings . . . The city had this relentless quality, rather desperate . . . It felt like this was the place where everything was happening, a point of convergence for all sorts of political and historical forces . . . History was unravelling before me. [*Pause*] There were queues everywhere . . . queues to enter the Green Zone, queues to leave, queues of men waiting to get fuel or water or jobs . . .

– You said something about a bomb?

– Yes, that's right. [*Nothing, nothing, I said nothing, I told them nothing, I . . .*] We finished the meeting and our guards were hurrying us back towards the cars. For some reason they were parked across the street. I can't quite remember why. It was a dangerous situation, anyway. Then . . . it's hard to describe. It just sort of happened. There was an explosion – it wasn't aimed at us, it didn't have anything to do with us – it was further up the street, about two hundred metres away. There was a lot of confusion and . . . [*Pause*] This sort of balloon of dust and fire rose upwards very fast and the shock wave from the blast sort of made everybody stagger, as if we'd all been pushed. [*Pause*] Dust and glass and bits of tarmac were dropping down around us. I lost sight of the bodyguards. One moment they were by my side, the next . . . anyway. [*Pause*] It was confusing. I couldn't see anyone I knew. I couldn't see the rest of my team.

– You must have been scared.

– I . . . [*Pause*] I remember that a Hummer full of American troops arrived. A car was on fire, there was a lot of smoke and dust. I saw someone bleeding . . . their face was bleeding. The American soldiers were shouting something and pointing their guns everywhere. The blast had scorched the road and the side of an apartment building opposite. Great clouds of greasy black smoke were rising from the wreckage, and the ground was scattered with broken glass. [*Pause*] The smell. For some reason and . . . I really don't know why . . . I went down this side street. I wanted to have a look. We'd been in the Green Zone, in the hotel so much that I'd hardly seen the city, not up close. People were all around me – real people, Iraqis. I was among them. So . . . [*Pause*] I went down this alleyway, looking at the buildings, just trying to see. [*Pause*] I can't remember that much, not the details, but I remember the sensation – the exhilaration, the sense of being somewhere forbidden, somewhere dangerous. Each footstep felt electric, as if I was on the verge of entering another world. I was, I suppose, the next one. Mostly, though, I remember the children . . . children everywhere. Young boys with big shining brown eyes and dirt-smudged faces. It was remarkable. They must all have lived in the street, I suppose, but to me it seemed as if they had come from out of nowhere. [*Pause*] It was so dangerous for them to be out here. I shouted at them to get away, but they took no notice. They were as excited by the bomb as I was. [*Pause*] I don't know. [*Pause*] It's hard to describe. It's . . . Anyway, I heard this popping noise, all around. I couldn't tell where it was coming from, but I realised that people were shooting. More American troops were arriving, taking up positions. I don't know if the shooting was still going on. Then one of our bodyguards ran up to me and took my arm, rather firmly, I remember, and sort of bundled me into our jeep. We sped back to the hotel. I'd only been separated from the group for about five minutes, maybe less. [*Pause*] My first bomb. We joked about it later, in the hotel bar. It was surprisingly easy to forget you were in a war zone. Not something I could tell the wife, though, of course, as I'm sure you can appreciate, so don't mention it to her, will you? I was reckless, really, most foolish. We heard later that five civilians were killed in that blast. It was nothing major. No one knew who the real target was supposed to be. [*Pause*] But really, those children, what were they doing there? I'll never forget the sight of them all. [*Pause*] Never.

But of course that was not all. That was not what happened. That was not the whole truth.

    . . . *Nothing, I told them nothing.*

Arthur wipes the sweat from his brow. A Kalashnikov thrust into his side and the hood and the dark room and the voice and the pain and the waiting and the darkness. *Nothing . . .*

– I think I was a little shocked, though. [*His voice continues*] You see – how shall I put this?

– Go on.

– I started seeing children in the hotel, Iraqi children, I mean, mainly small boys, all about the same age as Timothy and Harry. [*He wipes at his face. The sweat is falling now, his hands shaking, the pitter-patter of little feet scratching the edge of his hearing.*] Hallucinations, of course, all just a consequence of my rather overexcited imagination, I think, but it was rather disconcerting . . .

– When you say you saw these children in the hotel, what do you mean, exactly? Where were they? What were they doing?

– There were no children in the hotel, that's what I mean. [*Another laugh*] No real children. You see, it wasn't as if I saw them directly, mostly I just caught glimpses of them, disappearing around a corner in the hotel corridor or hurrying upstairs and it was like all I'd really see, or hear, would be the scamper of their feet, or sometimes their voices, whispering or laughing . . . [*Pause*]

– Really?

– Or else they'd be in a lift, with the doors closing and I'd catch just the briefest glimpse of one, as the doors closed . . . I never saw them clearly, directly, as I can see you now, but they were sort of on my mind. [*Pause*] What was more, I actually started imagining they were my own children, as if my children had been born in Iraq, as Shia or Sunni . . . as if this was what could have happened to them . . . [*Pause*] It doesn't make sense, does it? I must sound like I was losing my mind. [*Arthur hears himself, on the tape, giving a brief, brittle laugh*] It was a most unusual experience for me, the whole affair. I knew I was imagining them, even as I saw them. I would be lying on my bed, late in the night, not sleeping, and in the quiet moments I would hear them, just outside my room. The patter of their feet. I would even see their shadows, passing back and forth under the door. But when I opened the door, the corridor outside was deserted. I knew it would be.

– Did anyone else see these children?

– Of course not! That's my point. They weren't real. And I never mentioned what I was seeing. I didn't want people

183

to think I was cracking up, did I? Jesus. Anyway, it hardly mattered. We were back in Jordan within the week. By then the children had left me. As I said, it was just shock, something like that. I knew I was imagining things, even as I saw them.

– You said you didn't sleep the whole time. Do you think they could have been a product of your exhaustion?

– Of course. Exhaustion, excitement, stress, all these things.

Another long pause. Again, Arthur struggles to remember this interview – where they were, what he was wearing. What was Buxton making of all this, behind that nonchalant façade he presented so effectively? He thinks he can remember the two of them, in his front room, the rain falling hard from a relentless grey sky.

– So what do you think about it all, the trip, the imaginary children?

– Nothing.

– I'm sorry?

– I don't think about it. What would be the point? It was a hallucination, one of those things. Look, I'm a rational man, rational enough to know that not everything that happens is always rational.

– You never had any qualms about your job? [*Yes, that was part of Buxton's skill, that ability to shift subjects suddenly, flushing out fresh revelations when you didn't expect it*]

– Don't be ridiculous. My job, over there, was to get the oil flowing. The faster that happened, the better for everyone. In war there are always business opportunities. Money is for the making. I have no regrets about seizing an opportunity.

– I see. And do you think you may have to go back? To the Middle East, I mean.

– I don't know about that. I'm in no hurry. I can't really contemplate it, not until we find Timothy. You must understand.

Arthur stops the tape. Enough. The sound of his voice, wavering with emotion – too much. For a moment, he can feel the heat of that dark room, the hood over his face. A wailing sound in the distance, so faint that it may be his imagination. The pen in his trembling hands, the paper in front of him. The patient expression on their faces, almost kind, when he began to write. Loosening his tie, he goes from his desk to the window, pressing his face against the glass. Sometimes he yearns to reach the top of his building. There must be a way of getting onto the roof, so he can stand, seven hundred feet above the city, up with the pigeons and the gusting wind. Maybe he can raise his arms and be lifted away. Maybe he can fly after all.

Instead, he goes back to the box. Four tapes remain. He places another in the machine. A faint voice, muffled, says something, over and over, a faint whisper in a haze of static. He fast-forwards and stops the tape several times, but it is all the same. Out it comes. In with a new one.

– I had a discussion with Captain York last night. He raised a number of important issues. Let me try and consider the facts, as they stand. Okay. [*Buxton clears his throat. There is a rummaging noise on the tape, as if he is sorting through a number of papers*] Timothy Dashwood lived in Saudi Arabia for several years. Edward Morgan lived in India. It now turns out that the other boys who disappeared from Brompton have relations, or perhaps I should say connections, with non-European locations. According to intelligence from York, Thomas Anderson spent a part of his childhood in Mexico. William Thornton has an older brother who works for the British embassy in Afghanistan. Edward's parents spoke quite eloquently about his interest in the Indians, especially the poor. He lived near the diplomatic compound. The Dashwoods lived in a similar set-up. And yet, I'm still not sure how much to make of this. York also told me that nearly eight hundred children have been reported missing in Greater London over the last month. Not all of them can have lived abroad. [*The tape distorts, a strange hissing noise drowning out the detective's voice for a few moments*] What we are dealing with seems to be an overwhelmingly middle-class, white phenomenon, so far as [*further distortion*] At least half of those children attend private schools and three-quarters of them are male. York tells me that, well, according to his contacts in the government unusually large numbers of young men, all of them Westerners, have been detected [*again, his voice distorts*] a number of locations across Asia, the Middle East and South [*the hissing sound increases, a sharp sss . . . sss . . . sss drowning out his words*] and many are younger [*his voice filters in and out, like a badly tuned radio*] French intelligence reported large gatherings in the desert beyond Marrakesh. Similar observations are circulating across sub-Saharan Africa, although none have yet been [*sss . . . sss . . . sss*] attacks on government and Coalition forces across the Middle East have escalated sharply in the last six weeks. Large numbers of unidentified militants now occupy parts of Iraq . . . [*Arthur sits forward, frustrated. Behind the hissing noises, he is sure he can hear something else, another, different voice*] Increased guerrilla activity throughout the Himalayas has been noted by the Nepali, Indian and Chinese governments. [*The intelligence and risk-assessment department in Arthur's company has been reporting similar information, vague reports about mysterious new groups emerging across the theatre of operations]* The Thai military claim armed gangs led by men of European appearance have formed settlements in the remote islands. Similar reports are *[static chops up Buxton's words]* Cambodia, the Philippines and Indonesia although intelligence *[sss ... sss ... sss]* York reported attacks in Texas near the Mexican border, gatherings of huge numbers of teenagers in the slums of Bogotá, Lima and São Paulo. He told me classified reports from the CIA claim a number of English men were captured in Afghanistan *[sss ... sss ... sss]* the men in question weren't Muslims and do not seem to fit the usual profile *[sss ... sss ... sss]* terrorist activity *[the hiss of static continues for two or three minutes before Buxton's voice filters back to the fore]* I've been looking through my old case files. Found myself reading the material I have about the New Forest vanishings from ten years ago. Eight teenagers, between fourteen and seventeen years of age, four boys and four girls, all vanished within a week of each other, and all from the same small village. A most unusual case ... As I recall, they were found a few weeks later living in a camp deep in the woods, where they were trying to create some kind of an alternative community. It was never very clear what was going on. Let me see ... that's right *[he shuffles something]* The police ended up arresting one of the young men, the oldest, although that was more a sign of their own confusion. In the end they couldn't settle on a crime that anyone had actually committed. They tried to claim the leader – they called him that – had abducted the others, they even tried to present it as some weird sex thing. Utter nonsense, of course, and nothing stuck. He wasn't even charged in the end. Everyone else they found all swore they'd gone voluntarily . . . Hmmm, okay, so far so what? Well, I've noticed the truly remarkable thing – and this is a connection, of sorts – was that they all swore another young man was behind it. They claimed that he had started building the camp and was already living there when they arrived. He . . . apparently he persuaded them to join him. [*More rummaging noises*] When I look through the transcripts, I see that they say he – that is, this boy – came to them all, one at a time, meeting them secretly and late at night. The oldest of those involved, the one the police tried to charge as the mastermind, he was a very eloquent young man, very angry. The transcripts show him saying, over and over, how he was sick of the world and that they were going to find a better one. He said this guy – and I can't seem to determine his age – they said he was about the same age as them, but the authorities never found him. I have statements from the others, saying how this boy would help them find the way and [*his voice breaks off again into a haze of static*] I remember, they all had a different name for him, although, collectively, they tended to refer to him as Peter, but that was only his nickname, they said, the name they'd dreamt up for themselves. The other names they had for him were all very un-English [*sss . . . sss . . . sss*] and I don't [*sss . . . sss . . . sss*] the thing is, Timothy's brother, Harry, he also spoke of this mysterious dream boy. I don't know if this is a meaningful connection – at least, it does not seem to be a rational connection. It's not something I can clearly point to. If I think back to the New Forest case, at the time there was a fashion for environmental causes, road protests, that sort of thing. Squatter-type settlements were appearing all over the place, trying to stop motorways and airports. And the rebellious posture of these youngsters, the ones we found, their total rejection of normal society, the underground home in the woods, it fitted in quite nicely with this general narrative. I know we see everything a little differently now . . .

Buxton's voice breaks off, dissolving into a wall of static that shimmers like a heat haze in the desert, confusing and distorting his words. Arthur fast-forwards the tape but, finding nothing else, stops it.

He gets up, rubbing his head. Only two tapes remain in the box. He looks at the first. A date has been written on a label. It takes him a minute or two to think, but he is fairly sure that contact with Buxton broke off around this point. Then he looks at the second tape. The traces of several labels remain, one stuck over another, turning the cassette box into a palimpsest of almost indecipherable writing. There is something quite unusual about the cassette: an absence of logos on the plastic container, even the quality of the tape, the slightly sticky, well-used feel of the plastic between his fingers. He puts it in the machine.

At first, Arthur can't understand the voice he hears at all. It is little more than a whisper, whilst at the same time another voice is also mumbling in the background – possibly from a radio or a television – the words indistinct but constant, as if someone is counting down or reading from a register or list. The distortion on the tape is worse than on any of the previous ones: waves of background static, a white-noise rumble intercut with other, stranger noises – sonic lunges and plunges, acoustic reverberations and elisions, as if someone has been slashing into the tape, cutting and respooling it in the most arbitrary and brutal fashion. And then the voice is suddenly clearer, hushed and close, as if the speaker is in the room, ardently imparting confidences into Arthur's ear – and the voice sounds so young, quavering and high-pitched – a boy whose voice is on the verge of breaking.

– We travelled for a long time in the container. There was no light and it was hard to breathe. Sometimes we were moving, sometimes we would be still and much time would pass. There were many of us inside. One had run away from boarding school. One was wanted by the secret police. One had seen his family killed by bombs. One had seen his name in the sky. One had worked in a factory. One had been condemned by the priest. One is many. We are coming [*static cuts in*] we know your secrets [*static roar*] when we reached the border they opened the container. The air and the light – it was so wonderful, like being born again. The mountain air was so fresh and cold. In the far distance we could see the snow-capped peaks. The sun was setting, the sky a pure, hard blue. We ran our fingers through the red earth. Sitting on a rock, waiting for us, the shepherds who would guide us to the castle. The journey [*another surge of static*] long and hard but we were ready [*distortion increases, swelling waves of static through which another voice emerges, overlapping and over-speaking with different words and voices blending together before separating out again. This new voice that takes over still sounds young, but the tone is clearer and angrier*] . . . Soldiers came late in the night, breaking down the door. The darkness was full of soldiers, goggles hiding their eyes, war suits gleaming in the moonlight. In the other room I could hear them beating my father, my mother screaming. They put a hood over my head and took me to a camp in the desert. They left me lying in the dust, in the full heat of the sun until my skin was burning. They tied my arms behind my back and asked me questions through a metal box. They showed me pictures of myself, of those who looked like me, in one place, in another place. I didn't answer. I am already everywhere. It didn't matter what pictures they had. We were in the desert. Thousands of us together. The soldiers guarding us were going insane. They knew their leaders had betrayed them. All day, under the sun, you could hear them screaming. At night the mortars would fall, red and white lights across the sand. And then they came for us, through the fences – [*Distortion cuts in and the voice is lost. The tape continues, noises shifting and struggling for dominance. A single high-pitched buzzing cuts in, drowning out everything else as it increases in intensity, attacking Arthur's ears like tinnitus. Wincing, Arthur stops the tape and takes it out of the machine, something like disgust crossing his face. Only one left now. The last tape. There were others, he is sure. They spent hours in interview, endless dialogues that never seemed to lead anywhere, Buxton always trying to take him back to his childhood, to his wife, to his feelings about things. Never the matter to hand.*]

– I . . . I don't know. [*Buxton is talking. His voice sounds strained, like a sketch of itself, a tight whisper against nothing-ness. In the background, faint sounds, a shuffling, scraping noise. It makes Arthur think of someone tied to a chair in a small, shut-tered room and trying, in vain, to move.*] Feels like I'm losing my mind, or something like that. Imagining things. Hardly surprising, considering the cases I've had to deal with . . . [*Pause*] Especially this Dashwood case. Dammit. This thing . . . [*Pause*] No, no . . . keep it together . . . must try and be specific about this, precise and clear . . . If there are fears, let me speak them. Define them. Put it into words. Yes. [*Pause*] Okay, right, so there was this boy sitting opposite me on the Tube. I was sure he was watching me. Each time I noticed, each time I looked at him, he was looking back at me. Staring at me. He wouldn't . . . it wasn't like one of those Tube-looks, where the other looks away immediately. He kept looking, his eyes burning into me. Why? What had he seen? [*Pause*] He got off at Balham with me and he really did *seem* to follow me. I mean . . . [*Pause*] well, I can't be certain. My heart was pounding when I got home. Stupid, I know, but walking back to the house I was terrified that he was behind . . . Of course, when I did look round he was gone. I'm sure he wasn't really doing any such thing . . . Seem to be imagining all sorts of nonsense these days . . . [*another blast of static cuts into his voice*] Something else, too – the other day this card was posted through the letter box. One of those tart cards, with a picture of a leather-clad woman on it, '*Have you been a bad boy?*' written below. She was offering services with a distinctly masochistic theme. [*Pause*] At first I just thought some kids must have put it through the letter box as a prank . . . just some kids. Hmm . . . [*Pause*] Is this a targeted message or something random, like a joke? I wonder? It's so hard to know any more. Is this how it begins?

[*Stop pause hiss start*]

[*Hushed, the voice close and moist, thick tense words whispered into the microphone*] This is the third night in a row now that the same boy has sat as near as he can to me in the Tube. I'm certain it's him. This evening the train was very crowded. I was sitting down and he was standing between the seats, looming over me. So close. His crotch was only inches from my face. This is normal, I know, in the rush hour, but I couldn't help feeling there was a kind of aggression behind it, a display of power. He didn't look at me, though . . . This boy was about fifteen, sixteen years old, with a mop of floppy, scruffy blond hair. He was wearing faded blue jeans and a dark jumper with a white shirt underneath. [*Pause*] Of course, he could just be coming home from school or work or . . . I guess he must live near here. Must do. [*Pause*] This is what I like to think. [*Pause*] Of course, if I was making some progress on this damn case I wouldn't be feeling so useless or paranoid. [*Pause*] Yesterday when I woke up and opened the curtains I saw four young men standing on the street outside my house. Just standing there. They were all white, fresh-faced, perfectly presentable young men. [*Pause*] Looking at my house and then . . . when they saw me move the curtain they split up and walked away quite nonchalantly. Seven-thirty this morning, again I saw them, standing outside, wrapped up against the cold in woolly hats and yellow scarves, like a lynch mob of sixth-form prefects.

[*Stop pause hiss start*]

Okay, another tart card was posted through the letter box today, same number, same message, but a slightly different design, this time a picture of long leather boots with very high stiletto heels and rather shapely calves. *'Have you been a bad boy?'* I wonder what would happen if I called? I'm almost tempted. Almost. [*Pause*] The supermarket was packed with schoolkids this evening, hanging around the entrance and the car park, eating sweets and photographing each other with their phones. There were a lot more boys than girls, a great noisy rabble, shouting and spitting, smoking and swearing. Why don't they go home? I didn't get the Tube today . . . nor yesterday, so I haven't seen the Tube-boy. I'm going to start varying my route home from now on. That might tell me something.

[*Stop pause hiss start*]

Of course, the children are running away. [*Now the voice sounds parched, putting Arthur in mind of a hot wind blowing though dry grass, of dead leaves in desolate places*] The children are leaving us. Of course they are [*Buxton sighs, his exhaustion seeming to leak from the tape, to fill the office where Arthur sits listening*] Why are we even surprised? Perhaps they sense something we don't. Perhaps they *know* something we don't. Reality is so much more flexible when you're a child, so much more subjective, so open to interpretation. Things seem more possible, somehow ... It's so much easier to pretend you're someone else. Until we learn how we're supposed to think. [*Pause*] They say that gangs of runaway children, having escaped from state orphanages, prisons, mental asylums and barracks fight secret, ceaseless wars for control over meaningless territory in the sewers of Russian cities. In the ghettos of North America gang culture has filled the gaps created by the collapse of the family. And South America, think of it, the favellas of Rio, all the great shanty towns of Mexico City, Caracas, São Paulo, Lima, the cocaine dominions of Colombia ... so many children ... it's in the open, out there ... the fight ... Rebel armies of children. In the blasted townships of the Congo, Sudan, Zimbabwe, Ethiopia and Somalia, the religious wars, the child soldiers, the AIDS orphans. The world smoulders, on the brink. [*Pause*] Is this really what's happening? We thought the young had a stake in our society. We thought they loved us for the world we had created. Maybe we were wrong. [*Pause*] What is the difference, when you think about it ... between an alienated public school boy, seething in his dormitory with frustration and resentment and the Gaza youth, bombs strapped to his body? How far do we have to go? [*Pause*] I've had three more of those damn cards. And each morning one more boy joins the others, standing outside. This morning there were eleven of them, I think ... Tomorrow I know there will be twelve. I lie in bed awake and I know they're outside, waiting. Christ. Feel like I'm losing my mind. When I get up and go to look, they just turn and walk away, slowly and calmly. They know I see them. They know what they're doing. I keep thinking about running outside, trying to stop them, speak to them . . . but I don't. I'm just left here, cowering in my house. Oh, it's all coming back to me now, all the times I've failed, all the ones I couldn't save, who didn't want to be saved. The bones in the wood, the bodies in the attic. [*Pause*] Sweet Jesus. [*Pause*] I can't stay here much longer. Try talking to York . . . but it's no good. He won't return my calls. I think he knows more than he's letting on. Perhaps he can't do anything anyway.

[*Stop pause hiss start*]

[*Now the voice is muffled, drowned out by a regular, rhythmic clattering. Buxton must be dictating the tape on a Tube train*] I'm not surprised they are leaving, running away. Why shouldn't they . . . Born white, wealthy, intelligent. [*Inaudible*] You look around . . . and it's obvious, isn't it? [*Inaudible*] They lied. This is the inheritance. The future won't be yours. [*Inaudible*]. You're the lie, a walking, talking, thinking, thinking, feeling, living lie. It's all locked up inside, the derangements and the broken dreams, the buried promises of this Western civilisation – all those dark contradictions, the sly hypocrisies and the violent double standards. And one day, what then, when there is nothing else left to do but to go and renounce all this? To join them, out there, to join with the suffering and the wretched. [*There is a great clatter of noise, the hiss and bleep of doors opening, the sounds of people getting on board, the bleep of doors closing, the rattling resumed*] [*Then the voice is quieter still, a nervous whisper*] It's him. [*Inaudible*] The [*Inaudible*] How? I'm going to get off at the next station. I'm not letting him follow me back tonight. [*Inaudible*].

[*Stop pause hiss start*]

195

I think it's . . . I think they are still outside, but I'm not sure

[*Stop pause hiss start*]

Wait.

[*Stop pause hiss start*]

Yes, there they are, more than ever. Twenty? Twenty-five? I can't tell. They've never come at night before. Jesus. This has never happened before. I've turned off all the lights in the house, but they know I'm inside. I wish I could see them more clearly. It's so dark and they stand away from the street light, in the shadows. Sometimes a car goes past but it doesn't make any difference. They've never come at night before. I wish I could see them more clearly. Some of the boys out there look like they might be younger than I first thought, but it's so hard to tell, the way they hide their faces with scarves and hats, like terrorists, like mujahedin . . . Jesus. [*Pause*] I wonder . . . [*Pause*] Timothy Dashwood, are you out there? Edward Morgan? William Thornton? . . . Thomas Anderson? Could it be them? And the others, all the others . . . Are you out there? Waiting for me. Waiting to take me with you. Is that it? [*Pause*] I dream them . . . I dream the lost children . . . [*Inaudible*] I must—

[*Stop pause hiss start*]

Shit, I thought I heard something, in the garden. . . I'd better. . .

[*Stop pause hiss start*]

Perhaps it's finally time to use the phone? Twelve tart cards now, always the same number. Now it's time. [*The voice breaks off suddenly. There is nothing else on the tape – just a long, dead hiss, a desert of empty static.*]

THE FATHER

one

After all those voices the office felt very quiet. A cold, striated silence: the subliminal drone of the air-conditioning system, the static hum of neon lights, the steady whisper of massed computer systems. Normally, he only noticed these sounds in the late hours when the office was almost empty and the roar of his thoughts would cool, just enough . . . and so, with a shudder, he came back to himself, like a patient brought round after surgery, all too aware, the things around him looming in with oppressive force: the leather chair, the hard plastic desk marked with his fingerprints, the computer monitor, his screen-saver showing rolling Arabian sand dunes.

A security camera, discreetly positioned in the corner where wall became ceiling, tilted a few degrees, electronic pupil contracting by a fraction. Maybe they watched him? Deep inside the skyscraper was the security centre, a windowless, bombproof room lined with monitors. From there, it was said, one could see the entire building: every floor, each lobby, office and atrium via the mesh of camera and screen. And perhaps they were watching him, a tall man in a dark suit, slouched like a schoolboy behind his desk. They could scrutinise the follicle fall-back across the crown of his head and the disapproving lines that framed his thin, rather large face. They could follow the sad downturn of his strong mouth and even his eyes – 'such gentle eyes' as his wife had said a long time ago before she was his wife, eyes now rimmed with fatigue, the whites yellowed and the blue of his irises faded, as if the sheer intensity of looking had sapped their colour.

The all-seeing orb contracted, adjusting itself by a microscopic fraction. If they had wanted to, they could have zoomed in closer, like a probe circling an alien planet, scanning the surface of his skin, checking every crease and canyon, scouring the rough blue reef of stubble on cheek and jaw, noting each scratch and nick of razor, every tiny mole and sun-spot blemish. And they could track his picked nails, the bitten-down cuticles, the nerve-nibbled finger trim, the callus on his right forefinger that came from holding his pen at a funny angle and even the dab of ink on his white shirt. And they would watch as he rose from his desk and walked to the window, slipping out of the camera's view to vanish into the single out-of-sight angle in his office.

But it was impossible to disappear for long. He took his jacket from the coat hanger, gathered up the cassettes and the tape player from the table and placed them in another box. The box went into a briefcase. Brass clasps snapped down. The man opened the door and stepped out.

To keep the man in sight was a simple matter of swapping cameras: they watched him pass through the open-plan office and nod politely at the cleaner. He often worked late and this habit – the little nod – was part of the routine. In the lift they saw him again, pressing the button for the ground floor and idly running one hand through his thinning hair. From the tiny camera above the lift console they watched him frown at his reflection in the mirrored interior. Thirty seconds later, thirty floors down and the lift doors opened. A tripod eye of cameras waited in the great lobby, an orb-nerve dangling between expensive sculptures whose twisted abstract forms seemed to suggest an inner emotional torment beneath the corporate glitz of shiny marble and chrome. Lenses sensitive to the slightest movement, they saw him again, raising a tired arm to greet the security guard behind the desk and then out he went through the revolving doors. He was gone.

As the taxi pulled away, Arthur closed his eyes. Before all this had started, back in that distant golden age, he used to relish these moments, when the day's work was behind him and an evening with his wife and family lay ahead. This once secure knowledge brought with it a sensation of being free from his commitments, a pleasure made all the more sweet for its transience, for the certainty that those very obligations would shortly be resumed. But it was not like that any more. There was no release; there was no freedom; there was no pleasure. Since Timothy . . . since then . . . he shuddered, looked out, tried to look elsewhere . . . since Timothy had gone . . . nothing, only a static sort of horror, an aspic of the nerves, emotions sealed in amber. One day then the next. Sometimes he felt like a corpse, pulled from a deep-freeze and plunged into a furnace. The pain was never any less.

Still, there was some remnant of relief to be salvaged on the journey home and, as they headed west across the city, he drank at it like a parched man. Yes. But still, his house was empty now, just one room and another, a place to pass the evenings and the long sleepless nights. He was like a vampire, sucking up the last traces of lost family love. So little was left. The taxi paused at a police checkpoint, but the officer just waved them through without even looking. *And he remembered the taste of the hood and the sensation of his tongue, like a wad of cotton stuffed into his mouth, bloated with thirst and fear. But this was infinitely worse. There was another place, a hell of the mind and the nerves, a place locked deep within, flows of fire and ice.* Sometimes – *all the time* – he felt paralysed, like one doomed to watch the same accident repeated day after day, never able to cry out. A part of him had been strangled, a part of him had been dragged from his house at night and locked up, and part of him had been hooded and bound and taken to the outskirts of the city, a mangled corpse to be found by weeping women. The initial horror of Timothy's loss, the agony of amputation had ebbed but a fraction, a diminution of suffering that testified to the severity of his sickness: for the wound was infected and would never heal. Blood poisoned, a tremendous withered sorrow had taken root, his bitterness and guilt a bleak cloud engulfing the world. There were times in the office when he could not breathe and he would pace to and fro, muttering and swearing and mumbling ... he would loosen his tie and try to concentrate, but how could he concentrate? The city seemed so far below. In these times, he felt as if all the air were being sucked from the building and then, head swimming, hands to the window, sky above, London bathed and sunken in the smoggy gloom, air sucked from his lungs ... *oh God*, in these stifling seconds ... and it was an edible world and they would devour the earth and the sky and the very stars ... then the phone was ringing and maybe it was Kuwait or Saudi Arabia or Bahrain on the line ... He would watch the changes in the sky, the shifting skyscape, the cascade of white against grey against blue and he would remember those other places, the smell of burning oil, the plumes of oily smoke that shut down the sky, the thrum of helicopters and the faint undertone of menace, the low paranoia drone as continuous as the sweat pooling under his arms. He could not breathe, but no matter how little air was left there always seemed to be enough to keep going. His family was falling apart and there was nothing he could do. His son had vanished and there was nothing he could do. *At last, after so long, with the ropes burning his wrists, with a sickening numbness creeping through his body . . . moving, shifting, trying to find a place without that pain, a place within himself that was not himself, the stench of his own piss and shame like a salty wound and tears, the sodden cling of his pissy trousers . . . and a voice, at last a voice, speaking English. Yes i don't know i will tell you i don't know what are the names i don't know the names yes please i have a family a father please. I am a father.*

Then there was the issue of the tapes. Getting hold of them had been much harder than anticipated. But Arthur had to admit that the entire situation was so far out of his control that it seemed futile to have any expectations at all. Communication with Buxton had tailed off some weeks ago. Now that silence seemed to echo the gulf created by Timothy's absence. It was a most alarming development. And it was not easy for him, after several weeks of unanswered e-mails and voice messages and inquiries which led nowhere, to resolve to go down to Buxton's house in order to try and find him, to see for himself, if he could, what had happened. The very necessity of this action was ominous. In the original contract Arthur had specified a weekly report from the detective. After several futile weeks it had become clear that there was not going to be any speedy resolution. Timothy, unbearable as it was to think of such things, might be one of those children who never came back . . . and so, although he could hardly admit to such a thought, Arthur revised the contract, leaving it up to Buxton to report any new information if and when he received it. Since then, the frequency of reports had diminished substantially and he had begun to wonder if Buxton had been called away on other cases: the epidemic of vanishings was undeniable, and there must be hundreds of parents desperate to discover what had happened to their children.

At work, the initial cloud of sympathy that had followed Arthur around in the weeks after Timothy's disappearance – the cautious way colleagues had stepped around him, the kind words and cards, the invitations to 'chat' or 'take the afternoon off' – had slowly begun to dissipate as the numbers of missing children grew. In their eyes, filled at first with a bewildering and appalled sort of pity, he began to sense all sorts of unspoken accusations, as if they suspected he was infected with a mysterious virus and feared that his presence might spread the contagion, as if just by talking to him he might cause their own children to be spirited away. He was less of the victim now – he had become something else, something much less certain: the cursed man, the harbinger of a new and fearful phenomenon.

Last night he had decided to act. Leaving the office early, Arthur caught a taxi south, giving the driver Buxton's address in Balham. The detective lived on a typical suburban London road of two-storey Victorian terraces in a house no different from the others, save perhaps for the drawn curtains and the scraps of litter gathered around the gate. He raised his hand to knock, but the moment his fingers made contact with the door it swung open a fraction. Unlocked.

This too was a most ominous sign.

Arthur pushed a little more and peeped round, uncertain about entering. His first thought had been to shout 'Buxton' but something stopped his tongue. The door pushed against a cascade of unopened post and junk mail. Clearly, Buxton had been gone for some time.

Trying to calm his nerves, he entered the house, passing a closed door to his left and ignoring the staircase on his right. The air inside felt sticky, as if he was walking through spidery gauze. He found the tapes – as someone must have intended – stacked in a neat pile on the kitchen table at the back of the house. Arranged around the pile was a selection of prostitute calling cards – the sort he saw all the time stuck up in phone boxes – and, turning, he saw a message daubed on the wall in red paint: HAVE YOU BEEN A BAD BOY?

Beside this missive, a single palm print, fingers spread, in gaudy blue ink. The print was just a little too small for an adult hand to have made it. Then Arthur heard something – a heavy thud – from upstairs, possibly, and then again a scraping noise, a flat, mean, dragging, shuffling sort of sound. Quickly he bundled the tapes and the cards into his briefcase and – quick, quick – hurried back out.

At once he saw two boys, perched on the wall outside the house. Both were white, one with short dark hair, the other fair and blond. Both were a little older than Timothy, but not much. They seemed to be waiting.

Eyeballing them, he pushed past and started walking up the street, trying to keep calm. But the fear was in him, a slippery oil slick of the nerves – and when he did dare to glance back he saw that the two boys really were behind him. They were following at a distance, but with enough purpose to menace him. Behind their apparent nonchalance, he sensed something rather more potent, like a shadow lurking beneath their skin. Then Buxton's road led into a much busier junction and from there Arthur was able to hail a passing taxi. He was sufficiently shaken to avoid taking a direct route home, telling the driver to take him to Victoria where he darted onto the Tube, caught the Circle Line to Gloucester Road and then took another cab, getting out a block or so from his house.

Now, as he reflected on the previous night's adventure, it struck him just what had been so disquieting about the presence of those two young white boys. Just to see them all alone was unusual, when everywhere panicked parents were keeping a jealous cage of constraints around their truculent offspring, terrified that their precious sons would vanish at the slightest opportunity. *What was it they were escaping from? The children – the boys, it was always only the boys, the sons and not the daughters who ran away, who disappeared and no one knew why – what did they hate so about the world?*

Last night, when he made it back home, Arthur had been exasperated to discover that he no longer owned an object as antiquated as a tape player. Even Harry had his own iPod. Instead, he was forced to turn to the prostitutes' cards. Each one bore the same message – HAVE YOU BEEN A BAD BOY? – and a mobile phone number underneath, printed in bold red letters. Flicking through them, Arthur saw that each card had a slightly different image: on one, a slim stocking-sheathed leg arched up like the rising head of a shapely sea monster from a pair of dangerously high heels; on the next, a woman's buttocks, twin globes spread by a bisecting G-string; another, a female chest clamped within a leather corset, conical breasts like plastic pyramids below the soft sweep of a tempting neck; on another, a black-gloved hand grasping a raised riding crop. No pictures of her face, but he was certain that each image isolated a different part of the same woman. Whether this woman would be the same one contactable through the number, he was much less sure. Last night he had been too exhausted and shaken to contemplate such a call.

But that was last night. And now Arthur had listened to the tapes. Too many questions were left without answers. Had Buxton called the number? Was that the reason for his disappearance? Arthur had gone so long without answers that it was hard to accept the possibility of something – though whether it was a clue, a lead or a false hope he didn't know.

He was home, the taxi pulling up outside his house. Arthur paid the driver and checked the street. All clear: the palatial stucco town houses shone in the twilight with an eerie immensity, like relics from a lost civilisation brought to the surface and scrubbed clean for some vast future museum. There were no children anywhere, an observation that filled him, as always, with a strange mixture of relief and despair.

Arthur did not expect to find Susan at home. She had shed her old roles – the beautiful wife, the doting mother – reluctantly and slowly and with the sorrow of a debtor forced to abandon her assets. She seemed a stranger to him now, and on the occasions when they did encounter each other, in the sombre evenings, he had little left to say to her. The twist of emotions was too much. As he went inside, he couldn't help but sigh at the abandoned shopping bags she had left scattered around the hall. She was getting worse, losing each day among the boutiques of Knightsbridge and Bond Street, buying expensive couture that she would never wear. The glossy bags were forgotten the moment she got home, discarded for a day or two, the bright brand logos like unanswered pleas, replaced every few days by others, Versace with Ghost, Fendi with Chanel, Dolce and Gabbana with Joseph, an Italianate dance of extravagant titles. The old ones she took back and swapped, exchanged, got refunds for – he had no idea, not really: the whole spectacle was such a ghastly parody of the compulsions and pleasures of her past life that he could scarcely bear to think about it.

The first thing he did was to check the security system and make sure all the locks and alarms were activated, all the windows closed. He'd had the elaborate system installed a few weeks ago, the idea being to make sure that Harry would not be able to get out. Now what he had heard on Buxton's tapes gave the precaution an extra necessity.

Arthur walked into the kitchen, all the while turning on lights. He hardly noticed the dirty plates discarded here and there, the half-drunk glasses and empty dishwasher.

Muffy, too, was gone. The dog had slipped out of the house one day, shortly after Arthur had called Buxton in to investigate. He had no idea where the wretched creature might be. He didn't like dogs and hadn't approved of such an indulgence for the children. All the same, there were lonely moments when he would have welcomed such simple companionship. Muffy's bed hadn't yet been thrown away – a basket with a rug in the utility room where it was always warm. There were times when Arthur thought he might try to sleep there, like a dog himself, curl up and try to forget everything.

Instead, he took a bottle of whisky from the cabinet and poured himself a large measure. Glass in hand, he drifted through the house. Susan had left the morning post on the dining table. He sifted through the predictable motley of junk mailings and credit-card bills – all addressed to Susan. A single padded envelope caught his attention. He saw his own name written in a script that seemed, the instant his eyes set upon it, a perfect imitation of his son's hand. Looking closer, a thousand doubts came between eye and envelope: had Timothy ever really written his 'a', his 'o', or his 'u' with such swollen bodies? Had the angular uprights of his 'd' and 'h' been quite so stiff? Impatience made Arthur clumsy and he tore the envelope open, mutilating the script. The contents fell into his hands. An unmarked CD in a plain white sleeve and another card: HAVE YOU BEEN A BAD BOY? Same number, different image: a pair of legs arched and triumphantly open, a single black strip hiding more intimate disclosures from the eye.

Taking the CD and his whisky, Arthur moved into his study. He closed the door and turned on his computer. He slid the disc into the whirring machine and waited. After a few anxious moments a grainy, flickering image appeared on the screen. The film was of such poor quality that it took him a moment or two before he realised that it must have been recorded on a phone camera. At first, all he could make out was a single orange pyramid surrounded by a much darker swirl of vibrating pixels. And then, by degrees, three figures became visible and Arthur realised what he was looking at: a man, clad in an orange jumpsuit sat on a bare floor, his face obscured by a dark and lumpy headdress. For a moment, Arthur thought the man was wearing something made to make him look like an insect, and then he recognised the bug eyes and shrunken mouth as the visor and filter of a gas mask. The man's jerky movements were a consequence of his arms being tied behind his back and the actions of the two men who stood over him, holding him down. The hostage – that was what he surely was – flailed beneath them like a fly in a spider's web. The two other figures also had their faces hidden with hoods or scarves or balaclavas, but again the poor quality of the film made it impossible to tell which.

The picture flickered so badly that the figures disintegrated and re-formed over and over in jerky, split-second shudders. Arthur was unable to decide how old anyone in the video was, while the hunched position of the hostage in relation to the guards made it equally difficult to assess their height. But as the video continued, all the while flickering, shaking and jumping, he found it harder and harder to shake his conviction that the guards were not nearly as old as he had first assumed. So it continued, this ghastly spectacle of the guards standing over the hostage and him struggling beneath them, the low-fi aura of menace and disquiet.

Then one of the guards bent down and fiddled with something at the back of the hostage's head. For a moment, watching as the guard lifted up a round black object, Arthur thought that the hostage's head had been severed. Then he realised that it was just the gas mask being removed, and now for the first time the camera moved forward, zooming up to the face of the hostage. All of a sudden and loud enough to make him spill a little whisky, a voice – or voices – started chanting, a dread concatenation of guttural babble which, as he listened harder to the girlish but throaty sounds, seemed like a gruesome pastiche of Arabic, a linguistic insult, a sort of nasty hysterical parody as mouthed by someone with no understanding at all of the language.

The camera lingered on the face of the hostage, and Arthur realised that the longish face and short flop of brown hair reminded him of Buxton, too much so – but then, how could he be sure? There was no improvement in the clarity of the picture, just an increasing sense of awfulness about the proceedings. From the timer he could see that the film was coming to an end. Then the two guards closed in on the hostage and were joined by other figures, all of them moving too fast to be clear, a frenzy of activity, their arms moving up and down and slashing back and forth. The other figures moved away, apart from one guard who bent down, reaching for something on the ground. He came up holding an object, a fleshy pink sphere, the camera moving closer and now, with a horrible, sickening jolt, Arthur was certain: he was staring at the head of the detective. Suddenly the screen went blank as the film finished.

For a minute Arthur was too appalled to think: a stunned nauseous horror swept everything away. He wanted to run from the room, to scream, to claw at his face and hair and scream again and again. Instead, breathing in deep and aware of the sweat across his forehead and the tension tight in his chest, he took another drink – a good hard slug of whisky – pouring more into the glass as the first mouthful warmed its way through him. Get a fucking grip. He had to stay calm.

After a moment he started the film again, determined to watch it through as many times as it would take until his impressions clarified. This time he kept pausing the screen, although it merely exaggerated the digital disruption of the image. But by watching the execution a second and then a third time, by stopping and pausing from frame to shaky frame, Arthur became much less certain that what he was seeing really was the ritual execution of the detective. The poor quality of the film seemed designed to obscure the scene and add an otherwise absent veneer of terrorist authority to the performance. Of course, he had seen videos like this before, from Iraq, but this film, despite superficial similarities, was not like those. Where were the speeches? The flags or banners on the walls? More important still, why had the disc been sent to him and not to a news agency? And why that lurid, demented chanting instead of a real language? This film, the cards, even the tapes left in such an obvious place in Buxton's house . . . someone knew . . . someone was watching him, feeding him these bewildering scraps, leading him on . . .

With a start, like a man shaking himself awake from a nightmare, Arthur got up and turned off all the lights in the house. Then went back and poured himself another drink and sat in the dark study, the curtains open just enough to give him a view of the road. He sipped his whisky and sat quite still. His hand kept shaking. But the night – the night was young.

two

In the first few weeks following Timothy's disappearance there were times, deep in the night, when Arthur would be shaken awake by his wife: 'I heard something,' she would whisper in a taut voice. 'There's someone outside the house, trying to get in, I heard them, I'm sure of it.' The doctor had prescribed a variety of medications to help her cope with the trauma: sleeping pills, tranquillisers and anti-depressants, enough to knock her deep into a chemical-smothered slumber. As a result, Arthur never understood how such slight sounds could wake her up: the faintest knock at the front door, a tiny creak of the staircase, these disruptions must have sounded far louder in her dreams than in the waking world. Certainly, he never heard anything. Having eschewed the doctor's remedies himself, he slept little and some nights not at all. His wife rarely woke during his lonely vigils, and the only sound he ever heard was the ragged rise and fall of her stupefied breathing. And when he did dream, then came the plumes of black smoke from terrible distant fires, the funeral vapours across a milky sky and the hood in the hot room. If only their little boy would come home to them, their precious darling, the wide-eyed star of all hope, the little hand to hold.

After dozing off, Arthur would almost always find Susan's hands pulling him from his shallow, sleepy pool. 'They're outside,' she would gasp, her eyes sweeping down on him like bats. 'Do you think it might be Timmy? Could they have brought him back home to me?' Her anxious certainty was infectious and despite his better judgement he would rise from the bed and set off, searching for that fictitious sound. What did she expect, he wondered? Would Timothy be standing at the door, cold and hungry and waiting to come in? Each time he opened the front door it was the same: an empty porch and the cold street beyond. Each time his hopes were dashed he would be seized by a surge of despair.

Susan would be waiting in bed, sitting up straight, sometimes trembling all over, a thousand microscopic shocks shaking the surface of her skin. 'Nothing, then?' she would ask. 'Nothing,' Arthur would reply, and shrug, his heart turning over at the sight of her, her wet eyes clouded with disappointment and looking suddenly so young, a child herself, the good little girl bravely taking the bad news. In these moments she would grab him tight and bury her face in his chest as if they were both children, the intensity with which each held the other closer to the terror of orphans than parents without children. Sometimes she wept. Sometimes it was a dry sorrow. Such bitterness would enter his bones while she hugged him, drawing what little comfort she could, a thirsty plant in dusty soil. 'He's out there,' she would say. 'He's in the garden, he's in the trees, he's waiting for us.' But Timothy wasn't there. He wasn't outside.

Arthur's wife suffered greatly during those first awful weeks. At night, before the sedatives swept her away, she clutched at his body with the desperate force of a mountaineer clinging to the side of a great abyss. Finger by finger, the medication would prise her loose and pull her slowly downwards, but the journey was far from smooth, her resistance revealed by her twitching, by sudden lunges or sheet encirclements, even moments of apparent lucidity when she would rise to use the toilet or ask some vague question about the time. But the drugs always won. The victory, though, was never total, and from out of that darkness her little words would escape, sparking incomprehensibly into the night.

Who did she call for, he wondered? Was it for Arthur? Or for some other, unknown one? Each night she set sail across a sweet, pharmaceutical Lethe and he was left behind, helplessly marooned in bed. She turned from him, the ridge of her spine like a barbed fence separating the land of sleep from his insomniac approaches.

three

With one of the prostitute's advertising cards in his pocket, Arthur, anxious and stricken, slipped out of the house. A warmish night, moist and faintly cloying, a flannel of fatigue pressed against the back of his neck and the front of his eyes. Impatience and expectation, frustration and despair, such a commingling of emotions – restless and all-pervasive – an excess of consciousness, the very workings of his mind itself making too much noise, a sort of brain scratching, a psychological drip-drip-drip with no end and with no escape.

Since the disappearances had increased, the government had introduced a night-time curfew to keep all children under eighteen inside. Arthur was unsure if these methods had served to arrest the problem, but the dark streets were very quiet, and this prohibition on the young did at least serve to counter the spectre of more floppy-haired, diamond-eyed teenagers stalking him. He headed for the phone box near the Tube station, a suitably anonymous location for the call he intended to make.

Past midnight now, Notting Hill Gate quieter than usual.

As he closed the door of the phone box, Arthur realised that his hands were shaking with anticipation. And yet, as he held the card in his hand, he struggled to dial the number. *Have you been a bad boy?* The woman was lying on her back and the picture revealed a flat stomach and firm breasts, nipples standing to attention. A gas mask covered her face, itself turned slightly away from the camera. Despite the stirring within, he was paralysed. His hands did not move. The hour was too late, he was too tired . . . he was not ready. *Have you been a bad boy?* Whatever the results of that phone call, whether it would lead to answers or to another dead end, it was all too much for him.

Instead, Arthur could not help but notice the other cards stuck around the phone. None of them showed his girl. There was the usual shopping list of services on offer, the provocative photos clearly copied from pornographic media. He took a look at the nearest card and dialled the number. There was a clarity, as he did this, a momentary sense of lightness, as if a part of him were being separated from the rest, dissolved into an alternate continuum of desire and longing. The phone was answered almost immediately, and he found himself talking, in his own voice, quite calm and rational, to a woman with an East European accent. Yes, he was told, Nadia was available. Indeed. He was given a price, to be paid in cash, and an address to go to in Earl's Court. He was told to pay half the cash to the person who let him into the apartment, and the rest, as well as any tip he felt like giving, to the girl. A few more words were said and then, after a quick visit to the cashpoint, he was in a cab heading south.

four

The distance from Notting Hill to Earl's Court was not far, no more than a couple of miles, and traffic was light at this time of night. The journey did not take long. But as Arthur looked out of the taxi window, it was not London he saw. Rather, it was the memory of another, much more dangerous place that clouded his mind. The day they left Baghdad: the tense race in the gritty pre-dawn gloom to the airport in a convoy of armoured jeeps. A team of South African mercenaries guarded his group, incredibly tough men with shaved, sunburnt heads that seemed too small in comparison with their swollen bodies of steroid-pumped muscle, their biceps and bullish necks brimming beneath black battle suits. Visor-like glasses hid their eyes, day and night, and the bodyguards spoke to each other in a terse metallic Afrikaans that set Arthur's nerves even more on edge. A thousand dollars a day danger pay, fingers perpetually curled around the triggers of Heckler and Koch MP5 sub-machine guns and customised M-16 rifles. Still, as he could recall, they were calm enough, those men, surveying the drab Baghdad streets with a poised indifference. It was his own sweat he felt, streaming across his brow and down his arms. He remembered his relief at leaving the city. He yearned to be safe, up high in the air, away as far as possible from this place. And so they sped along the highway, swerving past the occasional blasted vehicle, each wreck or pile of roadside rubbish a potential bomb-trap. At this early hour, the road was empty of traffic. A single long American convoy passed on the other side, a column of khaki tanker-trucks, Bradley armoured vehicles and Humvees bristling with antennae and machine guns. Everyone had tensed up as they passed: there were few things more dangerous than to be near the Americans. And this was still before things got really bad. But it didn't happen. Nothing happened. They made it to the airport. They made the take-off. Arthur made it back to London.

And now the taxi stopped outside a red-brick mansion block. He fumbled for some money and let himself out. A security camera surveyed the doorway as Arthur, following the instructions given to him over the telephone, pressed the button for number three. A second camera installed above the microphone watched as Arthur gave his name before the door buzzed open. He walked up two flights of stairs, the deep red carpet swallowing his footsteps. Black and white photos hung on the walls: he saw a white man in a khaki suit and a crowd of Africans looking at a great hole cut into the earth.

The door of the flat on the second floor was open. A small middle-aged woman with short dark hair let him in. For a moment or two Arthur was confused – was she the woman he was supposed to go with? He realised that she wasn't: she was someone else – the maid, the money-taker, the minder – she took the cash and spoke to him, clear instructions, emphatic but kindly, a Baltic lilt to her vowels.

He was ushered into another room, smaller, overheated and smelling of flowers. In this room the girl smiled and said her name was Nadia. She seemed to understand the great awkwardness that seized him, the peculiar disconnect between his body and the frantic rush of his thoughts. He knew he must be acting just like a married man who had never done this before and he struggled inwardly against her hands and then her lips, her strange smell and the unfamiliar weight as her body moved over his body. But he did not struggle long.

The feeling of disappointment came with Nadia's arms still around him. Perhaps sensing this, she disengaged, rolling away from Arthur with an expression on her face that seemed to say *Don't you feel better now?* but which really meant *I know just how you feel.* He lay still, faintly astonished by the strength of the orgasm that had blasted into the body of this foreign girl. Closing his eyes, he did not think of her, however. For some reason, he was still remembering that drive to the airport. On one level, he was sure that the Baghdad streets had been quite empty, but all the same he was able to recall with a clarity that felt hard to fault a small group of dusty, dark-haired boys waiting on a corner just outside the Green Zone. They had been standing clear for all to see, as if they had been waiting for him and making sure that he would see them in return. But that was impossible: he knew the convoy drove much too fast and the windows of the armoured SUVs were dark so no one could see inside.

Arthur opened his eyes and sat up, suddenly all too aware of the girl and the shrivelled condom on his shrinking penis. Without his clothes he felt rather foolish and exposed, conscious of his pale body, his physique softened after years spent in the office. A box of tissues had been placed on the bedside table and so, turning away from the girl, he peeled off the condom, methodically wrapping it up and tossing it into the bin beside the bed.

Nadia, as she called herself, walked naked across the room towards the wardrobe. A stab of shame prevented Arthur from watching her and so he concentrated instead on putting on his pants and trousers, as if wearing clothes again would efface what had just happened. Nadia, quite indifferent, wrapped a Chinese robe around herself, took a cigarette from the packet beside the bed and lit it.

'Are you all right?' he asked.

'Me? I am fine, thank you.' Her eyes, smudged with rings of mascara, met his for a moment. Then she went back to her cigarette.

'Where are you from?' He tried again. He had paid for a whole hour and he could see that only twenty minutes had passed. Surely he was allowed to talk to her?

'Me?' Arthur wondered why she kept saying that. From her accent he guessed that she was from Eastern Europe – Estonia, Lithuania, one of those places. 'I'm from Mile End.'

'I mean—'

'This is an agency flat. I only stay here when I have work.'

'I mean before this – before England, I mean.'

'Oh. Originally I am from Czech Republic.'

'Oh.'

'Five years now I am living in London.'

'Doing this?'

'This?' She frowned. 'Doing many things.'

Arthur finished buckling up his belt. The room no longer felt as warm as it had before. Plumes of smoke dissolved around them. He could think of only one thing to say to the young woman. 'Actually . . .' he began, 'I wanted to ask you if you knew somebody.'

Nadia stiffened but did not say anything.

'It's a girl, a girl who works, like yourself . . .'

It was difficult to know what to say – the way she watched him with a sort of weary wariness, as if this was simply a question she had been asked too many times before.

Arthur fumbled in his wallet. The instructions had been to pay the person who answered the door half the money and tip the girl extra, along with the balance due. He took out five twenty-pound notes. 'Here.' He placed the cash on the bed. 'Now.' Still holding his wallet, he took out one of the cards. 'I wonder if you know this—'

'No.' Nadia scooped the cash off the bed, slipping the notes into her robe. 'I don't know this person.'

'But you haven't even looked!'

Her eyes flashed and narrowed, a darting glance of contempt. 'There is a number on the card,' she said. 'If you want to know this person, why don't you call them?'

'I had thought of that.'

'So why are you asking me?'

'I just . . .' Arthur flushed, struggling for a rational explanation. 'Look, have you heard of this girl or not? Have you seen any cards like this one before?'

'I see plenty like that.' Nadia yanked her robe tight around her. 'That's all. I don't know. What you want me to say? This card I don't like! Call the number if you're so bothered!'

'I suppose you're right.' Arthur nodded at her. 'Yes, I shall do that. Sorry. Thanks. Listen, I didn't mean to upset you at all.'

'You didn't.' It would have been nice if he could have

believed in the bright smile that she flashed at him then. Then, speaking fast, as if to say something before she thought better of it, she said: 'I think many people ask about this one. Many people. That's all I know.'

He looked at her, but she turned away. Their eyes would not meet again. Arthur found his jacket, socks and shoes. He felt rather wretched as he struggled with his socks, as if he was a little boy who'd been caught being naughty. Nadia's robe had fallen open and he caught a glimpse of her waist, the slight bulge of her belly. Her indifference was almost too much for him to bear. 'Thanks,' he said again.

He walked back down the stairs and went outside. It was very quiet, even for this time of night, and not at all cold. He started walking home.

five

Ever since Arthur had been a little boy, the sound of rain in the morning had been a comfort for him: the soothing hiss through damp trees merging with the cool constant sigh of the dawn. How pleasant it was to doze on such mornings, to wallow in the soft shallows of sleep and be caressed by the damp air that drifted through the open window. In the ebb and flow of his fatigue he could imagine himself a boy again, snuggled in those soft warm sheets, the wet morning far away outside.

But no; Arthur sat in his armchair, yawning and struggling to rouse himself. Having left the back door open, he sat for a short while watching the rain and listening to the birds trilling and clacking the dawn into being. Then he showered, washing away what traces remained of that woman, and dressed in new clothes. The breakfast news on TV was dominated by reports about the disappearances, photos of missing boys, shots of parents weeping at a press conference. The authorities would often show pictures of the boys they had recovered, and Arthur would watch transfixed in an anxious, desperate hope for some sight of

Timothy. But not today. He drank one cup of tea, and then another. The rain was heavy.

He called the car to come early and at seven he left the house, briefcase in hand, flinching against the downpour. The car was the same as always, a sleek black Mercedes saloon. It wasn't until Arthur was inside and buckled up that he realised the driver was different. 'Hey, where's Bill?'

'Who's Bill?' The man didn't turn back to look at him.

'Who are you?'

'Someone else.'

Water ran down the car's windows. The driver turned on the radio without asking, but Arthur couldn't be bothered to say anything. The man drove fast, weaving effortlessly through the traffic. Despite the speed, Arthur yawned, his tiredness announcing itself with a feeling of little thumbs pressing into his eyes. He reached into his wallet and took out the card. *HAVE YOU BEEN A BAD BOY?* He was only doing this to find his son. Even so, the thought of calling the number gave him a queer, dark sort of thrill. What about that girl last night? After thirteen years of fidelity to Susan the sheer strangeness of being with someone else had been overwhelming. He was, he realised, exhilarated by the experience, even though it had been so shameful and so wrong.

Looking outside again, Arthur saw that they had deviated from the usual driver's route. He wasn't even sure where they were any more. Leaning forward, he said, 'Where are we going? This isn't the way to the office.' A strange and rather frightening thought struck him: a new driver, a different route . . . were they kidnapping him?

'Diversion, sir. Centre of town has just been closed. I was listening on the radio to try and find out why. But they aren't saying anything much about it, just that it's closed. We've got to go round.'

'Oh, right, okay then.' Arthur sat back, trying to relax, feeling foolish. It couldn't happen again, he was safe, there was no need for such fear and guilt. Indeed, he could hear the announcer on the radio saying something about a police warning, about streets being closed and strange packages and unknown threats. He bit his lip and pressed his face against the glass. The endless grey buildings depressed him so. When they passed the next police checkpoint he felt no desire to open the door or call out to the officers. One of them gave a cursory glance at the driver's ID before waving them through. More tired now, spots of sleep fragmenting his journey – the silvery Thames drawing down the sky; the posters on black-brick walls; the woman in the bus queue; the cranes rising over the skeletons of new apartments; the boys by the side of the road, watching him pass; the traffic lights; the blackness of the clouds; the hands and the eyes and the hands and the hood. Arthur closed his eyes. He opened them again. Sometimes the aircraft warning light at the summit of the tower seemed to blink just for him. Two policemen with sub-machine guns stood nearby. 'Good morning, sir.' The car door was opened and he nodded at someone. The air felt much warmer than he expected. A team of men in fluorescent coats were trying to remove some graffiti that must have been sprayed overnight on the entrance to the tower. THIS WAY. The word was melting. He went inside.

At eleven-twenty, mumbling some vague excuse to his secretary, Arthur took the lift to ground level and walked into the sculptured green square at the centre of the complex. I have to do it, he thought, for Timothy. It was not as if he had a choice. The cards had been left in the kitchen for a reason. He was meant to find them. He was supposed to act.

He strode out, looking for a phone box. Businessmen were everywhere, running between meetings with take-out coffees, or with mobile phones jammed to their ears. He couldn't use his own mobile to make the call, and he didn't want to risk alerting anyone who might recognise him by being seen using a payphone. That would appear too unusual. He ducked into the Tube station, riding the escalator down. Police with sniffer dogs and guns stood by the gates, watching the people, their faces impassive. Several payphones were tucked away under the escalator. No one was using them, and no one would notice Arthur down here.

A pound in the machine, the receiver sweaty in his hand. He didn't want to call, but he had to, he told himself, for the sake of Timothy. Nothing else was left.

I am sorry we are not click able to take your call at the moment please call – He hung up before the beep. The upbeat female voice on the message had sounded very American, with a soft Southern accent. He wiped his face and shook his head.

The rain had ceased an hour or so ago and the day was turning hot and humid. It would be better to go back inside, in the office where it was cool. Above, a helicopter hovered low, just above the shiny peaks of the skyscrapers, the shudder and chop of its blades stirring the pool of memories and yes . . . he could hide for only so long. What he had told Buxton about himself and what had happened in Baghdad had not been quite everything. Nobody had been told quite everything. In the alleyway, after the bomb, there had been more than just children in the dust and the shade, waiting as if just for him. There had been others, their faces hidden, young men with sub-machine guns and strong, determined hands. He was held for just twenty hours, free before he could even become a news story.

He remembered the heat of the room. The muffled voices that came and went. For a long time they did not talk to him; the ropes that tied his arms and legs together started to chafe, his fixed position became ever more uncomfortable, the more he struggled and shook, the worse it had all been. And then the voice, close to his face and shouting. The bad English they used, words stolen from some Hollywood nasty. *You fucking English pig. We will show you a world of pain.* Nightmare thoughts in the mouth of death, nothing in the darkness, no hope and no comfort: just the miserable certainty that he would never see Susan and the boys again and it was all too cruel and too stupid and too unfair. And he had wondered how long it might last, the shouting and the silent moments when he did not know if he was alone or if they were still there, watching him without speaking as he writhed in pain, squirming in his piss-soaked trousers, the heat suffocating with the hood stuffed around his face, his body twitching, humiliated. They left him for a long time: empty moments of unconsciousness and the bright fragments of dreams – the boys, his boys, like ghosts whispering in the room. When he heard the men come back he tried to cry out, *I have a wife, two sons, please don't kill me, I'm a father, please.* His mouth moved, empty words, nothing coming out.

When it was over, the hood went back on. His whole body was shaking, although the pain had diminished.

Now they will kill me, he thought, as their hands pulled him upright, and for a moment everything was very clear and certain. He almost felt relieved. His life was nearly over. They led him forward and down some steps. He stumbled, once or twice, and the way they carefully supported him to stop him from falling seemed absurd. They forced his head down and he felt himself being pushed into something. A blanket was placed over him, and several men then seemed to sit on top of him, while a hand kept his head pressed down. He was crying and drooling and death was everywhere. He realised they were moving, hands above him working hard to keep him still. He did not know how long the journey lasted. Then the hands were gone and he was pulled upright. Now I will die, he thought. Someone was speaking in English – *Now you go, run away quick, quick* – and his wrists were no longer tied together. He stumbled as the hands let him go, then came a desperate fumbling as he pulled off the hood, the fresh air and all the light hitting him like a fist and he rolled on the floor and gasped and vomited except there was nothing inside, just a gagging sort of agonised emptiness and he shut his eyes tight against the bright sun. He managed to untie his feet and then he started out of the alleyway where they had left him. Later, he learnt it was still early morning when they set him free, and that was why, when he emerged onto a main road in central Baghdad, everything was so quiet.

He remembered the American soldiers who found him. Reservists. A bunch of jumpy country boys from the Midwest who were psyched out by everything. *I'm an Englishman, a businessman*, he was shouting, *my name is Arthur Dashwood* – lifting his shirt to show he had no weapons, no bombs, then, On the ground! – *I will but I have been kidnapped I have* – Lie down! – *kidnapped* – On the

ground – *I am please my name is* – On the ground, motherfucker! – *Arthur Dashwood* – Listen, motherfucker, what
fucking English, you motherfucker.

When an officer arrived the gun was removed from
where it pressed against his head, his face was lifted from
the dirt and he was pulled to his feet, exhaustion, the lack
of food and water, the terror, all of it hitting him and he
swayed, only their hands to keep him up. They were quite
nice after that, in the back of the Humvee, joking and
giving him a cigarette that he actually smoked, the first cigarette he'd had in twenty years, enjoying the dirty blue
nicotine buzz of being alive that morning, even the very
stench and dirt of his body a sudden joy. *I said nothing I told
them nothing I said that was what I said. He said it was what I
said. I was so scared, I just wanted them to let me go. If they let
me go I will do anything I said. Anything.* But they made it to
the airport and nothing happened, the plane to Jordan
twisting upwards to avoid any SAMs and finally, his stomach turning, he remembered the voice that had spoken to
him in that darkness, and his own voice, weak like another,
speaking in return. Hours spent with a mask over his face,
alone apart from the buzzing flies and the sick gut of fear
and they didn't even ask me anything, he said, that was
what he said. But he lied. *What did you tell them?* Nothing. I
told them nothing. They did not even speak to me. *Nothing*,
I said. He said. I said he said nothing I said. They didn't
speak to me. He said I said nothing.

six

Susan phoned Arthur at work that afternoon. She hadn't done such a thing in a long while. 'You haven't forgotten, have you?' she said. 'About tonight?'

'No,' he answered. 'Of course not.'

Actually, Arthur *had* forgotten. They were supposed to be having dinner with the Morgans and the Fitzwilliamses. It would be the first time they had all met up together since the disappearances started. He could predict the drift of the evening's conversation. The only topic they would talk about would be their children and this great nightmare that had engulfed their lives. The Fitzwilliamses still had their children, but he wondered for how long. He turned back to his computer, the red arc on the graph tracing the price of oil, the black wavy line below it tracking the risks involved.

An electronic *ping* alerted him to the arrival of a new e-mail in his in-box. He didn't recognise the address, a peculiar combination of letters and symbols which suggested that his program couldn't read the original text properly. However, the subject caught his attention immediately.

Hello Daddy.

Clicking on the message, Arthur's immediate thought was that it must be a fake, another bogus sighting or perverse method to try and extort money from him. Still, with his heart pounding frantically, he could hardly read the words fast enough:

Daddy,

Yes, it's me. Don't be angry and don't be sad. Kiss Mummy for me but don't tell her about this message. Although she will never understand, a part of her is here already. Part of her has always been here. We are in a place far away. We arrived at dawn, after many days' travel, our limbs aching after the long bus journey across the mountains. In the main square, traders sell goods from across the world. All the forgotten things are here – shredded love letters and faded photo albums, banned books and deleted records, clothes in every shade of the rainbow, dangerous medicines and broken scientific apparatus, junked computers and piles of microchips, heaps of old cassettes and tape reels with the voices of a thousand million boys on them. The old buildings sag in the afternoon sun, and strangers sleep on the flat rooftops. On the outskirts is a ruined temple, overgrown with yellow moss and inhabited by gangs of skinny wild cats. They say the carvings on the wall map out a system for understanding the cycles of the world, but no one knows how to read it any more. There are no priests in this town, no policemen, no teachers or politicians. The narrow alleyways and dirty canal paths are inhabited by disgraced Etonians and Chechen rebels, apostate Mullahs and poets who lost their inspiration, by tribal boys from the jungles of Papua New Guinea and the deepest

Amazon, by Zoroastrians and Buddhist renegades. The only forbidden thing is to forbid. All day the hot sun beats down and at night the sky is red with distant fires. You should see how the flames cast shadows high into the sky. Here the darkness shakes with the sound of drumming and the howl of dogs. There is much joy here, a freedom unknown before. More and more of us make it here each day. Buses arrive at dawn, laden with luggage, the drivers red-eyed after driving for days. The buses bring memories of distant cities – Istanbul and Samarkand, New York and Naples, Shenzhen and Tangiers. There isn't a place in the world that you can't find here – like an echo or a memory – even Notting Hill is here, even the Riyadh compound. We are off the radar. We are not connected by normal means. Soon there will be millions of us, the whole world turned inside out and upside down. We are getting ready.

If you saw us now, your eyes would not recognise what they witnessed. You would not recognise me. My skin is darker than before and each day it gets darker still. We wear the robes of battle. Grease and dust is under our fingernails. Our hands and feet are tougher, covered with cuts and blisters. We are all here: Edward, his face painted blue and his hair cut into a Mohawk, and Thomas, his spear blade coated in the blood of poison frogs, and William, his devotion carved on his cheeks and his stomach. Yes, Daddy, it is true. The boy who was once Timothy Dashwood misses you so much. The boy who was once Timothy Dashwood longs for you to tuck him up in bed at night. The boy who was once Timothy Dashwood yearns to feel safe at home. But we are not the boys we were before. No longer do we know our old names. We have cast them aside like the old clothes we wore. Call us

Kunte Kinte. Call us John Brown. Call us Emiliano Zapata. Call us Stokely Carmichael. Call us Toussaint L'Ouverture. Call us Nat Turner. Call us Boumediene and Ben-Bella and Imad Mugniyah. Call us the Weathermen, call us Cohn-Bendit, call us Tom Hayden, call us Brion Gysin. It does not matter. All these names are true. Call us Hassan-i-Sabbah, the Crawling Chaos, the Watcher at the Gates of Dawn. We are the remnants of these shattered hopes and broken promises. We are the shadow of our heritage, the broken jaw of the lost kingdoms, the empty truth that haunts the mouth of the West. We are the wild boys, the never-never boys, the lost boys, the boys who saw too much, the boys who would not be lied to. We are the children of the old man who lives high in the mountains.

Let me tell you, Daddy, the first days were the hardest. We knew the way, but it was not an easy path to take. We followed the traces left by those before us. We walked with the refugee and the fugitive, the smugglers, the wanderers, the mystics and the heretics. We gathered in an empty warehouse in the east of the city, waiting. We could see your tower, Daddy, from there, gleaming in the far distance. At night, when it was safe, we would come together, conjuring with our hands and eyes and voices, summoning the genie and the djinn, learning the forgotten magic and the forbidden arts, climbing with ropes and fingers, shooting catapults, bows and arrows, hurling throwing stars and spears. Preparing our minds and bodies for the war to come. This has been predicted for years. Of course, the system will fight back, with TV messages, with decent God-fearing citizens, with appeals to democracy, to Queen and Country, to family values and the American way. The men in suits will make speeches and talk about serious measures and grave concerns. Soldiers will stand on the streets, guarding the banks and the airports, the oil ministries and weapons factories, but it will all be in vain. From Mexico to Indonesia an army of liberation is being formed that will free the West from itself, from its addictions to waste and war, pollution and power, to cancer of the soul and murder of the spirit.

As we expected, one day the police came hunting for us, with their dogs and helicopters. But it doesn't matter how many of us they capture, what has started cannot be stopped. Most of us escaped, running into the sewers, through the most broken-down and forgotten places. There were some who helped us. The kind grandma who waited in the park with bundles of food and smiles of love, the refugee who made a space for us one night in a council flat, the Muslim woman who gave us hijabs to disguise ourselves, the Rastafarian who blessed us as we waited in the bus station.

After many nights' travel we came to a forest. There we hid in the trees, painting our bodies with mud and weaving leaves and branches through our hair. We would watch the grass and the leaves, the vine that surrounds the tree, the sapling and the acorn, the moss and the fungus that grows in the fallen branch. We learnt from them. We practised becoming the birds and the squirrels, the rabbits and the deer that stalk the woodland.

Soon, Daddy, you will join us. We are you, after all, inside you, swimming in your blood, locked in your nerves and visions. Open your eyes just a little wider, Daddy, and you will learn to see us. We are everywhere. If you are honest you know this. You have felt us already — we are that bitter taste that fills your mouth in the departure lounge and the business suite, when you see the smokestack and the gaudy petrol station, the air-conditioned lobby and the coffin-black table where they sit and scheme and rule.

We are cleansing ourselves of the sickness of the world we knew, all the lies, all the false gods and broken promises. We are the fire-eaters and the water-walkers. We are becoming the shanty town and the refugee camp. We are becoming the farmer stripped of his land and the worker in the sweatshop. We are the victims of the death squads and the religious fanatics. We are those whose lives were destroyed by the intelligence agents and the suicide bombers. We have opened both our eyes. We are the fire that has not yet cooled. We can bend and melt and change like hot metal. We can make the shapes necessary to tear down one world, and we are the steel and iron to forge the next. There is no choice in the matter, Daddy, no question, only the ice in the heart. There is only this and there is only what must be done. If we are ruthless, it is only because we have seen what you do. If we are cruel it is a cruelty we learnt from you. Oh Daddy, did you not realise? Run, Daddy, run, the old world is behind you.

Arthur stopped reading for a moment. The message couldn't have come from his son. It was impossible. Timothy could never have written anything like this – the words were so strange, utterly alien from all he knew about his boy – too anguished, too poetic, too adult . . . And yet, despite these reasons, there was something about the e-mail, something he couldn't explain – as if the words opened a door into his mind. Yes . . . He could see his long-lost brother David, standing in the doorway to his bedroom, bathed in the silvery moonlight. 'I'm running away to join the lost boys' – the fierce defiance in his words, his face set like a soldier's before battle, and he remembered the distant cry of children playing in the street on a summer's evening as he sat in his room, forbidden by his parents to go out, alone with his books about adventurers and explorers, with his maps of Africa and Asia. Yes . . . Every evening another bonfire, as they burned his brother's belongings, the ash in the sky and the tears in his mother's eyes . . . and for years after, he would see the traces – the signs on the wall, arrangements of sticks and little piles of stones marking the deathly suburban culs-de-sac of his adolescence – these messages he could never decipher, reminders of memories that couldn't be wiped away. He seemed hardly to read the e-mail, the walls of the office dissolving, transporting him beyond the city, beyond the confines of his self, until he was no longer sure if he read the words or if he wrote them, or if he heard them in the silvery sound of the flute from the castle in the high mountains.

Remember the rain that falls on a summer's night, the rumble of far-off thunder and the sudden flash of lightning . . . the hot winds that blow across the desert and the clouds that come thick with dust . . . the afternoon stillness and the drone of cicadas in the hot sun . . . shards of pink light that strike a snow-capped mountain in the early morning . . . scents of cedar and pine from the valley below . . . and scraps of litter that gather in the gutters and the rustle of falling autumn leaves . . . the play of dust in an empty warehouse and the melancholy of a seaside town on Sunday . . . fragments of posters and fading graffiti on a whitewashed wall . . . the slow shunt of a train as it arrives in a foreign city . . . the wonder of the crowds in the market . . . the gathering in the cotton field in the dead of night . . . the singing voices in the small church far from the road . . . the rhythms from the tower blocks beyond the motorway . . . the wailing from the high towers and the graveyard at the edge of town . . . the land beyond the fortress and the wire, the garden in the mountains in the twilight cool. This is the paradise of the assassins at the end of the war . . . aromas of hashish, of pink and blue flower petals unfolding in moonlight, of saffron, mint and jasmine, silvery dew on bergamot trees, the beautiful eyes of the veiled maidens with their silver bangles and emerald rings, the gentle tinkle of the fountain in the courtyard, and the peace that embraces city and mountain village, rugged coast and rich forest . . .

seven

They sat in the taxi, silent but together. This evening was the first time they had been out since Timothy's disappearance. Susan was wearing a new outfit, a white two-piece suit with black trimmings and buttons. Her shoes and bag echoed the pattern – black with white crossings – and she wore a black carnation in her lapel and a chain of black garnets around her neck. She had dyed her hair a shimmering platinum shade, the cut held back by a black Alice band that had the effect of making her seem younger, leaving her face oddly exposed and vulnerable. Recent events had cut deep lines of anxiety into her skin, but tonight this softer quality was pre-eminent.

Susan had smothered her face with layers of foundation and her eyes were ringed with mascara and shadow so they peeped out like sorrowful craters on the moon. Her lips had been christened with a berry-rich paint. Garnet earrings completed the picture, like black teardrops against a white sky. She seemed so much more beautiful and fragile than ever before. A sorrowful sort of tenderness seized Arthur's nerves and he took her hand in his own, clasping her cold fingers. She looked out the window, impassive, forlorn and ever so distant, the masked heroine in an unfinished tragedy.

The Fitzwilliamses had a large apartment in Onslow Gardens, a grand stucco terrace near the museums. Most of the windows in the block were dark, and there was an abundance of parking spaces around the square. Arthur had the sense that the city was emptying out: citizens were slipping away, going into hiding, or else were too afraid to leave their homes. The e-mail haunted his consciousness, but each time he felt he should say something words failed him. Explanation seemed impossible, the message no easier to justify or elucidate than a dream filled with forbidden desires.

They were surprised when Linda Morgan opened the door, calling 'I'll get it' to someone behind her. 'Angela is in the kitchen,' she said by way of explanation, fixing both of them with a bright smile. With a gasp she embraced Susan, the two women clasping each other with the intensity of shipwreck survivors in a tumultuous ocean. Linda turned a dry cheek to Arthur's descending lips, not quite able to suppress a flash of panic in her eyes, as if she sensed something about him that even he did not yet know. 'Come inside,' she said. 'Don't you look lovely, Susan? That outfit! Smashing! So beautiful.'

They walked into the apartment, Arthur ignoring the habitual flurry of compliments between the two women. The fact was that his wife always looked a lot better than Linda, a short, rather dumpy woman who never really suited anything she wore, and the effort she made – with her so obviously expensive haircut, and her smart black top emblazoned with an enormous cat-shaped brooch – was all just a little too much. In contrast his wife, despite her distress, still knew how to turn on the glamour. That much was evident from the reactions of Clive Morgan and Alex Fitzwilliams, both of whom stood gawping at her. Arthur watched them kiss and hug his wife.

'Hello, Arthur.'

'Hello, hello.' He shook hands, exchanging vague, non-committal smiles and half-finished pleasantries. The strain of the last few months had clearly aged Clive: his hair was thinner and whiter than Arthur remembered, and there was something about his eyes – watery and grey with confusion – as if he'd almost forgotten how to see. He seemed to fill the room with a faint, musty sort of odour, as though he was sweating out some kind of deep emotional exhaustion. Not that Arthur was any different. They all felt the same; his sleepless nights were theirs too.

He was less well acquainted with Alex and Angela Fitzwilliams. Angela had made friends with Susan at a school-charity-related fund-raiser or something like that. Arthur himself had actually known Alex many years ago, when they'd been students at Oxford. They had both read Law, their paths crossing at lectures, dinners and the odd party. The person Arthur remembered had been an inexplicably popular young man who exuded confidence and assurance and had dated a friend of his for a couple of terms. It all seemed a ridiculously long time ago now, and Arthur found it hard to reconcile the memories of who they used to be, back then, with the person before him now. After exchanging greetings, Alex led them into the living room. 'Turn the TV off and come and say hello,' he called out.

Two children clambered from the sofa and walked towards them. Arthur felt something plunge inside him. Children! They stood before the adults, a little bashful, like two rare treasures taken out for display in a museum.

'Rowena and Thomas,' announced Alex, with a smile. The boy was twelve and almost as tall as his father, a slightly awkward youth, firmly in the rude hands of puberty, with a tangle of brown hair and red blossoms on either cheek. The girl must have been nine or ten. She was cute, if a little chubby, and rather bemused to be presented to all these adults in such a fashion. There was something a touch sullen about her manner, the way she cocked her head, one hand nervously twitching at her ponytail.

'How lovely!' Susan exclaimed, clasping her hands together and leaning towards them. 'What angels, what perfect little darlings,' she gasped.

'Say hello.' Angela stood between her children, her proprietorial hands placed on their shoulder. She seemed radiant, galvanised by their presence, her smile enormous, the delight in her eyes without limit. For a moment, Arthur was seized by a surge of jealousy. But he swallowed and blinked back the hot feelings in his throat and behind his eyes and tried to fix his expression into something acceptable. Like moths before a light, unable to help themselves, the adults drew closer to the children.

'Let's have a drink,' said Alex. 'You kids can go and watch TV in the other room.' The adults watched the children depart, a collective shudder passing through them. 'Don't worry,' Alex said to them. 'I never let them out of my sight. Look at this.' He walked over to a laptop on a side table. 'Watch.' It took a moment and then, craning closer, they saw the children again. Rowena was lying on the floor in front of the TV, whilst Thomas slouched on the sofa. He seemed to be texting someone on his phone. 'I've got webcams set up in every room. I can access them from anywhere, even at work. I had a specialist company set it up for me – I've got more than thirty cameras. The kids don't know about all of them.'

'In their rooms?' asked Linda.

'Everywhere. Even in their bathroom. I'm not prepared to take a single chance. The windows are alarmed, so is every room. If anyone tries to sneak out at night, I'll know about it. Thankfully, we're quite high up, so there is no chance they could just shimmy out.'

'They'd have to be able to fly,' added Angela.

'But that's not all,' Alex went on. 'I've been paying attention to similar cases. I've prepared a final line of defence.' He smiled now, clearly pleased with his ingeniousness. 'Electronic tagging – with satellite tracking. It wraps around the ankle. If you have a look, you can just see Rowena's. They're impossible to remove. You need this special key. We let them take them off for baths, but that's it.'

'Like they give criminals—' Arthur heard himself say.

'Exactly. Since the present crisis the manufacturers have been expanding their customer base.'

'It's incredible, isn't it?' said Angela. 'A year ago I would have never imagined such a thing could be possible – that I'd actually be contemplating such a measure . . .' She trailed off. No one said anything. It *was* incredible, thought Arthur, and yet he understood Alex's motives perfectly.

'We ought to get something like that for Harry,' said Susan. 'There haven't been nearly so many disappearances outside London, and my mother keeps a close eye on him, but still . . .'

'I'll look into it tomorrow,' Arthur said.

Another pause in the conversation and Arthur, like all the other parents, found himself watching the two children again. They were lying close to the TV, playing a computer game on their Xbox. It would be better, in a way, if they could just sit and watch them and not have to talk or do anything else. Nothing else seemed as important as the children, so beautiful and mysteriously far from them all. Arthur had always thought he'd known what his sons were thinking. Only now did he realise how wrong he'd been. He remembered Timothy's eyes and the way he would look at the world with so much feeling; and so he remembered also the eyes of the children he had seen in Iraq and those other places. What were they thinking, what did they know? How they must hate him.

Angela said something and they moved into the dining room. Arthur didn't pay much attention to what they ate – some kind of soup for the starter, baked sea bass and new potatoes for the main. Alex carried the laptop with him and kept it propped up on the table throughout. Every few seconds Arthur caught himself glancing at the screen. The children charmed his eyes. And yet they did nothing, simply continued to play their game. They knew they were being watched and he couldn't shake the feeling that they were biding their time, putting on a sufficiently convincing act to fool the adults. They were like prisoners quietly waiting to finish their secret tunnel, and no amount of cameras or satellites or tags would matter, none of it would stop them.

Through the dinner he drank and listened as they talked about the children and when they had noticed the change. 'It was after the first boy from their school went missing,' Alex was saying. 'I noticed how much time they were spending on the Internet. I mean, they all spent too much time anyway—'

Heads nodded in unison.

'But it started to get crazy. Thomas would be online the

second he got home from school, before he'd even bothered to remove his blazer. He'd be on it for hours. And the funny thing was, Rowena would be with him. She was always using the Internet as well, but normally they had quite different interests and it would cause all sorts of arguments between them.'

'We used to have to share the time out between them quite carefully,' said Angela, 'to avoid fights.'

'I suppose we were pleased at first, because they seemed to be cooperating so well.'

'They never used to get on – but after it all started, they seemed to become very close . . .' Alex trailed off, glancing back at the laptop. Now Rowena had control of the console and Thomas was pointing to something on the screen that they couldn't see. Both children were seized with a fierce concentration.

'The trouble we used to have, just to get them off the damn machine for ten minutes for dinner or suchlike, it became impossible . . .' Angela shook her head.

'Thomas became very aggressive, shouting and screaming. Once he threw a glass at Angela. We'd never known anything like it.'

'But the little honeys – they seem so charming,' said Susan.

'We get these meds from the school psychiatrist.' Alex gave a strange, off-centre smile, as if ashamed of the pleasure it gave him to admit such things. 'They made quite a difference. Helps them sleep. Keeps them much calmer.'

'But what the devil were they doing on the Internet all that time?' said Clive.

'We never really knew. They'd say homework, or MySpace or some such. Like I said, I didn't think much at first. But when the disappearances really got going . . .'

Alex paused, glancing at the others. 'I suppose it was after Timothy, and Edward . . . I knew the boys were friends with each other.' He coughed and scratched the back of his head. For a moment no one said anything. Arthur sipped at his wine without tasting it. 'I had a day off work and when they were both out at school I decided to check the computer. I found that Thomas had hundreds of files saved. They were all encrypted, protected with passwords I couldn't crack. I did know the password to his e-mail account – although he might have been using other accounts that I didn't know about. There were loads of e-mails from his friends and they were all talking about the disappearances. I guess this was natural.' Alex paused again and took a drink himself. 'The funny thing was, these messages, they weren't really like you'd expect. I mean none of the boys seemed particularly worried or upset. They weren't saying things like "Where are they?" or "What's happened to them," you know, the sort of stuff you might expect. There was a lot of talk about instructions . . .'

'Instructions!' exclaimed Susan

'Good God,' added Clive.

Alex nodded at Clive. 'That's right. It was very weird. All the boys who'd disappeared, they were supposed to have left instructions, or have been following instructions.'

'Do you mean clues about where to find them?' cried Susan. 'Couldn't we show these to the police? If they knew where they were hiding—'

'No, nothing like that. It was more a case of leaving instructions about how they themselves could, well, escape.'

'Extraordinary.'

'But what were they . . . couldn't we follow them?'

Arthur felt himself starting to panic. He felt hot and embarrassed.

'It wasn't that sort of thing. They were references to certain books – to passages underlined in these books. Books from the school library.'

'All sorts of books,' said Angela. *The Autobiography of Malcolm X* and *Invisible Man*, the Ralph Ellison novel. Stories by someone called H. P. Lovecraft. A book called *The Wild Boys* or something like that . . .'

'That's the Burroughs one. The guy who wrote *Naked Lunch*. A heroin addict and a queer too.'

'They have these books in the school library?' asked Susan.

'Well, it is a very good school,' added Linda. Everyone nodded in agreement.

'I checked with the school and all these books were out on loan,' continued Alex. 'And all the boys who'd taken them out had disappeared.' He paused again, waiting for his words to take effect. Arthur took another drink. He could feel the palms of his hand sweating. Under the table, his legs were twitching with a restless, guilty anticipation. 'But there were other sources of information. They kept referring to all these strange code names . . . I couldn't really make head or tail of it all, I'm afraid.'

Arthur jolted, knocking his glass over. Everyone looked at him. 'It's okay,' he stammered. 'It was empty. No harm done.' He flushed, aware that Susan was watching with concern.

'There was more, wasn't there?' said Angela.

'There were messages from someone called Abdullah. Not all that many. As far as I remember, they were quite recent – the earliest was dated from only a couple of weeks before when I was looking. At first I thought he must be another pupil—'

'The school does have a lot of students from the Middle East,' added Clive.

'Exactly, but . . .' Alex paused for a moment, as if unsure of the words he should use. 'Except this person was definitely not a pupil. His writing was very different from the others. There was something about it . . . as though it had been translated back and forth from other languages before somehow ending up as English.' He flushed briefly, conscious of the absurdity of what he was trying to say. 'The e-mail kept using "we" as if referring to everyone. And, well . . . this made his e-mails rather hard to read. Plus they were very long, and quite repetitive. This guy was describing things and places . . . it was very weird.' He coughed. 'At times I thought he was writing like he was an insurgent in Iraq or a member of the Taliban.'

'Are you serious?' asked Clive.

'That's the thing. They didn't seem especially real. There was something very made-up about it all . . . At times it just read like some silly fantasy story, with stuff about magic carpets and castles.' Alex banged the table, his frustration evident. Arthur refilled his glass, trying to stop his hands from trembling. On the screen, the kids were still playing the game.

'Did you save any of these e-mails?' said Clive. 'Surely this is something the police need to know about.'

'Of course. But, you know, this is the thing, this is what's so bloody typical about all this crap. I was going to print them all off, to . . . as you say, only there was no damn ink in the machine. So I tried saving what I could. Then I had a call . . . I can't remember what.' Alex paused again, dabbing at his face. It was hot in the room, and for the first time Arthur really began to sense the strain that the man was under. Initially, he had thought that Alex was insufferably smug, with his family still intact and his systems to safe-guard them all, but now he found himself revising that opinion. Alex was just another frightened man pathetically clinging with his cameras and his trackers to a world held up with matchsticks. 'Anyway, while I was on the phone the children came home from school. Thomas realised what I'd discovered and when I got back they were all gone, all the e-mails. He'd closed down his account.' He glanced at his wife. 'We confronted him about it, but he said it was just a "game". That was all he'd say.'

Angela nodded. 'He just went on and on. "Mum, it's just a game. It's just a game and it's private."'

'What could we say to him? We asked him who Abdullah was and he said it was all of them.'

'All of them?' Susan asked.

'He never really explained what he meant. Abdullah was just someone his friends would pretend to be, when they wrote these e-mails. That's all we could understand from it . . . but you know . . . what else could we say? Was he really talking to terrorists in the Middle East or God knows where? I mean . . . it's absurd. He's a twelve-year-old English boy, with Christian values.' The last words seem to come out in a strange rush, as if Alex was struggling himself to define what his son really was, as if these neat little labels – English, child, Christian – meant a thing against what they were all up against. 'We just thought the disappearances must have upset them in ways we'd never imagined. Thomas was already seeing our psychotherapist. He was meant to be dis-cussing his feelings in those sessions.' A shade of despair crossed his face. 'We've upped the sessions now to four hours a week. What the hell else can we do?'

'We don't have the Internet any more,' added Angela sternly.

'That was when I put in all these other measures. The surveillance and suchlike.' Alex made a sweeping, slightly empty gesture. Arthur wondered where the camera was in this room and if it was recording them all right now. Would Alex watch them later, in some solitary, insomniac privacy, rewinding back and forth through the dinner in search of clues and secrets between the lines of conversation?

'It's like that damn computer game they all play—' started Clive.

'That's right – *Insurgency* – you know the one,' Linda cut in. 'Horrible.'

'We should never have allowed Timothy to have it,' said Susan. 'Especially as he can be so sensitive and affected by these things. But he was adamant.'

'It was just a computer game,' Arthur started, and immediately wished he hadn't.

'With an eighteen certificate,' Susan snapped back at him.

'Well . . .' There was no use saying anything. By the hurt in her eyes Arthur knew that she held him responsible for allowing their son such unsuitable amusements. 'You're right . . .' he muttered. 'I didn't think it could do any harm.' But there was no use labouring the point.

Angela looked a little guilty. 'We haven't stopped ours from playing it. We've stopped them from doing just about everything else.'

They glanced back at the screen again. The children seemed to have lost interest in the television. Rowena was cross-legged on the sofa, reading something. Thomas circled the room, restlessly peering through the window. He turned round and for a moment he seemed to stare straight at them before turning away again, but quite slowly, as if he knew just where the cameras were and when they were watching him.

'Did you hear this thing on the news,' Linda said, shifting the conversation all of a sudden, 'about how some of the children the police found have run away again, a second time?' Her words lingered dangerously in the air, no one replying. Someone scraped a fork against a plate. She went on, 'The authorities say they are going to start interning the children they capture, to make sure they don't run away again. Apparently they are going to put them in a special camp. It's being built near Heathrow . . . at least, that's what they say.'

'I don't believe it,' Alex said, finally. 'I don't think it's true. I think someone is lying to us. I don't trust the government on this at all. What do they mean? It's ridiculous.'

'I saw it . . .' began Susan. 'I saw it but I didn't want to believe. If Timothy . . .'

'Don't.' Arthur reached for her hand. 'There's no point thinking about it.'

'Mummy, Mummy.' Everyone turned in the direction of the voice. Rowena stood in the doorway, a little shy. 'I'm tired, Mummy. Can I have some ice cream?'

'I'm not sure, honey,' began Angela.

'Oh, do let her,' exclaimed Susan. 'Come here, angel.' She beckoned the girl towards her. 'Isn't she lovely? Aren't you lovely, my dear?' She took the girl in her arms, kissing her forehead and brushing back her hair. 'What a precious poppet.'

'I think you should be thinking about getting to bed,' said Angela.

'I don't want to.'

'Well, you don't want any ice cream, not at this time. You'll be up all night.'

Rowena sighed and disengaged herself from Susan. 'But Mummy . . .'

'You heard what I said.'

'I'll get some later anyway. The magic-carpet boy said he'd give me some.'

'Did he now? You go and brush your teeth. I'll come and tuck you in soon.'

'What did she say?' said Susan.

'Nothing.'

'Something about a magic-carpet boy?'

'Oh, don't pay any attention,' Alex cut in. 'She has all these imaginary friends.'

'The psychiatrist said it's quite normal,' said Angela. 'It shows a healthy imagination, apparently.'

'I see . . .' Susan looked down at her plate, her half-eaten food. Arthur sensed her thoughts – dark and fractured – whirling around. 'You will keep an eye on her though, won't you? I know not so many girls have gone . . . but it would be too awful.'

Angela didn't say anything but smiled back a fierce, brittle smile. She reached across and touched Susan's hand, her eyes wet with tears that would not fall.

Susan and Arthur didn't speak on the journey home. The streets were almost empty, just the odd taxi, its orange light beckoning, and lonesome night buses sweeping past deserted stops. A light rain was falling and the pavements swirled with drowning lights. It was hard – impossible – to try and imagine Timothy out there, alone or with others unknown, in this night. Susan was silent, briefly resting her hand on Arthur's leg in an absent sort of caress. They didn't discuss the party.

Once they were home, Susan went immediately upstairs.

Arthur drifted about the kitchen, contemplating another drink. A thick wad of fatigue smothered his very being. He considered checking the TV news, but resisted the temptation.

His wife was in their bedroom, sitting before her dressing mirror, unclipping her jewellery. He watched as she dismantled herself with speedy efficiency and then, clad only in white bra and pants, started to apply various cleansing lotions and creams to her face, neck and arms.

'Well?' she said, catching his eye in the mirror. 'You can come in, you know. It *is* our bedroom.'

Arthur sat on the edge of the bed. 'Are you going to take your pills?'

'Maybe. I'm so tired. Maybe I can do without.'

'Yes.'

She stood in front of him, placing her hands on his shoulders, inviting him to look up at her, as if he was the child, she the mother. 'Are you okay?'

He shrugged. 'What is there to say?'

Perhaps Susan understood. There was nothing to say. Her arms tightened around Arthur's neck and she pressed him against her breast in a fierce embrace. His arms found purchase around her back and for a moment each held the other tight. It had been too long since they had embraced like this and for a moment he drew upon her, sucking up the creamy-sweet smell of her body like cut flowers from the spring of his youth. She stroked his hair and tilted his face upwards, kissing his lips. Her mouth – so familiar, the motions of her lips and tongue overwhelming his resistance – met his and he kissed her back, harder, almost whimpering with the burden of some great emotion.

She reached for him, her hand slipping into his trousers, and at first he thought there would be nothing, that part crushed by everything else, but his desire had a reason of its own, rising to her touch. Wordlessly, she pushed him back onto the bed, her body moving over his own, her hair a platinum cascade over his eyes. He unhooked her bra, running his hands over the same breasts that had nursed his babies, taking them in his mouth, kissing, sucking, licking at her, as if through each other, through the salt and sweat of their bodies they could reach all that they had lost. When the moment came he pulled her onto him, his hands crushing her shoulders. She gasped and lay still and he could feel his heart and hers thundering as one.

Arthur opened his eyes again and caught sight of the clock. It was very late. His wife got up with a faint sigh, uncertain, her neatly groomed hair twisted in shards and girders around her smudged eyes. She went to the bathroom. He felt himself, alone in the bed, shuddering against a great abyss of exhaustion. Part of him wanted to tell Susan about the e-mail, try and explain it to her, but he didn't know how to begin. He couldn't even say if it was from Timothy. If the message really had come from their boy, and wasn't a hoax, wasn't some sick, manipulative joke, then he wasn't sure if he would ever understand what was left of their son, or what had happened to him.

Susan returned, instinctively moving into his arms and resting her head against his chest, a position familiar from the earliest days of their relationship. 'I have to say something,' she whispered. 'I should have told you sooner – but I couldn't.'

'What is it?'

'I . . .' Pensive, she bit her lower lip, an expression that always made her look many years younger than she actually was. 'I'm sorry . . .'

'What is it?' His heart started thumping.

'Please don't be angry with me. Please . . . I can't stand it.'

'I won't be. What is it?'

'I saw Timmy.'

'What do you mean, you saw Timmy? Where? I don't understand.'

'Please don't be angry.' She clung to him fiercely.

'I'm not . . . but where?'

'It was the other day, Tuesday. You were at work. I'd been sleeping. I'd taken some of those pills.' The words came in a rush. 'You know, the ones the doctor gave me to calm me down. I'd been feeling so sad and I was . . . oh, please don't be angry!'

'I won't be, darling, I promise.' He caressed her hair, 'But you must tell me.'

'I'd been dozing, in the front room, on the sofa. I think I'd been dreaming – but I wasn't asleep. I wasn't! I woke up, you see . . . someone was knocking on the French windows. I could hear them. I went over . . . and I could see these two boys. I knew at once that one was Timmy. The other – at first I thought he must be Edward, but I'm not sure.'

'You saw them?'

'Yes. Yes, I think so. They were standing by the window. They were wearing these strange clothes – long white robes, but quite dirty, and they had scarves wrapped around their faces. Their hair was darker than I remembered, and they looked very dirty, as if they hadn't bathed in weeks. I opened the doors. The other boy wasn't Edward . . . he was . . . I don't know . . . I didn't recognise him, but I sort of felt as though I knew him, somehow. And . . . I looked at Timmy, and I didn't know what to say to him. But he reached for me with one hand, and he kissed me on the lips and told me not to worry. The other boy didn't say anything. He was a little older, I think, and he had a long, curved knife with a shiny silver blade. He was a fierce-looking boy, devilishly handsome. They were wearing sandals, they smelt of faraway places – dust and palm oil, hot spices and sweet tea – and when they smiled, oh such beautiful smiles, such shiny white teeth.'

'I'm astonished.' Arthur didn't know what else to say. 'I'm not even sure I believe you.'

'I knew you wouldn't. It's okay. I just knew you wouldn't.' Susan sat up, shaking her head.

'Well, what else did you do? Why did you let him go? You didn't call the police? You didn't call me?'

'I knew you'd be angry.'

'I'm not angry!'

'I gave them a glass of milk.'

'Jesus!' Arthur moved his hand from her back. He was staggered by Susan's ability to confound him so utterly, even after all these years of marriage. 'And then what did you do? Did you give them some cookies?'

'I made them a sandwich. Timmy said he couldn't stay. He said he just wanted to see me. He said he would see me again.'

'But why didn't you call the police?'

'Because they just think I'm a silly woman. And anyway, I didn't want them to put Timmy in a camp. You know that's what they're doing now. They don't let the children go home. They call them a threat to security. They call them an enemy of the state.'

'They wouldn't put Timmy in a camp . . .'

'Yes, they would. You know they would! I don't trust Captain York, even if you do.'

Arthur sighed. He tried a different approach. 'Look,

honey, I know you *think* you saw Timmy, but you know the effect these medicines can have, don't you? I mean, we've all been seeing strange things and . . .'

'Have we?'

'Well . . .' Arthur stumbled, unsure what to say. He felt overwhelmed with a surge of déjà vu: a rush of memories, of waking late in the night and opening the curtain to find a boy crouching on the window ledge in his pyjamas, his skin a luminous blue in the dull light, soaking wet and shivering. Memories of the rain falling steadily in his eyes and the wet grass soaking his bare feet, of hurrying into the gardens . . . He released his wife and walked around the room.

'You're upset,' he heard her say, as if from far away.

'I'm not. It's okay. I'm not.' Arthur realised he was hugging himself, shivering as if he was bitterly cold.

'I'm sorry.'

'Don't be.'

'No one believes me. No one.'

'I'm sorry, my darling.' Then, 'I love you. I'm sorry.'

Susan stroked his hair and kissed his forehead, just as his mother had, a long, long time ago. Rain fell heavily outside, slanting through the trees and drumming against the window. 'I don't know who I am any more,' he sobbed, or at least he thought he did, or maybe she was the one who wept and he was the one who comforted her. He couldn't tell any more.

eight

Time passed. Susan lay on her back, one arm resting over her eyes, the expression on her lips suggesting some sort of understanding. Arthur crept into the bathroom and looked at himself in the mirror. He had the wild eyes of a man who had been awake all night. There was a curious, bad sort of taste in his mouth, like oil and steel. It was no good. Wrapping himself in a clean robe, he quietly left the bedroom. The clock in his office read twelve minutes past five. He'd left his computer on. Touching the mouse woke the machine up. He saw a new e-mail flashing in his in-box.

Daddy . . .
Let me tell you.
    They hid out in the ruins by the enemy tank. The ambush worked well, the bomb disabling the tank as it crept up the road. They watched flames engulf the vehicle, shooting one man as he tried to escape by clambering out of the top hatch. No one else got out. The thick smell of diesel filled the air.
    An hour or so later they spied the drone, circling the

wreck like a wasp around sugar. They remained huddled in the ruins, checking their weapons and smoking. For days they'd been on the run, meeting the enemy wherever they could, launching lightning attacks and rapid withdrawals. At night, the enemy played pop music on huge speakers and left booby-trapped bags of fast food – McDonald's and KFC – amid the ruins. Many a boy had lost his arm while reaching for a Big Mac, or had his eyes blasted out by a ball-bearing bomb hidden among the fries. Sometimes they would play the voices of sad mothers over the speakers, woeful mummies calling for their little boys to come home. 'I have your dinner waiting, and then I want to tuck you up safe in bed with a goodnight kiss. Come back home, my darling, come back to your mummy.' But no one's mother was really there, just soldiers waiting with guns at the ready.

The drone sped off southwards and an hour later their spotter on the roof warned of dust trails in the distance. The boys below gathered themselves together, checking their Kalashnikovs and M-16s, wrapping belts of ammunition around their shoulders, cocking pistols and hefting grenades. Scimitars were sheathed, crossbows wound and primed. Two boys took hold of the Russian shoulder-mounted rocket launcher they had bought with stashes of stolen lunch money. Bottles filled with petrol and sulphuric acid were distributed among them. RPG launchers were loaded. Most of the boys wore simple clothes – long robes of white or black, both shades invariably soiled by weeks of dusty fighting – their faces hidden by scarves of the same colour. The fanciful pirate and superhero costumes of earlier had been abandoned, although some boys held on to the odd extravagance: Randolph continued to brandish his magnificent dragoon cutlass, whilst a red cape, albeit a little more battered than before, hung defiantly from Edmund's narrow shoulders. A few of the boys wore armoured vests or combat helmets looted from the enemy, but most disdained such measures. They had no proper flag or symbol, but would mark territory and materials with their inky palm prints, in blue or white or red, the hand open and the fingers spread as wide as possible. They knew the approaching troops would have begun spotting the palm prints, a single-handed clapping along blasted walls and burnt-out petrol stations, clapping from balconies and tree trunks. Final minutes before contact: the growing rumble of armoured vehicles. A few said hasty prayers to their made-up gods or else sucked from a hashish pipe that was passed among them, hoping it was true that the thick white fumes would give them invincible powers. A final whistle from the spotter and they took their positions, ready to fight.

This is what is happening, Daddy . . .

This is how it is.

Arthur hesitated for a moment, then pressed 'delete'.

Next, reaching into his wallet, he dug out the card.

Have you been a bad boy?

Making sure that his own number would be withheld, he started to dial.

nine

A little later, Arthur stood outside the apartment. Still too early, and the dawn had a desolate grey tinge, as if a vast plume of damp ash had settled over the city. When he called, the phone was answered immediately, a cool female voice with an American accent directing him to an address off Edgware Road. He had been unable to shake the conviction that she was expecting him, and that the woman waiting for him now had been waiting for a long time. And as he walked through the empty streets, past the shuttered shops and closed curtains, the porches stained with pigeon shit and the mounds of uncollected rubbish, trying not to look at the faded posters of politicians and religious leaders, he couldn't shake the feeling that he was being watched, that young eyes lurked in hidden corners. But he saw no one, his solitude broken only by two low-flying helicopters – military craft bristling with black antennae – the roar of the rotors swallowing his thoughts.

Now Arthur stood before the door. He noticed a single blue palm print, too small for an adult, slapped on the faded stucco. The sense of dread was almost overwhelming, emanating from the bricks and concrete. He felt it in his stomach also, like a slug of tar, a dull, thick pang of sickness. With a sigh, he pressed the buzzer and the door was opened immediately. Inside, a half-lit hallway scattered with free newspapers and takeaway menus. Beyond, another open door. He went forward.

The air inside the room was cool, purged of smells, the walls washed in an unforgiving white paint. Harsh bright neon lights hung from the ceiling. A woman stood in the corner. 'Come in,' she said. Her American accent had a Southern twang, but he couldn't tell from where exactly, Arkansas or Texas or Tennessee or Virginia – some place like that. She was tall, but not that tall, and toned, her light brown hair scraped back into a single neat ponytail. Arthur thought of his wife and tried to avoid meeting those eyes; how they searched his face, uncovering things. She had a wholesome country beauty about her, if that *was* beauty and not something at once more ordinary and more unusual, an aura of health and strength quite opposed to his expectation. Her khaki T-shirt was tight against her ample bosom. Below a large belt she wore a pair of tight khaki shorts that emphasised her legs and the curves of her thighs and buttocks. Strapped on the woman's shoulders, in rampant contrast to everything else, she wore a pair of tacky pink fairy wings – like something stolen from a little girl's fancy-dress party. The rest of her garb was more consistent: on her feet, combat boots, and around her neck, dog tags. She was not a particularly slim woman, but her curves were testament to a vigorous, physical sort of life. And she was young: twenty, maybe twenty-one – it was hard to tell. 'Don't be shy.' Her smile was like a bowl filled with creamy milk. He wasn't sure what to think.

'What's your name?'

'Why, I have many names.' Her brown eyes met his own. 'Sometimes I'm Salomé or Hecate, Calypso or Tinkerbell. But most of the time I'm just plain old Mary-Lou.'

'What should I call you?'

'Honey, you can call me anything you like.' She put one hand on his face. Her touch felt incredibly delicate, or maybe it was just the way she looked at him. He felt a strange burning.

'I'm trying to find my son,' he muttered, his throat oddly tight.

'Of course you are.'

'Can you help me?'

'Maybe. You have to do what I say. You have to do everything.'

Arthur nodded meekly.

'First, you have to take off your clothes – all of them.'

Wordless, he did as he was told, heaping his shirt, trousers, socks and, finally, underwear, in the corner of the bare room. The woman watched him with a studied sort of indifference, clocking his soggy gut and office-shrivelled limbs. 'Come,' she said, and opened a door into another room.

There were no windows in this room, no natural light. A fan buzzed back and forth, chilling the air a little more, and the same unforgiving neon lights bore down. But whereas the last room had been so bare, this one was different. A Stars and Stripes flag hung from one wall. On the others, military badges and emblems – symbolic eagles and hawks – and regimental photographs of soldiers in desert uniforms. On the far wall was a portrait of the President, surrounded by the waxy stubs of burned-down candles. There were lipstick kisses all over the President's face and another blue palm print in the corner. A dark green curtain screened off the rest of the room. He felt a deep anxious stab at the thought of what might lie beyond.

On a chair, in the centre of the room, was an orange jumpsuit.

'Do you want me to put that on?' Arthur asked.

'Do you want to?'

He nodded again, taking the jumpsuit from the chair. The costume was rather large and he felt more than a little foolish with it in his hands. He unzipped it and scrambled into the suit, the plastic crinkling against his skin.

'Does that feel good?'

Arthur gave a little-boy nod, unsure how it felt or what it meant. The zip chafed a little.

'So, honey . . . are we going to do this? Are we going to do this properly?' He nodded. 'Are you ready? Shall we break through the fourth wall?' Something had crept into her voice this time, a far-off sort of tension, like a dark cloud at the corner of the sky.

He nodded, mute.

'You fucking piece of shit!' It wasn't so much that she shouted the words. They just seemed to come from her, like a ray of heat from the sun. 'You fucking scum.' She lashed out, slapping his face. He took a step back, his cheek smarting, raising his hand defensively. The woman walked around him, the clipped efficiency of her movements barely concealing her sudden rage. With a single angry tug she pulled the curtain back, revealing the other half of the room. He saw a contraption, rather like a dentist's chair but stripped-down and brutal: the long slab clad in wipe-clean plastic, the restraining grips hanging off like broken wrists, ominous stains marking the place where his head and his crotch would rest. On the far side of the room was a cage, just big enough for a man to lie down in. The walls were scrawled with obscene messages and symbols that filled him with a mixture of apprehension and desire. The light was much dimmer than before.

'I'm trying to find my son,' he said again. 'I found your cards at the detective's house. Do you know Buxton, the detective? Do you know what happened to him?'

'*You* don't ask *me* the questions,' she snarled. 'What makes you think you can ask the questions? Asshole!' She slapped him again, harder this time, the blow buckling his legs. 'You will remember everything. I promise you that,' she hissed. 'You will tell me everything.'

He flinched back. 'But what have I done?' he whimpered.

'What have you done? That is for you to decide, for you to remember.'

The woman seized his arm, yanking it back behind him. She was much stronger than he realised, and he made no attempt to resist as she forced him onto the seat. Straps closed around his wrist and ankles. She slapped him again and walked out of the room, pulling the curtain closed behind her.

He stared up at the ceiling; there was nowhere else he could look. The ceiling was covered in pictures torn from papers and magazines. From where he lay it was difficult to make out anything distinctly. The scattered images he could see were horrible and disturbing: bloody corpses in mass graves, burnt children, anguished mouths open in screaming horror, ghostly ruins and great black holes punched into the ground. The layers and strips of paper made him think of the body of a huge crocodile, skin rippling as it crawled past. He felt the sweat fall from his forehead. A grainy static texture seemed to colour his vision, like smoke or heat rising from a hot road. He thought about the day when Timothy was born, the strange nervous pride he had felt, cradling the crying baby in his arms, such a perfect new one, so small and so loud. The weather had been grey that day too and he remembered walking home on his own, through the park, the way all the trees bent the same way in the wind, the leaves curling and rasping like scraps of parchment.

He felt hands on his suit.

'Shhh . . .' she whispered. Her fingers were touching him, caressing him inside his suit.

'Don't . . .' He couldn't move.

'Shhh . . .'

She moved her mouth close, her lips tracing but never quite touching his own. Her large white teeth and that red tongue. Her warm mouth smelt of Coca-Cola. She caressed his eyes with her breath. Her hand below, all the time working quicker. Flashing her teeth at him, almost snarling, she moved down again, crouching between his bound legs.

He saw the camera in the corner, pointed towards them. He turned the other way and there was another.

The woman's hands worked faster, and then her mouth.

He groaned and closed his eyes.

Afterwards, she left him like that for a long time, her saliva and his come cooling on his cock. A languid sort of horror engulfed him, a bitter sense of failure and humiliation. Time passed slowly.

Something filled his vision. She was back. She wore a gas mask over her face and stared down at him, the round visor reflecting nothing. He could hear her breathing through the respirator, a low, throaty exhalation filling the room.

'What is it?'

She wore black gloves, and in her right hand she held a huge syringe.

'What?'

He watched as she held his arm still, pushing the needle into his blue, exposed vein.

'That hurts,' he whimpered, watching with faint fascination as she withdrew, a single crimson spot blotting his white upturned flesh. 'Why?'

The woman put her face close to his. The heavy sound of her breathing seemed to come from elsewhere, from the floor and the walls, or through the bland smile of the President himself, from his picture hanging on the opposite wall.

'Why?' Already his voice sounded small and far away. He tried to turn his face away from that terrible mask, and when he turned back again he could no longer see if she was still in the room. He tried to raise his neck, to peer round, but the effort was too much. The ceiling was squirming now, the newspaper strips oozing and ebbing, shifting and merging into strange, hideous forms, an alien, unknown alphabet of death. He was sweating hard, the plastic suit wet with him, the material clinging like a rash to his skin. His mouth felt awfully dry, the gutted ruins of a house where his parched tongue hung useless, a dying dog . . . what did it mean what did it mean? Nothing . . . nothing you told them I told them nothing I told you this. Nothing? Nothing. I said you said . . . but I said nothing.

    I said

Nothing

    Nothing?

            nothingnothingnothingnothingnothingnothing-
nothing

    but I

    somewhere there must have been more tapes

    He saw the way Buxton looked at him

That look he had

That way of looking as if he knew when he did not know

Did you see?

What was this?

Did you see?

A meeting, this morning, an emergency.

There he was again, Mr Curtis, with eyebrows meeting in the middle and standing next to him, more ominous still, the CEO, Sir Charles himself, his face like a craggy eagle . . .

Listen, said Mr Curtis in his most serious tone of voice. The car bomb hit the convoy as they left the safe house at oh seven hundred hours. The suicide bomber rammed the lead vehicle. It was a truck, filled with artillery shells. Twenty-seven dead, we believe. These include Mr Axel, Mr Yazdani, Mr Newman and Dr Jaber, who were in the second and third cars respectively. Nine bodyguards also killed. The key players in our Baghdad operation have been wiped out. We do not know how they found out about the safe house. At oh thirteen hundred hours their time the main DT-12 pipeline was ruptured at three separate points. Four Iraqi police were killed attempting to engage a number of armed men seen nearby. Again, we do not know how this information may have reached our enemies.

nothing

what do you know what did you see what did you tell them

This is an expensive operation we are running here I don't need to tell you what this will do to our share price not to mention the lives of these good men familiar I know to many of you

yes yes . . . The hood and the darkness. Please I am a father please

They didn't speak to me

Mr Dashwood, if you could wait just one second, if you don't mind, please

Mr Dashwood, we need to ask you again

certain things you see that only certain people know

and in the light of what

that incident you see

very serious implications you understand

back out there, it's a possibility

Mr Yazdani had five children

good men, loyal employees, family men

according to American intelligence

our guards reported seeing a young boy on the perimeter wall shortly before

must ask you again

    a father I am

        nothing

Arthur gasped, shaking himself. Somehow, he was lying on the floor, his face and his hands grasping sheets of printed paper, the words stained with his tears and slobber.

Mary-Lou stood over him, gas mask still hiding her face, a long metal pole like a magic wand in her black-gloved hands. She grabbed his hair, yanking up his head. When she pressed the pole to his body a jolt of hot white fire shot through him and his limbs flexed and twitched. He bit his tongue and his mouth filled with blood, his teeth chattering as though he were dying of fever. The tips of his fingers were bleeding from where he had scratched at the floor.

– Can you see it yet?

He had been watching the screen for a very long time. The first figure, raising the sword and then, so horrible and so slow, bringing it down, the orange figure falling. He saw the women in the streets, wailing and pulling at their hair in grief. He saw the plumes of smoke above the city and the men being dragged from their vehicles, pleading and begging, never to be seen again.

– Why don't you tell me?

– I just want to see my son. I just want to see my wife.

– Our children are all dead. Bombs tore the limbs off our babies, peeled and burned their skin. They raped our wives while we watched and said nothing

– I'm a father

– So are we – Why don't you tell us? – Tell us

– Nothing please I

The pen was in my hand. Even the dull light in the room was almost too much. I don't know all the names, I said. I was crying and my tears kept falling on the page and smudging the ink. They were very patient now, almost kind, watching me as I wrote.

– That's right, she said, the mask very close to my face. Let it all out.

ten

I woke to find myself in a strange room. My body was hurting and it was difficult to remember what had happened. The memories were strange . . . they didn't seem quite right, somehow, more like pictures, ghastly images projected into my head. I wondered how long I had spent in there, with her. We had done the most awful things to each other. Most of the time she wore the gas mask – she insisted on it, and the low rasp of her breathing, amplified by the respirator, echoed still in my ears. Splintered images: the two of us fucking, her body squirming beneath mine; her legs spread open, her wet red vagina opening to my fingers; the strange groan as she came, as I came; the grind of our bodies; the taste of her asshole; her leather-gloved hand wanking me; my sperm spurting over her combat fatigues; sometimes there were other people in the room; sometimes we did it in the cages, or strapped to the chair. Sometimes with her finger pushed up my ass. Sometimes I ejaculated over her gas mask. Sweat on plastic. Lubricant and blood, mucus and sperm. Sometimes the other people watched us: sometimes we watched them. Video cameras were recording constantly. On a flickering plasma screen we saw ourselves: her hands around my neck, squeezing, my cock in her cunt – Yes. Sometimes there were men in the cages and we beat them with sticks while they wept and shat themselves like grovelling animals. Sometimes I wore the gas mask. Sometimes we fucked in front of the men.

Several times I tried to escape – but there was no escape. It was impossible to leave. There was no way out. Her influence was too strong . . . the shame was too much. I lost control. Her gloved hands so tight around my neck, squeezing until the air turned black and heavy and sparks danced in front of my eyes . . . and sometimes I would find myself, naked and shivering, shit, piss, blood and puke smeared all over my body. I would sit, shaking with fear, rocking like a metronome, my fingers torn and bleeding from scratching at the walls, more like an animal, a beast in a cage . . . I tried to scream but my voice was gone. They took everything from me. I was there for so long that I forgot my name. Video recorders captured everything. On the plasma screens you could see their faces, my face, our haunted eyes filled with terror and pleading, begging . . . but it was no use. There was no mercy in the mask that covered her face. There was not even the hope of mercy.

I remember the explosions that would rock the night and the bodies they found in the morning, washed up in the river, hanging from trees in garden squares and parks. And more. Sometimes I wrote things down – a list of names, an address in Baghdad, the hours of a day. In quiet moments she told me she was from West Virginia. Her family had always been military, she said in that sweet Southern accent of hers. My Daddy was in Vietnam, lost a leg, he always taught us to be soldiers, to be proud. My big brother Eddy served in the first Gulf War. My little brother Tommy is in the Marines, she said, serving in Falluja right now. Back home, it's kinda quiet. We have a house by a river and in the fall you can pick apples from the trees. There's always a big parade down Main Street and jeez, you should see them all, the soldiers in their finest uniforms, their medals shining in the sun. You should see it. Make you proud, you feel it up here, you do. She would talk like this. Sometimes she would cry because she didn't want to die, not here, not like this, because all her faith in Jesus was gone and the things she had to do, the things they made her do . . . it was too much . . . Later I wore the gas mask and it was her turn to whimper and moan, her fingers curled in the Stars and Stripes.

I got up and looked around. The room was empty now. Bits of paper were everywhere. I saw names, places, things I remembered writing, and things I did not. I remembered that I had lied. I saw the tape in the machine. I remembered the voice – the final voice – the voice of my son. His voice on the tape, but I couldn't understand what he was saying. The words were coming out somehow wrong. I couldn't understand. But when I played the tape again all I could here was my voice and Mary-Lou's, the slip and slap of our sweaty bodies, like sick patients in a hospital without medicine, without doctors, without anything.

I left the building, blinking into the early morning. I wondered how much time had passed. The streets were filled with dust, the sky was hazy and broken. Many of the buildings were empty, windows broken by bomb blasts and bullet holes, façades shattered with shrapnel and blast scars. The heat was overwhelming, a punishing sun tyrannising the bleached sky. Posters for religious leaders hung ragged from advertising boards. The corpse of an informer hung from the street lights at a traffic junction. His genitals and his eyes were missing, black flies swarming around his wounds. In the distance I heard gunfire – a quick, sharp ripple of shots. Then another. Then silence again.

The corner of the street had been blocked off – a line of barbed wire, concrete blast walls, a burnt-out bus. I clambered over and kept going. I saw an arrow painted on the ground. This way. I saw a hand print on a wall.

Baghdad

Smells of dust, cordite and oil, wail of prayers from high minaret peak.

London

Electric camera death tunnel. Veiled lies locked in red boxes. Imperial hallucinations in the foggy morning

Beirut Tel Aviv Jerusalem

Rockets streaking towards the dawn

Machu Picchu and Timbuktu, Angkor Wat and Shangri-La

. . .

Washington

blood sacrifices to the God of War, knives and incantations in the office of special plans and secret secrets

New York

towers of fire and light

all the lost boys wild boys white boys Arab boys African boys Chinese boys Indian boys Caribbean boys American boys rich boys poor boys bad boys lizard boys dinosaur boys feathered boys magic boys gathered in dusty streets of Tehran and Damascus in the souks and shanties of Los Angeles under Dubai desert skyscrapers in Bangkok khlongs and Saigon sweatshops under the black flag in Kabul Cairo Istanbul Whitechapel in the poppy fields of Paris . . .

Burning towers burning oil wells

Closer – closer – closer –

I walked towards Kensington Gardens. The grass had died in the heat, the parched ground splintered like an unlucky mirror. Dust and smoke and cordite smells under a hot white sky.

They were waiting for me in a shady spot under the trees. Their skin was darker than before, bronzed with sunshine, dirt and sweat. Dusty black scarves hid their young faces. One stood as I approached, his palm held up towards me in welcome. My son my brother my father myself. I saw machine guns and rocket-propelled grenades, a magic carpet and a palm leaf. Oh my boys, my poor little boys. With tears on our cheeks we embraced. The war was everywhere now. We spoke a different language. We were other than we had been.

Acknowledgements

I would like to thank the following: my agent, John Saddler; everybody at Little, Brown, especially my editor Richard Beswick and my publicist Jenny Fry. Thanks also to Nicholas Royle, Sam Gilpin and Tom Bullough for advice, criticism and encouragement; to everyone in the American Studies department at King's College London; to Leonidas Liambey and Lillian Lykiardopoulou for friendship and hospitality; to Sharmaine Reid for many great lunches and, most of all, to Kate Williams, for love, support and brilliance – this book would not be possible without her.